Praise for *Ex-Heroes*:

'My 2 favorite things, zombies and superheroes . . .
Hurry with the sequel to *Ex-Heroes*!'
Nathan Fillion, star of *Firefly* and *Castle*

'It's *The Avengers* meets *The Walking Dead* with a
large order of epic served on the side.'
Ernest Cline, author of *Ready Player One*

'Zombies? Check. Superheroes? Check. Awesome? Check.
Ex-Heroes has it all. You're in for a treat!'
Mira Grant, *New York Times* bestselling author of *Feed*

'Superheroes. Zombies. Gripping. Action-packed adventure.
Stories of overcoming personal and physical challenges.
Cinematic-quality fight scenes. These are just some of
the things you will find in *Ex-Heroes*.'
Wired.com

EX-HEROES

Peter Clines

DEL REY

5 7 9 10 8 6 4

First published in the US in 2010 by Permuted Press
This edition first published in the US in 2013 by Broadway Paperbacks,
an imprint of the Crown Publishing Group, a division of
Random House, Inc., New York.

Published in the UK in 2013 by Del Rey, an imprint of Ebury Publishing
A Random House Group Company

The Random House Group Limited Reg. No. 954009

Addresses for companies within the Random House Group can be found at:
www.randomhouse.co.uk

A CIP catalogue record for this book is available from the British Library

The Random House Group Limited supports The Forest Stewardship
Council® (FSC®), the leading international forest-certification organisation.
Our books carrying the FSC label are printed on FSC®-certified paper.
FSC is the only forest-certification scheme supported by the leading
environmental organisations, including Greenpeace. Our
paper procurement policy can be found at
www.randomhouse.co.uk/environment

Printed and bound in Great Britain by Clays Ltd, St Ives plc

ISBN 9780091953621

To buy books by your favourite authors and register for offers visit:
www.randomhouse.co.uk
www.delreyuk.com

EX-HEROES

Prologue
NOW

KATIE HAD BEEN on the walls of the Mount for two hours, leaning against the Earth, when St. George dropped out of the sky wearing a leather flight jacket.

She held out a fist without looking up and he rapped his knuckles against hers. They didn't speak for six minutes, and she used the time to finish cleaning her rifle. Half the reason she volunteered for the walls was so she didn't have to talk to people, and he knew it. She finished with the weapon, reloaded it, and adjusted her sunglasses. The rifle settled against her shoulder as she finally looked up at him.

St. George was in his midthirties, a solid six feet tall with pale eyes behind tinted lenses. Like a lot of people in the Mount, he was lean, with a body more used to surviving than being well fed. Unlike most people, he had thick brown hair that stretched down past his shoulders. It took way too much effort to cut it, she knew, and it wasn't like it put him at extra risk.

"You're early," she said at last.

He shrugged. "Slow day. I'm doing the rounds in reverse."

"She won't like that. That's the kind of thing's going to get you in trouble."

"Maybe."

She tossed a pebble over the edge and tried to pick out the rap it made on the pavement from the chattering below. "You still going out tomorrow?"

A single nod from him. "We're going to head north again. Try hitting some of the apartments and smaller shops toward Los Feliz." He looked down at the exes milling on the streets and sidewalk below. "Nice crowd today."

"You should've been at the Van Ness gate yesterday. Almost twice as many."

"Any problems?"

She shook her head. "Stealth authorized ten rounds. Only one miss."

"One's enough to piss her off."

"Yes it was." Katie glanced at the moving figures on the street. She counted two dozen exes below on Gower. Nine male, fifteen female. Just the other night she'd gotten in a heated, after-sex discussion with Derek about whether exes even had genders.

"They don't mate," Derek had said. "They don't use the parts for anything, so calling them male or female is pointless. They're all just 'its.'"

"So if you don't have sex, you're an it?"

"Well, not if you're choosing not to have sex, no. But rocks don't fuck. Neither do chairs or blankets or exes. So they're its."

Katie wondered if St. George was fucking anyone, or chose not to. Or if he was an it. The heroes still tended to keep to themselves, even the friendly ones. Still, she was guessing he'd be pretty awesome.

"Anything else?"

She handed her binoculars to him. "Look up at the sign."

She pointed up Gower to the hills, where the most famous real estate sign in the world still stood.

He took a long look. Near the "H" was a small oval of darkness, maybe six feet across and ten high. It was like a dead spot on the lens, and it made the white, weather-beaten letter look more like a backward four.

"Midknight?" Katie asked.

"Yeah," said the hero. He sighed and smoke curled from his nostrils. "That's him all right."

"What d'you want to do?"

He handed her the binoculars. "Track him. He's not dangerous up there in the hills, but if he gets down into the city he could play hell with our night defenses."

"Why don't you just go take care of him now?"

"Hardly worth the effort, don't you think?"

It was her turn to shrug. "A dead ex is one less ex."

St. George took a long, slow breath. "Like I said, he's no danger to us up there. If he gets into the city, we'll get rid of him. It's a waste of time and ammo to do anything else."

"Sorry. Was he a friend of yours?"

The air hissed out of his nose as more smoke. "Only met him two or three times. But he was a decent guy."

"Don't get soft. Stealth'll have your head."

His lips twisted into a wry grin. "She's tried."

Katie snorted and looked back down to the street. Right below her one of the male exes, a guy in a gore-covered casual suit, was banging its face against the wall of the Mount, trying to walk through the concrete. "You heading over to Melrose next?"

"Yeah," said the hero. "Message for Derek?"

"Just tell him he's an idiot and he's still wrong."

"I was going to tell him that anyway, but sure."

She gave him a weak salute. St. George took a few running steps along the rubbery tar paper and hurled himself back into the air. He sailed away along the wall, heading for the gate a few blocks east.

Katie settled back against the oversized globe and watched the stumblers below. The trendy ex had managed to turn. Its shoulder dragged against the wall, and every other step sent its face swinging at the concrete again as it clicked and clacked down the sidewalk.

"Living the Hollywood dream," she sighed, and shouldered her weapon again.

Enter the Dragon

THEN

THEY SAY YOU never forget your first time.

It'd been about three months since the Incident at the lab. "Incident" was how they kept referring to it in the news and in the therapy sessions, and the word had been beaten into my head by constant use. There'd been a lot of publicity around me at first as the sole survivor of the explosion, but the news quickly shifted to focus on the twelve people who had died and the scandal of poor chemical storage. Of course, who could blame the University for not designing their building to resist a meteor strike?

Of the twelve victims, seven took a few hours to die. One took a whole day. There was a lot in the papers regarding the wave of chemicals we'd been exposed to. Things that could poison you, twist your body chemistry, or taint your blood. Even corrupt your DNA, according to some people. I also read lots of articles about that meteorite and the odd wavelengths of electromagnetic energy it threw off. Lots of stuff on Wired news about it for a few weeks. I think NASA ended up with it, farmed a ton of work out to MIT, and then it just sort of dropped off the radar.

I was in quarantine for a month. Three more weeks passed

and I faded back into obscurity, too. Well, George Bailey did, anyway.

Yes, George Bailey. My name's been my curse my entire life. To this day I've got no idea why my parents were so cruel. And, yes, I own the deluxe DVD edition and I prefer to watch it in the original black and white.

Anyway, it'd been three months when I noticed the strength. That was first. Physical therapy after the explosion had felt kind of easy and weights seemed a little lighter at the gym, but nothing amazing. One day I was running to beat the street-sweepers (if you live in the Koreatown area like me, street-sweeping rules your life) and somehow managed a fumble-drop-kick that left my keys under the car. I was stretching for them when my shoulder pushed against the frame and shoved my Hyundai a foot up onto the sidewalk.

Odd, yes, but it's amazing what you can justify when parking enforcement is closing in on you. It wasn't until a few days later, back at work, that something happened I couldn't ignore. I got pissed, lost my temper at a dumpster with a stuck lid, and kicked it through the side of the applied physics building. By the time a crowd gathered and security showed up, people already assumed some drunk had slammed it with his car.

Even that I probably could've rationalized somehow, but a week later I was taking a shower and had a rasp in my throat. One of those little tickles that're a bit too coarse, like you'd hiccupped a bit of stomach acid but it didn't quite make it to your mouth. I hacked to shake it loose and belched a cloud of fire a little bigger than a basketball. It melted part of the shower curtain.

I was smart enough to start testing my limits out of sight. People tend to be surprised how much empty space there is in Los Angeles. You can wander some parts of Griffith Park and you'd never guess you're still in one of the biggest cities in the country. So getting away to practice lifting boulders or breathing fire isn't impossible, but it still has some risks—especially when you're training yourself to vomit on command. I hate to admit it, but I started one of those fires that were on the news. Not the big one that threatened the Observatory, but one of the small ones that followed it.

Lifting rocks bigger than me wasn't too much effort. If I got my leverage right, I could get most cars off the ground. I got the Hyundai over my head twice.

This was the kind of stuff distracting me. Thinking about picking up boulders and coughing like a flamethrower. This was running through my head every day at work, at each meal and when I stretched out on my cheap-ass futon at night. It distracted me enough I tripped and fell down the stairs one morning.

Or at least, most people would've fallen. I coasted across the stairwell and floated to the floor. Once I was sure no one else was in the hall, I threw myself down the next three flights. Each time there was a weird little buzz, sort of a twist between my shoulders, and I felt light. I'd drift down and land with a tap of my feet on the floor.

Flight was sort of the last straw, in a good way. Maybe I'd read too many comic books as a kid or watched too many superhero movies as an adult. I don't know. Could be I was just stupid enough to think this had happened to someone like me, in a city like this, for a reason. That one man could change things.

I spent another three weeks up in the Hollywood Hills. I snuck into Runyon Canyon at night and threw myself off hills and cliffs. There's a bench at the very top of the dog path that turned out to be a great launch point. There are some great ones out in Malibu, too, like all those rocks at the end of Zuma Beach. I just needed to watch out for night surfers.

It's not real flight like Superman or the guy from *Heroes*. It's more like a hang glider, I think, where you have lift but no actual propulsion. I can soar pretty far and pretty fast thanks to my enhanced muscles, but I always come down.

A few crashes confirmed I was a lot tougher, too. My skin, my bones, even my hair. I wouldn't say invulnerable, but at the time I felt safe thinking "bulletproof." I spent one weekend trying to break my skin with sewing needles, an X-Acto knife, and even a cordless drill. Heck, the stove burner cooled off in my hand while I watched it.

The last detail was the costume. The ski suit from Sports Chalet was already silk-screened to look like red scales, and the gauntlets and boots were all black. The mask was two or three different things from Party City mashed together, enough so I wouldn't be looking at a copyright lawsuit. I had to reinforce the Halloween cape with the folding arms from a pair of umbrellas, which worked pretty well all things considered. The idea was to increase my hang time, as it were. Not all of us own a multibillion-dollar company with an R&D lab in the basement, y'know.

My first night out was June 17, 2008. A Tuesday. At this point it had been over half a year since the Incident. No news coverage in three months. It'd be tough for anyone to link my new identity to it.

I took the whole mess up to the roof of my apartment in a duffel bag. Didn't want to risk any of my neighbors seeing me. I changed in the shadow of the elevator tower and hid the bag behind one of the air vents. I'd never wear this costume under a shirt and a pair of jeans, that's for sure.

From the roof of that old building you could see all of Los Angeles. Griffith Park Observatory. The Hollywood sign. Downtown. Century City. Wilshire Center. And the pit my section of town had become. I didn't have to turn my head to see three or four cans' worth of graffiti and gang signs spread across the sidewalk. XV3s. Seventeens. All fighting over an area where people just wanted to live in peace.

I remember my heart was pounding, and a dozen things were running through my head. Bulletproof was still just an idea at that point, and I knew enough about guns from GTA to know all firearms are not created equal. Hell, looking back on it, an AK-47 wouldn't've been unrealistic to run into.

After ten minutes of telling myself how stupid this was, how ridiculous I looked, and that I was probably heading out to my death, I got a running start and jumped off the roof. I focused and felt the small twist between my shoulders. The cape caught the wind and the umbrella arms snapped open.

And I was flying.

I crossed Beverly and Oakwood, sailed over the hill, and landed on the roof of a Laundromat on Melrose, just past Normandie, six blocks north of my starting point. As far as I could tell, no one had seen me. I launched myself back into the air, and this time I kicked off a phone pole when I started to lose momentum, flying right over the 101 freeway. I leaned on the cape and swung back toward Hollywood.

I played around like this for an hour, figuring out my limits, when I heard the scream. Sounded like a woman. It took me a minute to get turned around, then another to get high enough so I could see the area.

There were three guys chasing her down one of the smaller streets. Well, not even chasing. Running alongside and teasing her. One of them kept grabbing at her, and she kept shaking him off. Even from sixty feet up, I could see she was scared and running blind.

I pulled the cape in tight, went into a dive, and let the wind pull it open at the last minute to swing me around. I stumbled a bit on the landing, but they were all so startled at me dropping out of the sky none of them noticed. One of the guys swore in Spanish. So did the girl.

While I'd been flying I'd been thinking up clever catch-phrases and opening lines, but now my mind was blank. At that point, though, I'd been psyching myself up for almost a month. I just started walking toward them without think-ing. I think I blurted out "Leave her alone," without even try-ing to disguise my voice. The words weren't even out of my mouth before two of them had pulled out pistols. They fired two or three shots each. The girl screamed. So did I.

It goes without saying getting shot hurts. Not as bad as it could've been—it was like getting punched, where there's pain but you already know on some level there's no serious damage. I staggered a bit, but I didn't fall.

They swore some more. The one without a pistol cracked and ran. One of the others emptied his gun into me. It stung like hell but now I was braced for it. I didn't move this time, and the bullets pattered on the ground at my feet. The third guy seemed to be in shock.

I took in a deep breath, tried to relax my tongue, and felt that scratch in the back of my throat. Another breath swelled my chest and I tasted the faint sizzle of chemicals mixing. I let it all out.

It was the biggest flame I'd ever made, and to this day I

still think one of the most impressive. A good fifteen feet of golden, burning air lit up the entire street, hitting the ground right between the last two men. Not even men. Teenagers. Kids in green bandannas who were screaming like little children as the cuffs of their jeans caught fire. I coughed once as my lungs hit empty and burped up a little softball of flames with some black smoke. They ran.

The girl was staring at me and whispering prayers over and over again. She was barely out of her teens. I think I freaked her out just as much as the other guys did.

I debated chasing the bad guys or trying to calm her down, but in the time it took me to decide either one became a lost cause. Then I spent another few seconds deciding if I should say something or go for the dark and silent persona. So many things I hadn't thought out. In the end, as the last of the flames hissed out on the pavement, I gave her a smile and a nod and hurled myself upward. A quick push off a lamppost gave me some extra "ooomph" and I flew into the night. Less than three seconds and I was a hundred feet up.

I glanced down and saw her still standing there in the middle of the street. She just stared up in amazement. I spread the cape, caught a faint breeze, and started gliding away. And then her shout echoed up to me.

"Thank you!!!"

And that's how I became the Mighty Dragon.

EX-HEROES   17

Two

NOW

ST. GEORGE BALANCED on the point of the water tower, the highest point on the lot, and looked down at the fake city.

It was just a couple of buildings and a pair of short roads, and from this angle their facades were obvious. But compared to the rest of the Mount, New York Street looked normal. Normal and peaceful. It wasn't unusual to find people wandering there, where they could walk two blocks on a sidewalk and pretend the world was still safe and made sense.

He'd visited the Mount twice. Before, when it was just a film studio. A friend of a friend had gotten him on the lot years ago and they'd spent an afternoon walking the choked streets and alleys. At the time, it had seemed like the most amazing place in the world. He remembered the fake city from that visit.

The second time had been at night, in costume. He'd stood on this very spot on top of the water tower and looked past the walls of the studio at the glowing expanse of Hollywood while the wind whipped his cape. He'd felt like an honest-to-God superhero.

It all seemed so long ago.

Just over the West building he could see the North-by-Northwest residential area. Close to a thousand people packed into less than a city block. Stage Fifteen, on the far side of New York Street, had a large cluster of tents set up on the roof. Scavenged solar cells, water barrels, and gardens covered the rooftops.

It had taken two months after they moved into the Mount, but most of the stages had been changed into mass housing. Now there were two dozen families living in each one. The plus side was they all had plenty of space and huge rooftops for private gardens. The downside was two dozen immediate neighbors and lack of privacy.

As they'd all quickly discovered, lack of privacy was the killer. Over a hundred fights broke out the first week. Two of them ended in deaths. Stealth had thrown the murderers over the fence at the North Gower gate. Their screams hadn't lasted long, but the lesson had.

He looked over his left shoulder. Far in the distance, half-way to the ocean, he could see the towers of Century City. They'd filmed one of the original *Planet of the Apes* movies there. Just off to the left, he could see a few thin lines of dark smoke trace paths in the crisp blue sky.

People could say a lot of negative things about the apocalypse, but there was no arguing the air quality in Los Angeles had really improved.

As a gust of wind came from the west, he turned from the film sets and hurled himself off the tower. He soared across what had once been a parking lot and pool for water movies. It had taken them two months to fill it in with all the potting soil and dirt they could scavenge from the Home Depot up on Sunset, plus a few drugstores, but now it was just under half an acre of farmland in the heart of the lot. Over a dozen people walked the rows of soybeans, spinach, and potatoes with watering cans. Their tired eyes looked up at the hero as he flew over them.

He passed another rooftop and let himself drop between buildings. He could see himself reflected in Zukor's mirrored windows before he landed on the narrow length of Avenue L. One of the guards in front of the hospital gave him a sharp nod, the other a lazy salute. The third man bowed his unusual head.

Gorgon had struck St. George as shifty and underhanded from the day they'd first met, probably because he always hid his eyes. He did it for everyone else's sake, but it still bothered people. A huge pair of mechanical goggles covered half of Gorgon's face. A spinning iris of dark plastic made up each lens, mounted in a rim the size of a can of tuna. He hadn't been as good about combing his hair or shaving since Banzai had died, and, wearing his leather duster, he looked like a Japanese cartoon character.

A seven-pointed sheriff's badge rode high on the duster's lapel. Someone had dug it up from one of the prop or costume trailers. After Stealth's lesson at the gate, Gorgon had taken it upon himself to patrol the streets, halls, and rooftops of the Mount. He wore the silver star with grim pride.

"Morning," he said.

"Gorgon. Surprised to see you here."

"Had to make a drop-off. Fight in the mushroom farm."

"Again?"

"The big guy, Mikkelson," said one of the guards. "Throwing his weight around again, yelling about starving."

"I put him down," said Gorgon. His head tilted a bit, a

twitch, and let the lenses catch the light. "He hit his head on one of the trays and cut his forehead."

"Still weird to see you here," said St. George with a half-smile.

Gorgon coughed. "I was the only one who could carry him up the damned stairs. You know what the Stage Five farm's like."

They all nodded.

He swept down the sides of his trenchcoat and gave the sheriff's badge a quick brush. "Anyway, I've got rounds to make and I'm behind now." He tipped his head to St. George. "Watch yourself out there this afternoon."

"Hey, yeah," said the other guard. He tipped his head after Gorgon. "Boss says all y'all's going out today?"

St. George nodded. "Sheets have been up for a few days. You didn't see?"

The man shook his head. He had a salt-and-pepper beard that added a dozen years to his face.

"If your shift's over by eleven, be at Melrose," said the hero. "We can fit you in."

"I'll be there." The guard shifted the rifle on his shoulder.

Another guard stood inside the door and gave him a nod. Zukor was the most heavily defended building on the lot. If an outbreak happened inside the walls, it would start here. Each emergency room had three armed guards and all the medical staff carried sidearms. If someone died, putting a bullet in their brain was a top priority.

St. George paused at the large sign dominating the right-hand wall. Each of the letters was four inches tall. He'd mem-orized it at this point, but its sheer size made him look every time.

WARNING SIGNS

FEVER – DIZZINESS – CHILLS – WEAKNESS – HEADACHES – BLURRED OR DOUBLE VISION – DIARRHEA – NAUSEA – CONGESTION – PALE SKIN – TROUBLE BREATHING

PERSONS EXHIBITING ANY OF THESE SYMPTOMS MUST PRESENT THEMSEVLES FOR TESTING AND QUARANTINE IMMEDIATELY

The Adolph Zukor Building hadn't always been the Mount's hospital, but Stealth had pointed out they needed something more central and better equipped than the small first-aid office off Avenue P. Deeper into the lobby was a statue of the man himself. St. George had moved it out of the way when they put the sign in.

He found Doctor Connolly in her office. Roger Mikkelson was sprawled across the examination table, his head wedged in place with two rolled-up towels. She tied off a fourth and final stitch in the man's forehead and mopped up some blood with a piece of gauze.

"Shouldn't you use anesthetic or something when you do that?"

A few streaks of silver highlighted Doctor Connolly's crimson hair, and fine wrinkles marked the edges of her eyes. She'd been a medical researcher when they found her in the remains of Hollywood Presbyterian. Now she was in charge of their small hospital staff. "Anesthetic's a limited resource," she said, "and Gorgon told me I had at least half an hour before he regained consciousness." She smiled and peeled off her gloves. "To what do I owe the honor?"

He gestured up to the lights with his chin. "We're going

to have to put you on solar for a while. Barry's coming out with us."

"How long?"

"Four or five hours, tops. Do you have anything critical?"

She shook her head. "Slow week." She nodded at Mikkelson. "He'll be out of here once he wakes up. We've just got a broken leg, a concussion, and a gunshot wound staying here tonight."

"Who got shot by who?"

"Zekiel Reid, Luke's brother. He nodded off on the Marathon roof with his finger on the trigger. Ricochet caught him in the calf."

"Idiot."

"Lucky idiot," Connolly said. "At that range he could've blown his foot off. If the bullet got him in the thigh, he would've bled out hopping here."

"You don't sound too surprised."

She shrugged. "We've been seeing more and more accidents from the wall."

"You think they're trying to get out of guard duty?"

"I think they're bored silly."

"Yeah. Who would've guessed survival would be so dull?"

"To hell with that," she snorted. "Who'd guess living in a movie studio would be so dull?"

"When I get back I'll see about setting up shorter shifts. I think Gorgon has a few people ready to go on active guard duty."

"Can I toss an idea at you? It's something I've been thinking about."

"Sure."

She settled back against the wall. "Back before Nine-Eleven, I did a semester abroad in Egypt. Cairo American

College. They were already nuts about security then. It took a serious effort to go anywhere and not have line of sight to a soldier or a police officer. Turns out they were having the same problem, though. All these men standing around for hours and hours every day with nothing happening. They were getting careless and having tons of accidents. Soldiers were shooting themselves in the leg or the foot. If they were on a tower they could even shoot people below them."

St. George nodded. "How'd they solve it?"

"They stopped loading the guns."

He smiled. "I don't think that'll fly with Stealth."

Connolly shook her head. "They gave them ammo. They just didn't let them stand around with it. They'd tape two clips together, one up, one down. That way the guns weren't loaded, but all they had to do was flip the clips over and they'd be ready to go."

"And you just happened to notice all that?"

"I was fifteen years younger, twenty pounds lighter, and traveling alone." She gave him a smirk. "Men talked to me about anything they could think of."

Across from them, Mikkelson groaned and twitched. A shiver passed through him and a slow hand reached up to feel his stitches.

"I hear it's like having one of the worst hangovers of your life," she said with a nod at the shuddering man.

"That it is. Any other news?"

"I think we've made a small breakthrough with the ex-virus. Nothing groundbreaking, from a practical point of view, but I'll know for sure when some tests finish up this afternoon."

He nodded.

Mikkelson almost fell off the table and swore under his breath. He stood on wobbly legs, took in a breath to start shouting, and saw St. George. The hero gave him a slow nod. "Problem, Roger?"

"I just wanted a couple extra mushrooms," he muttered. "I was hungry. What the fuck's the big deal?"

"I think when you take stuff that's not yours they call it stealing."

"They're fucking mushrooms."

"They're food. You want more rations, you bring it up at your district meeting."

"Whatever. What would you know about it? You don't even eat." He rubbed his stitches and pushed past them into the hall.

"You want to leave those alone," said the doctor. "Come back in a few days and I'll take them out."

He waved a dismissive arm back at her.

"Roger," St. George called down the hall. "This is two strikes for you. Next time it's not me or Gorgon. You'll have to deal with Stealth."

The big man gave them another glance, but his eyes softened. He shoved his hands in his pockets and clomped down the stairs.

Connolly glanced at St. George. "You do eat, don't you?"

"God, yes," he said. "I dreamed about ultimate cheeseburgers last night. A big pile of them, all warm and wrapped in paper. I'd kill for some meat these days."

She laughed. "One other thing?"

"Sure."

"Can you talk to Josh? I think it would mean a lot to him."

"Why?"

"He's getting depressed again."

"I mean, why would it mean anything coming from me? Heck, at this point you probably know him better than I do."

"I do," she said with a nod. "And that's why I think he still relates better to you than he does to me. Not to swell your head or anything, but he used to be one of you and now he's just one of us."

"Wow. How superphobic of you."

She smiled. "Did you just make that up?"

"No, I heard Ty O'Neill use it once. You know it's a hell of a lot more than just losing his powers, right?"

"I know," she said. "But there's only so much I can deal with. The dead wife I can relate to. Loss of godlike powers . . ." She shrugged.

He sighed. "Yeah, okay. Where is he?"

"In the infirmary. Doing his rounds."

"Ahhh," said George. "Spreading his cheer and goodwill to all the patients."

× × ×

The man once known as Regenerator stood by a hospital bed, checking his patient's chart. His right hand rested in the wide pocket of his lab coat and a purple stethoscope dangled around his neck. The young man in the bed was out cold, his lower leg bound tight with white gauze.

St. George cleared his throat. "What's up, Doc?"

Josh Garcetti glanced up from the chart. "Hey," he said. Without moving his pocketed hand he hung the clipboard at the end of the bed and held out his left. "Long time no see. What've you been up to?"

St. George caught the awkward hand and shook it. "Trying to survive the end of the world. You?"

"Same thing, smaller scale." He made no attempt at a smile. The two men were close to the same age, the same height, but even slumped Josh's shoulders were broader. Like so many people these days, his hair had gone gray years before it should have, and a few strands of pure white highlighted the mop. In white makeup, he could've passed for a somber Greek statue. In the lab coat, he was almost spectral. They walked back to the hallway. "Heard you're heading out later today."

"Around eleven."

"Who's going with?"

"Cerberus and Barry. I just came over to tell Connolly you'll be on solar all afternoon."

The doctor nodded and leaned against a set of file cabinets. A beat passed. Then another.

"You should come out sometime."

Josh shook his head. "No. Thanks for the offer, but no."

"I think it'd do you some good."

"How?"

"You haven't gone out once. Hell, have you even been near an ex since . . . ?" St. George paused again before giving an awkward nod at the pocketed hand.

"Not really, no."

"We could use you out there. You've got experience."

"I have experience in field hospitals," he said with a shake of his head. "I was never much of a fighter. Just good at not getting hurt."

"You were good at making sure no one else got hurt, too."

"No," he said. His face hardened. "No, I wasn't."

"Fuck. You know I didn't mean it like that."

He closed his eyes. "I know. Sorry."

"It's coming up on two years, isn't it?"

"Yeah. Eleven more days."

"You know . . ." said St. George as he edged out onto the emotional thin ice, "last year things were still pretty hectic. You want to get a drink or something? Talk? We could get Barry, Gorgon, maybe even convince Danielle to take the damned armor off."

Josh turned to the cabinet behind the counter and examined the contents with sudden interest. "Again, thanks but no. I'm just going to stay home. Besides, Gorgon wouldn't want to see me."

"It wasn't your fault."

"Let's just drop it, okay?" He massaged his temple with two fingers.

"You should really come out, though."

Josh opened his eyes. "Look, it's a nice thought, but let's face it. I'm too much of a distraction out there." He pulled his other hand out of the lab coat's wide pocket. "Everyone'll just be looking at the damned bite instead of watching their own asses."

As he raised the hand the sleeve sagged a bit and revealed part of his withered forearm. The flesh was pale and splotched with gray. Dark veins ran into his palm and met up with yellowed fingernails. The teeth marks were still visible, a semicircle of ragged holes just beneath his wrist.

For the first few months of his superhero career Josh Garcetti called himself the Immortal. He could heal from wounds in less time than it took to make them. Fire, bullets, broken limbs—he laughed at all of them. Then he discovered how to share his healing factor with others and he became Regenerator.

Then his wife died. And then the world went to hell. And then an ex bit his right hand. In one of the last field hospitals, as everyone pulled out and all the last-ditch emergency plans kicked in, a dead cop rolled over on the slab and sunk his teeth into Regenerator. Put him in a coma for three weeks, but it didn't kill him and he didn't change. For the past fourteen months his healing factor had done nothing but keep the infection from spreading past his biceps.

St. George tried not to stare at the hand. "You can't hide in here forever, Josh."

"Of course I can," he said. "What do you think we're all doing?"

They looked at each other for a moment. The hero made a noise that was half snort and half sigh, accompanied by a puff of black smoke.

"Look," said the doctor, "I've got some immunizations to get ready for and an inventory to do. It was good seeing you, George. Be careful out there, okay?" He worked the hand back into its pocket, gave a faint bow with his head, and walked away.

× × ×

St. George stepped back out into the open air. "Hey," the hero called to the guard with the salt-and-pepper hair, "what's your name, anyway?"

"Jarvis," he said with a grin. The guard gave a sharp, three-fingered salute. "Pleased to meetcha."

"Same. Melrose gate. Eleven."

"See you at eleven," echoed the bearded guard.

St. George gave him a nod and launched himself up to the roof of the hospital. Another kick got him up and over the stages to the east and headed toward Four.

Four had been a stage once. They'd found some plaques and paperwork that said shows like *Deep Space Nine* and *Nip/Tuck* had been filmed there. They'd stripped all the operating room sets there for Zukor, used the set walls for housing, and tied it into one of the Mount's nearby power houses with heavy cable from the nearby lighting warehouses. Now it reeked of ozone and the air danced on St. George's skin.

At the center of Four was the electric chair. It was a set of three interlocking circles forming a rough sphere, but the nickname had stuck. Each ring was wrapped with copper wire stripped out of three miles of cable. Five people had spent a month building it. St. George thought it looked just like an enormous toy gyroscope.

Floating inside the sphere was the blinding outline of a man. It was a reversed shadow, like looking at the sun through a man-shaped cutout. Arcs of energy shot from the white-hot figure to snap and pop against the copper rings.

"Morning, Barry," the hero shouted over the crackling of power.

The glowing figure shifted in the sphere. It had no eyes, but St. George knew his friend was looking at him. A voice made of static echoed over the electric noise. *Morning,* it buzzed. *You ready to head out?*

St. George shook his head. "Not yet, but I asked everyone to switch over early. Thought you might like a bite to eat and a nap."

God, yes, sighed the brilliant wraith. It shifted again and examined the building. *Where're my wheels?*

"Over by the door."

The outline nodded. *Catch me*, it buzzed.

There was a twist of lightning and the figure was outside the sphere. It sank to the floor and the concrete began to smoke. The shape grew dim, the air flattened, and a gaunt, naked man tumbled to the ground with the sudden *whuff* of a flame being snuffed out.

"Oh, Jesus!" he shouted. "It's freezing in here. Where's my clothes?"

"On the chair." St. George scooped him up, taking the dark-skinned man in one arm like a child.

"Get me over there, for Christ's sake."

"Wuss."

"Big man, picking on the naked cripple," Barry said. "Get me some damned pants."

They crossed the room and St. George lowered his friend into the wheelchair. Barry dug through the bundle of clothes and wrestled his way into the sweatpants. He'd been dressing in the chair for most of his life, so it didn't take long. He tugged a T-shirt over his stubbly head and wrapped himself in a fleece jacket. "No shoes?"

"What do you need shoes for?"

"My feet are cold."

"So put on the other pair of socks."

"Are they still serving breakfast?"

"Yeah. And I got you something to eat on the way." He dropped a shrunken muffin in the other man's lap.

"Thanks. Which truck are we taking out?"

"*Big Red*, I think."

"Good," said Barry through a mouthful of pastry. "The shocks on *Mean Green* suck so bad I can feel it in *my* ass. You know what?"

"What?"

"I think this is the best blueberry muffin I have had in my entire life."

"I'm sure Mary'll be glad to hear someone liked them."

"And I'm not just saying that because it's been four days. This is one spectacular muffin."

St. George spun his walkie in his hand. "You know what you want? I can call ahead, have something ready."

"I will have," he said with great thought, "a stack of at least five pancakes. Lots of syrup and whatever's passing for butter these days. Some potatoes. And any of those pow-dered eggs they've got left."

"That it?"

"We'll talk later about what I'm taking with me for lunch. So, what's going on?"

"How so?"

"You're transparent, boy scout."

St. George shrugged. "Just talked to Josh."

"Oh, joy. How'd that go?"

"Same as always. Self-pity, a little self-loathing, deter-mined to end his life a lonely martyr."

Barry pushed another lump of muffin into this mouth. "One thing you have to say about our brave new world. It's very consistent."

× × ×

Big Red was parked next to the guard shack. It was a twenty-four-foot truck that had been used for hauling set dressing back when the Mount was in the movie business. The new residents had cannibalized and customized it for scaveng-ing runs. They'd chopped off most of the box and built a new frame for it, making it into a gigantic pickup. It had a backup gas tank, a winch, and a cow catcher that had served as a battering ram once or twice. The double-cab sat four, another six rode in the bed, and a steel grille let two more ride on top of the cab. A petite woman with yellow and black stripes in her short hair was already there, seated on an old couch cushion. Lady Bee had an M-16 slung over her shoulder and a tactical holster strapped to one thigh. Someone once told St. George she'd been a movie costumer in the old days. She blew him a kiss as he walked past the truck.

Luke Reid was at the wheel, as always. He was a blond, broad-shouldered Teamster who used to drive trucks for a living before everything went south. St. George saw Jarvis in *Big Red*'s back, along with Ty O'Neill, Billie Carter, Ilya, and a few others he sort of recognized. They all gave him salutes and determined nods. Barry was already asleep in the giant truck bed, stretched out on a thick pile of furniture blankets with his wheelchair strapped to the wall next to him.

St. George walked up to the Melrose Gate and stopped a few feet away from the dozens of grasping hands reaching and clawing between the bars. The exes had the gate mobbed, as they always did. It was the only place they could still see into the Mount, see all the succulent, tasty people standing inside.

Although, no one was sure if exes could see anymore.

Almost no one used the word "zombie." They'd been "exes" since the first presidential press conference. It made them easier to accept, somehow. The ex-living. Ex-people. Most of them still looked human. Usually the uninjured ones and the newer ones that hadn't fed.

The former citizens of Los Angeles reached for St. George with discolored, rotting fingers. He could hear their joints pop as they moved. Dozens of jaws hinged open and closed, clicking their dark teeth together.

A curly-haired blonde whose mouth was caked with gore. A bald man with a gashed scalp and one ear. On opposite ends of the gate were a man and a woman in running clothes. By the left hinge, next to the female runner, was one with a face scoured down to the bare bone. A teenaged boy with a *Transformers* shirt and a clotted stump where his left hand should've been. A grandmotherly woman in a business suit stiff with blood. A black man near the break in the gate who stood still and stared back at St. George with blank eyes.

Their skin was anywhere from sidewalk gray to white, sometimes colored with dark purple bruises. Their eyes were all dull and faded, like cloudy glass. Many of them were just worn out. Flesh dry and cracking from months in the sun. Covered with injuries that would never heal but could never kill them.

St. George didn't recognize any of them. That always made it easier.

A huge blue and platinum statue thudded over to stand next to him. His head didn't even reach the stars and stripes stenciled across its armored biceps. The titan's androgynous lines made it hard to think of as anything but an "it," even knowing there was a woman inside. She looked down at the hero with bright lenses the size of tennis balls. "You know I hate doing this, right?"

He nodded. "You've mentioned it."

Cerberus turned her gaze to the crowd of exes. "Just so you remember on the day I finally snap. Where's Barry?"

"Asleep in the truck. You charged up?"

The armored figure gave a clumsy dip of her head. The Cerberus Battle Armor System wasn't built for subtlety. Of course, she hadn't built it with subtlety in mind. Even without the M-2s mounted on her arms, Cerberus could take on almost anything left in the world. St. George had seen the nine-foot battlesuit rip a vault door off its hinges, lift a cement truck, and wade through a swarm of exes without scuffing the paint.

The guards had already unlocked the gate's four reinforcing legs, and Derek and Carl stood waiting on either end of the long pipe resting across the Melrose Gate.

"Everyone ready?" shouted St. George. "Gate? Luke? Guards?"

They all nodded.

He leaped into the air and soared over the archway. As he sank back to street level outside the gate, his foot lashed out and an ex flew back. He grabbed two more by their necks and hurled them across the six-lane street.

The exes sensed life and the mob closed on him. Hands grabbed at him. Bony arms wrapped around his neck. A faceless thing that may have been a woman once bit down on his arm and lost two teeth.

St. George seized a wrist, swung the dead thing in a wide circle, and knocked down half a dozen more before launching it into the air. It clanged into the stoplight over the intersection. He slammed his palm into a breastbone and the ex flew back through some bushes into a wall. Another tried to grab his calf as it crawled to its feet and his boot broke its spine just above the shoulder blades.

"Still creeps me out, watching that," said Derek.

Carl stared out at the battle. "Seeing them pile on him?"

"Seeing them not do anything to him."

"Open it up," barked the battlesuit. Cerberus clenched her three-fingered hands into fists as big as footballs.

The guards hefted the pipe from its brackets and trotted out of the way. The gates swung open and Cerberus stomped out. Some of the clawing exes were dragged along, their arms tangled in the gates. She brought her armored fist around like a wrecking ball and shattered their skulls. Another punch crushed an ex's chest even as it sailed backward.

St. George flung off a dead man gnawing at his shoulders. The ex slammed into an old grandmother and they both tumbled away from the gate. Another one reached for him and the hero grabbed its elbow and swung it into the air. Its flailing legs knocked down three more exes before the arm snapped off and it tumbled away across the cobblestones. "Make a path!" he shouted.

Cerberus spread her fingers and brought her stun fields up. Her gauntlets sparked and snapped with white lines. The titan stomped toward the street and exes dropped at her touch. She left a path of figures wiggling on the ground behind her. "Bring it out!" she bellowed with a wave.

Big Red's engine growled and Luke guided the truck forward through the gate. The heavy tires crushed legs, arms, and skulls beneath them. A few exes flailed at the cab and the truck bed. None of them could reach that high, but the men and women in the back shoved them off with pikes and spears anyway. The salt-and-pepper man stabbed his weapon down through a chubby woman's skull and she dropped.

The guards pushed the gate shut behind them, the two sides meeting just as the truck cleared. There was a clang as the pipe dropped back into place, followed by the click of the legs dropping back into their brackets. Derek gave a thumbs-up through the bars.

"We're out," yelled St. George. "Cerberus, mount up." He swung his arms and sent two exes hurling through the crowd like a pair of bowling balls into a forest of pins. There were already four or five dozen more shambling down the street toward the gate from either direction, drawn in by the movement and the noise.

The lift gate carried the battlesuit up to the bed, then folded up behind her. Cerberus turned to watch their rear, and the truck swayed with each step. She turned her head and signaled the driver.

"Rolling out," called Luke. *Big Red* growled, swung to the left, and picked up speed as it headed down Melrose Avenue. Exes were battered aside by bumpers or fell beneath the wheels. St. George flew up and landed on the reinforced rack on top of the cab next to Lady Bee.

Guards waved to them from the Mount's walls and watchtowers as they headed off into the wasteland that had once been Los Angeles, destination for tens of thousands of dreamers every year.

Three
NOW

ST. GEORGE DROPPED down to the cab's running boards. "You still want to head over to Vermont and straight up?"

The driver nodded. "Nice and clear all the way to Hollywood Boulevard. That's where you wanted to start, right?"

The hero nodded.

Big Red rolled down Melrose. St. George and Cerberus had spent weeks clearing off the roads surrounding the Mount. Here and there exes stumbled out of open doors or from behind wrecked cars. They staggered and loped toward the truck with grasping arms, then forgot it when it was a block away.

"I've been thinking," said Lady Bee as St. George swung back up to the roof rack. "I bet Spider-Man would kick your ass."

He peered over his sunglasses at her. "What?"

"Spider-Man," she said. "If the two of you fought, he would totally kick your ass."

"Spider-Man's not real, y'know. He's a comic book character."

"Look who's talking."

"I never had a comic book."

Lady Bee swung her head and her rifle back and forth, watching the sides of the road. She was wearing a shirt a size too small under her motorcycle jacket, and whenever she turned to the left he caught a glimpse of the fire-red bra she was wearing between the buttons. "In that movie he held up a whole warehouse wall," she pointed out. "To save his girl-friend."

"That's a movie. It's special effects. They did it with computers and stuff."

She grinned. "Can you?"

"Can I what? Lift a wall?"

"Yeah."

"Guess it depends on the woman." He shook his head. "Probably not. The most I can lift is about three and a half tons. Maybe four if I'm worked up."

"So Spider-Man would kick your ass."

"Okay, fine. If Spider-Man was real, and we decided to fight for some reason, yes, he would probably kick my ass."

Bee nodded. "See? You're not that great."

"Whatever." He looked back down Melrose. "Is this your idea of flirting?"

"Maybe."

"I don't think you're doing it right."

"Maybe." Her head swung back and forth again. "You know, Superman would mop the floor with you. It wouldn't even be a fight."

× × ×

Next to Cerberus, a skinny brunette clutched at the pike she'd been assigned. The end was a gleaming spear tip, either from the prop house or the top of a flagpole. Her shoulders hunched every time a new ex appeared, and her knuckles whitened on the wooden shaft.

"Haven't come out often?" asked the metal titan.

She shook her head. "My second time since I came to the Mount."

"When was that?"

"Almost a year ago."

Cerberus dipped her armored chin. "Just remember, you're faster and smarter than them. Stay calm, don't do anything stupid, and it's almost impossible for anything to go wrong."

The girl nodded. "I'm Lynne."

"Cerberus."

"Yeah. I know."

They crossed Western without incident. The heroes had cleared the street by hand months ago, moving cars onto the sidewalk as searches expanded farther and farther from the Mount. As *Big Red* came up over a hill, looking down at the overpass for the Hollywood Freeway, Luke let up on the gas. "You see what I see?" he asked the men in the cab.

St. George stood up, getting a view of the road ahead.

Both sides of the overpass were clogged with automobiles. Cars and trucks stacked on top of each other and wedged beneath the concrete bridge. St. George could see a bright green cab, an LAPD squad car, and two motorcycles in the pile.

Lady Bee pulled a set of binoculars from the large mailman's bag she wore. "I count at least a dozen exes," she said. "All staying down."

Luke let *Big Red* come to a stop a few blocks away, across from a gas station. He glanced up at the hero on the roof. "You're the boss," he said with a shrug. "What's your call?"

St. George dropped to the pavement. "Safeties off, everyone," he called out. "Stay sharp until we know what's up."

The back doors of the cab opened up and the men slid out with weapons ready. Lady Bee stood up on top of the cab and swept the area with her bright eyes. Behind her the pikes clattered to the truck bed as more rifles swung up. Cerberus turned and lumbered to the front of the truck, her head even with Bee's. She glanced down at Barry, still asleep in his nest of blankets.

St. George took a few steps and then one leap carried him the three blocks to the roadblock. An ex lay there in a heap, a heavy Latino woman. A bullet hole pierced her forehead above her left eye and another one through her right cheek made half of her face sag.

He reached up, grabbed the axle of a Civic, and tugged. He braced himself and gave another hard pull. The Civic shifted back a foot with a shriek of metal. "They're in tight," he shouted over his shoulder.

He walked back to *Big Red* and checked the exes on the ground. Two were decapitated. One large male had his skull shattered. Gunshot wounds decorated the rest.

"They all down?" asked Lady Bee as she scanned the bodies.

He nodded. "We got an alternate route from here, Luke?"

The driver glanced up the cross street. "We can try going up Normandie," he said. "Haven't used it anytime recently, though. It's a narrow street. If someone blocked this, they could block that, easy."

"Also seems like that's just what we'd be expected to do at this point," said Cerberus. She'd turned up the volume of her speakers and her voice echoed.

"Then we go through." St. George looked up at her. "Can you clear it?"

The steel skull turned to the overpass. "You want it done fast or quiet?"

"A little of both, maybe?"

She nodded. "Give me ten minutes." *Big Red* trembled as she moved back to the lift gate.

"A couple exes coming up the road behind us," said Luke with a glance at his mirrors. "One's pretty close."

"You guys got 'em?"

The two men riding the lift gate down with the battlesuit gave St. George a quick thumbs-up. "Not a problem," said Jarvis.

Cerberus stomped across the open road to the overpass. One armored arm swung up, seized the Civic axle, and yanked. The compact car flew out of the stack and skittered across the street. Her metal fingers clamped on the squad car's rear end and dragged it free of the tangle of vehicles.

"You think it's the Seventeens?" asked Luke.

"Can't think of anyone else it could be," said the hero. "Although this is the biggest thing I've seen them try so far."

"Fire in the hole," called someone. A rifle cracked from the back of the truck. Half a block back an ex slumped to the pavement.

Cerberus dragged another car out with a squeal of metal on metal. She swung her arms and tossed it to the side of the road with a crunch. She'd dismantled half the roadblock already.

"Movement," said Lady Bee. "I've got three more exes coming from the south, two from the north."

"We've got two more behind us, too," said Jarvis.

Lady Bee did another sweep with her binoculars. "I count nine, all within two blocks. More past them. We've got five minutes, tops."

"We're moving in less than five," said St. George. "Let's not start wasting ammo yet."

Big Red's engine rumbled.

Cerberus shoved a blue Prius up onto the curb and kicked the last motorcycle away with a spray of sparks. A few blinks inside her helmet switched on the armor's night-vision scopes, and she examined the shadowy underside of the freeway overpass. Some jagged, green graffiti spelled out PEASY RULES. Nothing else.

Her footsteps echoed on the concrete pillars. Another set of blinks brought up the long-range lenses. She studied Melrose as far as she could see for signs of life or ex-life.

Nothing.

She plodded back under the bridge and into the sunlight again. "Clock's ticking," shouted St. George from the truck. "Everything okay?"

She gave him a heavy nod. "How's that look?" she bellowed back with a wave at the overpass.

Luke gave her a thumbs-up from the cab and *Big Red* rolled forward. St. George walked alongside until they reached the overpass. Cerberus was still gazing down Melrose. He rapped her on the arm. "Something wrong?"

Her head shook. "I don't know. Something feels wrong."

"How so?"

The suit swept its gaze back and forth across the overpass. "Not sure," she said. She shrugged her massive shoulders.

"Mount up for now. We'll figure it out." He hopped past her as she rode the lift gate back up. "You okay for power?"

"I've got another ninety-one minutes at peak, three hours of idling." She dipped her head at Barry, a fetal ball in the blankets. "Let him sleep. It's not like he gets to that often."

The lift gate locked into position and St. George leaped to the roof of the cab. Lady Bee gave him a wink and settled back on her pillow.

There was a gas station at Vermont, drained dry three months back by an earlier expedition. They were turning onto Vermont when Lynne, the teenager, stumbled to the front of the swaying truck. "Can I ask you something?"

"Yeah, sure."

"You guys are the only heroes left, right? I mean, you and the ones back at the Mount."

"As far as we know, yeah," said St. George. "We know some are dead and a few are exes."

"Were there any supervillains? You know, like in the movies?"

"Not that we know of."

"So who stacked up the cars like that?"

"We think it was the SS. The South Seventeens. They were one of the gangs from the Koreatown area, like the XV3s. There are other survivors in LA, but they're not all quite as civic-minded as us."

"No," she said, shaking her head. "I mean how'd they do it? How'd they cram them all under the bridge?"

Seeing the Big Picture
THEN

THE THIRD PUNK met my eyes and froze in midswing. I held his gaze, drained him until he dropped the baseball bat, then let my goggles snap shut. The little fuck fell over, twitched once, and whined like a hurt dog.

When my eyes first started to change, a few days after I got the blood transfusion from that creepy old woman in Greece, I thought it was kind of useless as superpowers went. Then I realized people couldn't fight me without looking at me. And that changed my view on things.

After stumbling into this night job about seven months ago, I had a solid routine down. Work at the agency by day. Grab dinner or hit the gym to work out, socialize a bit, and convince everyone I have a life outside work. Leave early because I say I'm working on a script, like half the people in town. Home to sleep until eleven. Patrol as Gorgon for four or five hours. Two-hour nap, and then back to work. Catch up on any lost sleep over the weekend, and be seen enough to keep people from wondering why Nikolai started wearing dark glasses for his sensitive eyes around the same time an optic-themed superhero appeared.

Of course, half a dozen comic-book types have appeared

all across the country these past few months, even some in Europe, and they're all a lot more interesting than me. Somebody flipped a switch and *wham*, superpowers are showing up everywhere. The Mighty Dragon was the first, but I think the morning after my first night out the big story was a man made of electricity in Boston. The Awesome Ape is in Chicago. Here in LA, in addition to the Dragon, there's some kind of monster terrorizing drug dealers in Venice Beach, and a dominatrix-ninja type cleaning up the Rampart district. Over in Beverly Hills there's an immortal guy who heals instantly from everything. Just the other night I heard about some kid down in Koreatown who's wearing a rainbow-striped karate uniform and bouncing around like a superball.

Wearing spandex or bright colors wasn't my thing, though. There's so much more practical stuff you can get when the agency you work for represents celebrities. The body armor? It's a gift for Colin—he's playing a SWAT cop and wants to get used to the weight. I know it's bending the rules, thanks so much. Reinforced leather duster? Hey, you-know-who has a weird fetish, what can I say. Storage locker under an assumed name? Ms. Lohan has some things she'd like to keep out of sight, but doesn't want to get rid of. Your discretion is appreciated, thanks. Custom motorcycle helmet? Military-style utility harness? Kevlar gauntlets? People hand you stuff so they can tell their friends someone famous touched it.

It was the end of my Christmas bonus and the start of my night job.

These three Seventeens were out for at least an hour. Stupid fucks, barely into high school and already throwing their lives away. I flipped them over and took their wallets. Then

I dragged them to a sign post and zip-tied them to it with their arms behind their backs. I took their driver's licenses and their cash (crime fighting isn't cheap).

"See this?" I growled. I held up the IDs. "I know who you are now. I know your names. I know where you live. In an hour I'll know your families, your dogs, your girlfriends. What I've done to you, I can do to all of them. And worse." The licenses vanished into a pouch on my belt.

Yeah, I stole the whole gag from *Fight Club*. Sue me. If I was that creative I really would be writing a script and I wouldn't have to finance all this with drug money.

The goggles were the hardest thing. I knew what I needed, but had no idea how to make them. Through a friend of a friend I found a retired prop-builder out in Van Nuys. Guy used to design and make stuff for all sorts of sci-fi films before everything went digital. I told him they were for a movie being shot somewhere in Hungary. He complained for half an hour about film jobs leaving Hollywood and then asked when I needed them by. He built the goggles from old camera irises and dark-mirrored sunglasses, and made three sets of them so I'd have spares. I got the blueprints and design notes, too, in case they needed to do on-set repairs. On the movie.

I walked back to my motorcycle and pulled a road flare from the saddlebags. It hit the ground a few feet from the punks, casting a flickering red light over everything. People ignore gunfights, screams, and drug deals, but for some reason everyone calls the cops if there's a flare burning in the street.

I gunned the engine, spun the bike around, and gave them one last flash, the goggles snapping open and shut just like a camera. Somebody told me the moment I make eye contact is a lot like getting hit in the back of the head with a baseball bat, just without the actual pain. Then comes the fear when you realize I've got you locked. When someone's in my sight, they can't blink or look away.

"Get out. You don't want me to catch you again." And I roared off in what I hope was a terrifying display of ice-cold bad-assery. It's worked so far. Half a year at the night job and I hear crime's down six percent in my territory.

Of course, that doesn't mean a lot. There's always two or three gangs fighting over this part of the city. Sometimes it's just tagging. Sometimes it's drive-bys. The City Council would brag in the papers that gangs and drug dealers and homeless people had been driven out of this neighborhood or that one. No one would ever discuss the fact they'd all just moved somewhere else.

So my goal wasn't to drive them out. It was to eliminate them. To make every current and potential member of the South Seventeens—a gang that proudly referred to themselves as "the SS"—run in terror at the sight of a green gang scarf or bandanna.

The bike shot down the street, slipping through intersections and around corners. I tried to cover as much ground as possible each night. The trick was to be seen as many places as possible, but never be moving so fast that people thought I wouldn't stop for something. There's a reason police cars seem to move at "hanging out" speed a lot.

I've also learned moving targets are harder to hit. There's a chip in my helmet where someone tried to blow my head off with a rifle. Knocked me off the bike, and that was when I learned my power can drain someone from a block and a half away.

I was on Pico when the sedan pulled in behind me. I got a good look at it in the mirrors. An old Caddy with a lot of power, a lot of seating room, and one dumb fuck sitting in the passenger window with a shotgun.

I gunned the throttle and pulled away. They picked up speed. Their car swerved a bit and I could hear them howling and laughing. Drunk or stoned to work up their courage.

A little more speed from the bike. A lot more from the Caddy. They were gaining fast. My timing needed to be pretty good for my next trick to work, but they were so wired I didn't think I needed to be perfect.

I let my speed drop and swung the bike to the left, heading for an alley a bit up ahead. The sedan swerved to cut me off, gunning its engine again, and I clamped hard on the brakes. The bike shrieked to a halt and spun around.

They oversteered and rushed past me. The guy in the window fired off a blast from the shotgun while one in the backseat shot a few rounds from a pistol. They were barely aiming and none of them came close.

They slammed into the corner of the building, right where the alley began.

Fifty-mile-an-hour impact with no airbags.

I pulled the bike up and let the goggles snap open. Didn't want to drain too much—all these idiots had hospital time ahead of them. Especially the shotgunner. He'd been thrown out and made a good-sized dent in a blue mailbox. I checked his pulse. His collarbone and left arm were shattered, but he was still alive, lucky fucker.

The driver moaned as I dragged him out the window. The steering wheel had slammed him pretty hard, fractured some ribs, and his face was cut up a bit from pieces of windshield. He cried and cursed in Spanish until the third time his head hit the trunk of the car. "I don't know nothing, bro," he spit out. "Leave me alone."

"You don't know nothing?" I repeated, denting the hood with his skull again. "You were looking for me, weren't you?"

"No, man, I swear." He tried to spin and knock my hand away, but he'd already seen my eyes. He was as strong as a ten-year-old and I had the energy of four people. I twisted him back and pressed his head against the trunk.

"Any second now I'm gonna get bored hitting your face on this car and we're gonna move to the sidewalk. You were looking for me?"

"Yeah," he nodded. "Yeah, we were."

"Was it Rodney? He still too chickenshit to fight me again?"

If my life as Gorgon was a comic book, Rodney Casares would be my archenemy. He would've been exposed to gamma rays, found an alien artifact, maybe teleported with a housefly or something. Then he'd get a costume, rob a few banks, try to take over the city once or twice. We'd fight a lot, he'd be foiled and get away at the last minute, all that nonsense.

Instead, here in the real world, he was what you'd think of as the top enforcer of the SS. They had some stupid title for him, but I made a point of not using it. He'd been in court once on murder charges, four or five on assault and battery. He hated my guts for draining his little brother while the stupid kid was out trying to earn his way into the gang with some small-time robbery and vandalism. Once his brother got out, the two of them came after me with a few other boys and I took out all of them. Rodney's tough, but he can't fight with his eyes shut. And there's not much better insult in that community than making someone look weak in front of family and friends.

The Seventeen's face shifted at the name and he grinned. "You don't know?"

"What?"

"Rodney's fuckin' out, bro. In the hospital. Probably dead already."

"Who was it?"

The driver shook his head. "Weren't no one, just some crazy bitch. Jumped on him outside the movies Friday night. She was all biting and shit. Ripped up his neck, chewed off one of his ears. Loco Tommy said she swallowed it."

"What happened to her?"

"What you think happened, man?" A weak hand came up and wiped away the blood pooling in his eyes. "Shot the bitch fuckin' stone cold. Word is she was so hopped up she took almost twenty rounds."

There'd been a piece on the news a few days ago of a woman with multiple gunshot wounds. Gang related. I never followed up on it until now.

One of the Seventeens in the back of the car groaned and fumbled his door open. I kicked it shut, slamming his head on the frame. He slumped back in his seat. The idiot on the trunk tried to leap up again, and this time I let the goggles stay open.

"So who sent you after me?"

He whimpered and his wide-open eyes watered up. I let the lenses close and shook him.

"Everyone," he whined.

"What?"

"Everyone's gunnin' to score on you." He managed a weak smile. "You're the guy who shamed Rodney. Take you out, that makes someone new top dog now that he's gone."

I flipped him over and pulled his wallet. We went through the spiel, I pocketed his license and the cash, and then knocked him out against the trunk. Ten minutes later him and his two buddies were zip-tied together in a ring, arms to feet. I fastened the shotgunner's unbroken arm to the mailbox and threw down a flare.

In the sudden burst of light, I saw something across the street. A woman up on the roof. Watching me.

My first thought was club girls. The hot, borderline-slutty ones who make a career out of being the girl everyone wants to dance with, buy drinks for, and take home—or at least out to your car. Some of them used to paint themselves with latex rather than wearing clothes.

The woman on the roof, her outfit was that tight and showed off that much. And she had a lot to show off. I say this as someone who deals with some of the hottest women on Earth every week as part of my day job. Black straps and belts crisscrossed her body, accenting her curves, a lot like the utility harness I wore. But mine was store-bought and I don't think there was a quarter inch of material in hers that didn't need to be there. Pushed back over her shoulders was a dusty, Middle Eastern–looking cloak with a wide, layered cowl. The black and gray stripes were urban camouflage.

The dominatrix-ninja.

One of the Seventeens moaned and I glanced away, just for a second. She was gone when I looked back.

I was tier three or so, enough that a two-story jump was just possible with a little effort. I took a running start, hit the center line of the street, and leaped.

I landed on the bleached tar paper of the roof. The goggles were open, draining anyone who caught sight of me, but there was no one. I looked behind some air vents and an access door. She'd vanished like some little ninja-stealth adept.

No big deal. All of the hero types must have been hearing about each other. I knew I was curious about the monster in Venice. The dominatrix had probably come down to this part of town looking for me. Maybe hoping she could be a sidekick or something.

My coat flapped in the wind as I dropped back down to street level. No time to play cat and mouse with another hero. If the fucking kid was right and there was a power vacuum in the SS, this part of LA was going to be hell on Earth by the end of the week.

Five

NOW

LOS FELIZ WAS northeast of Hollywood proper. With the trees, brick shops, and the two-screen movie marquee, it wasn't hard to pretend this section of the city was part of a small town somewhere.

Big Red trundled to a stop under the trees. The scavengers hopped off the truck and spread out to a practiced perimeter. The lift gate hissed down and Cerberus lumbered off onto the pavement. Lady Bee slid off the cab, landing with a *clack* of hard soles. She opened the jockey box under the truck and pulled out a bundle of canvas grocery bags.

"Everyone listening?" asked St. George. He nodded at Lynne. "Okay, for those who haven't done this often, and the rest of you who've heard them thirty or forty times—here are the rules. Groups of three. We check in every half hour. No one goes off alone. No one does anything alone, no matter what. You see something, you tell the rest of the group. You want to go look at something, go with the rest of your group. You need to piss, I hope you like company."

Jarvis squeezed off a round and dropped the overweight ex wandering out of the alley by the bookstore. The pallid woman fell face-first onto the sidewalk. They heard her nose snap on the pavement.

"And as Jarvis just pointed out," St. George added with a glare, "don't shoot unless you have to. The noise attracts them."

The salt-and-pepper man winced and lowered his rifle.

"If you hear a shot, or shots, don't panic. Don't run. That just gets people hurt. One of the easiest tricks to surviving out here is to walk. Use your brains, use your walkies, find out what's going on first. Don't run unless you know you need to run."

He looked at them until they all nodded their understanding.

"Okay, then. Ty, David, Billie, check those apartments up there. Mark, Bee, you take Lynne and search all the ones on this side. Andy, Jarvis, Lee, you've got ground-level shops. Luke and Ilya, stay with the truck. I'm going to mind this intersection here. Cerberus, that intersection up there is yours. Questions?"

"What about Barry?"

"Barry sleeps unless we need him."

Ty twisted a pair of canvas bags into a wide rope and yanked it through his gunbelt. "How long do you want to spend here?"

"I'm hoping we can do this block in two hours. Move east, then north. It'll let us hit most of these small shops."

"I think there's a Ralphs or Vons or something three blocks that way," Lynne said, nodding.

Cerberus shook her head with a faint whine of servos. "Grocery stores were the first things people hit," the titan said. "Assume anything with its own parking lot was looted at least a year ago."

"I'm hoping we can get all of this street and the block to the east done today," said St. George. "Sundown's at seven-twelve. Half-hour drive back. We should have the truck loaded and ready by six at the latest."

Billie slapped the tactical holster strapped to her thigh. "Let's do it."

× × ×

Mark banged on the stairwell door three times while Lady Bee pulled the fire extinguisher from its socket. Lynne watched behind them with her rifle ready. She nodded at the gray door. "Why do you pound on them again?"

He pushed the door open with his foot and waited. The stairwell was lit by random shafts of sunlight. "You haven't been out much, have you?"

"Not really. Too young before."

"Noise attracts exes, like St. George said," explained Bee. "Before you open anything—doors, closets, whatever—you make some noise. If there are any on the other side, they'll try to walk through the door to follow the sound and you can hear them."

Mark nodded. "Either that or they're far enough away you'll have time to shoot them." He stepped into the stairwell and gave a quick glance down and up. "Looks good. Down just leads to the emergency exit."

"Smells like shit in here," said Lynne.

"Lots of dead stuff in these places," said Bee.

"Exes?"

"A lot of it's just dead."

"Hey," said Mark, "more looking, less talking."

"Oh, you love it," said Bee. She leaned back and her eyes

and rifle followed the stairwell up. "What man wouldn't want a little time alone with two sexy singles?"

"One who knows there won't be enough time to enjoy them," he replied. He gave her a thumbs-up and she slid to the next landing.

"Body," she called. "It's down."

"Sure?"

"Yeah. Well eaten. Not enough left to move."

He gestured Lynne up the stairs and she joined Bee on the bloodstained landing. The corpse was a withered thing, a skeleton held together with strips of human jerky. Most of the fingers and toes were missing. A few scraps of stained cloth surrounded it. Lynne couldn't tell if it was a man or a woman.

Mark shuffled up behind them and swung around the small platform.

"Next flight looks good," Bee told him.

He gave her a nod and worked his way up to the next level. "Second floor," he called out. He banged three times on the door.

Lynne moved up the steps. "Exes are as stupid as everyone says, right?"

"Dumb as ants."

"So where'd the one go that ate this guy? Or woman. Whatever it was. It couldn't get out of here, right?"

The two scavengers glanced at each other. "Score one for the new kid," said Mark. He craned his neck over the railing and looked up and down.

"Anything?"

"Still nothing." He slid his bulky form up the next flight, his rifle aimed at the next landing. "Ahhhhh. Got a leak."

Bee gestured Lynne up the stairs.

Mark pointed out the dark streams crusted on the third-floor platform. He took a few more steps and peered across the landing. "Another body," he said. His free hand went up, back down, and traced a circle in the air. "Ex. It's down."

Lynne stood on her toes and leaned to see the body. "You sure?"

"Yep. Looks like it tried to go up to the fourth floor and fell straight over backward. Cracked its skull wide open."

"How?"

"Seen it before," said Bee. "A body can fall pretty hard when it doesn't try to stop itself."

"Back down to two," said Mark with a wave of his hand. "We've got a building to search and we're falling behind already."

× × ×

St. George jumped up as high as he could, crashing through the dried leaves of the trees. Staying focused on the small twist between his shoulders let him go up fifty feet, just a bit higher than most of the buildings. It still wasn't real flight, even with three years of practice.

He hung in the air for a moment, looking across the rooftops. There were a dozen solar panels the next block over. Some sun-bleached shirts and shorts on a jury-rigged clothesline. Three or four blocks away, a pair of exes pushed against the railing of a rooftop patio.

He sank back down and launched himself up again. The solar cells closest to him were cracked. They might not work.

The hero turned, his arms slicing through the air, and cast his eyes down Vermont. From up here he could see for miles, to the 10 freeway. If he focused a bit, he could see slow, staggering movement everywhere. Over five million exes in Los Angeles county, if Stealth's estimates were correct.

As he drifted toward the ground again, he saw the figure shuffling up the street. A dark-haired young woman in jeans and a T-shirt. She had one eye, and her left arm ended at the elbow. Something twisted and turned on the blacktop behind her.

He swung his legs and slipped forward, landing in the intersection past the trees. The ex swung its eye toward him and snapped its jaws while it stumbled forward. Its right arm hung back, its wrist connected to the small thing by a colorful cord. St. George saw the bright red Velcro and realized what the creature was dragging.

It was a child. Two years old at the most, leashed to the thing that had been its mother. Its clothes were tatters. Most of its face was raw and bloody from being dragged across countless miles of pavement, and he could see bone and teeth everywhere. The mother would come to a brief halt between steps, the dead child would roll and twist, and then be yanked off balance again as the larger ex shuffled on.

St. George's boots tapped against the road and the female ex raised its stumped arm to him. It strained to pull the other forward, and the dead child flailed on the ground. This close he could see the damp trail the small ex left as it was dragged.

The hero reached out and the woman closed her mouth on his fingers. It reminded him of a small puppy as it tried to bite, one without the strength to break the skin. The mindless jaws worked up and down and tried to gnaw through his stony skin. Its tongue was a coarse piece of ragged leather against his fingertips. A tooth fell out and clicked on the blacktop.

Ilya called to him from the truck. "Problem, boss?"

"No," he said with a glance over his shoulder. He braced his free hand on the ex's forehead and slid his digits free. Another tooth dropped. The dead woman pawed at his arm for a moment, like a kid dealing with a schoolyard bully, while he flicked the gummy saliva from his fingers. Then the heel of his palm chopped through the thing's spine, severing its head. The body collapsed and the head tumbled away.

The small ex—the child—was on its feet. It staggered at him on stumpy legs, gnashing milk teeth in its small mouth. He couldn't tell if it had been a little boy or a little girl. It stumbled past the headless corpse of its former mother, and its stubby fingers reached up for a hungry hug.

St. George sighed, drew his leg back, and drove his toes into the ex's chest. Thin bones cracked under his boot as the red leash snapped and the dead child was launched into the air. It soared up past the rooftops and crashed down a dozen blocks away in a splash of bone and meat.

He looked back at the truck and scraped the tip of his boot across the pavement. Ilya stood on the lift gate, looking back at him. "I hate the little ones," the hero said.

× × ×

One of the restaurant's big picture windows had been shattered. A body was draped over the sill. Its legs had been chewed down to gristly bones. Lee gave it two hard kicks to make sure it was dead.

The inside was messy, but not destroyed. A few chairs had been tipped, some glassware broken. Lee stomped his foot a few times and crouched to make sure nothing was hidden beneath the tables. Jarvis kept his rifle trained on the archway to the kitchen.

"Looks clear."

Andy slung his rifle over his shoulder and dragged the window-corpse into the restaurant. One leg fell apart as it bumped over the sill, dropping a few bones outside on the sidewalk. Jarvis blinked at him. "Whatcha doing?"

"Just showing a little respect for the dead," said Andy. "Figure it can't hurt." He laid the body out flat, dusted off his gloves, and crossed himself with his thin fingers.

"When you're done, grab all those salt-and-pepper shakers," said Lee. "And check the wait station."

"Yeah, whatever." Andy straightened up and grabbed the spices from the closest table.

Lee and Jarvis swung around the main counter, both rifles aimed low. Another body was sprawled in the narrow space, its face and torso eaten away. The floor was dark with old blood and old footprints. Jarvis kicked it in the foot. "Dead."

Something gleamed deep in the space beneath the cash register. Lee batted a few boxes aside under the counter to reveal a polished wooden stock. "Holy shit!"

"What's up?"

"Somebody wasn't getting robbed again, that's what I'm getting." Lee pulled the sawed-off shotgun out and set it across the counter. He dug around and produced two boxes of shells.

"Wow," said Andy. "Never struck me as that kind of neighborhood."

"Apparently no one told them," chuckled Jarvis.

Lee glanced into the kitchen. The back room was an open

space, split only by a rolling chrome table with a wire shelf on it. He saw a back door and a large freezer. "You want the kitchen, I'll play lookout?"

"You giving me the option?"

"Nope. Just being polite."

Lee pressed his back against the arch so he could see both rooms. Jarvis slipped past, keeping low. He reached out to tap the muzzle of his rifle on a shelf and the wire chimed and rattled. His finger tapped on the trigger guard five times before he moved to the back door. It was solid, with a heavy dead bolt locked into the frame.

"We're good," Jarvis said. He slung his rifle over his shoulder and checked the dusty shelves.

Lee turned his head back and saw that Andy had finished with the tables and was rooting through the small cubby of the wait station. A box of sugar packets dropped into his bag, along with more shakers.

In the kitchen, Jarvis tapped a large plastic bin with his foot. "This whole thing's flour. Still good, sealed up tight. Got an industrial-sized can of baking powder and some big spice jars, too. Haven't checked that first-aid kit or the fire extinguisher yet." He pointed at the steel cases mounted on the wall. "We've even got a cart."

"Nice. Call it in and let's get it out to the truck."

× × ×

Half a block behind Cerberus, *Big Red* rumbled to life and began inching up the street toward her. She brought all her sensors up to full and scanned the area. Looking north, east, and west, there were seven exes in range of her optics. The nearest one was three blocks away to the north, at Vermont and Franklin.

Another dead person stumbled out of an alley behind the 7-Eleven and into the street. It was just over a hundred feet away from the intersection where she stood sentry. The armor's targeters highlighted it and zoomed in.

It was a woman. Thirty, tops, when she changed. Long, brown-blond hair, pointed face, very thin. Her shirt sagged open to reveal a black bra and a trail of blood ran down her torso from her neck, accenting her tiny breasts. Her head hung at an odd angle, probably a broken neck, but her lips were still wet from a fresh kill.

Cerberus raised an arm, lining up a phantom weapon on the ex's skull. Despite the warning lights flashing in her visor, the armor still moved as if the massive M2 Brownings were mounted on it. It had been over a year since Stealth confiscated them, insisting the ammunition had to be saved for a real emergency.

The ex saw her move. Wiry arms creaked up, hands groping, and the shift in balance made it totter for a moment. Then its left foot shuffled forward and it staggered across the pavement.

If she still had her cannons, she could've turned its head into vapor. And the ex two and a half blocks north. Even the three she saw way up on top of the hill at Los Feliz, almost three-quarters of a mile away. She'd built the suit for that kind of accuracy. Five shots, five headless exes.

If she had her cannons. Like an amputee missing her limbs, her arms itched for them.

The grasping ex had covered half the ground between

them. It was working its jaws and the armor's mics picked up the *click-click-click* of teeth.

Without the cannons, all Cerberus had was up close and personal. She had to let the exes walk up to her, crowd her, claw at her as they tried to find a way past the armor. Even powered down, the suit was a match for undead fingers and teeth. But they'd try for hours and days and weeks because they didn't know they couldn't get through.

They had swarmed around her for two days that first time the power cell died. Thirty-one and a half hours in the armor as fifty exes pawed at her and groped her and stared with blind eyes. Thirty-one and a half hours before the Dragon and Zzzap found her.

The ex was less than ten feet away. Cerberus realized the woman wasn't wearing a black bra, but a whole lingerie ensemble under her clothes. A corset or merry widow or some such thing she'd never bothered to learn the name of. Its mouth was glossy with red lipstick.

"Someone had hopes for their last night." The towering battlesuit coughed out a grim laugh. "Guess you didn't get eaten the way you wanted, eh?"

She reached out and set one armored gauntlet on the ex's shoulder. The other one came down on its blond head, the huge fingers wrapping around it. Her wrists flexed, the ex's skull came away from its crooked neck with a sound like dry wood, and the body slumped to the ground.

Cerberus held the blond head out at arm's length, letting the black fluid leak out of it while it snapped its jaws at her. When it stopped draining, she tossed it down the road. Her targeting software tracked every bounce, turn, and spin.

"All clear," she called out over her radio. "Bring it around the corner."

× × ×

David pushed the apartment door open with his foot and counted to five. He stomped his foot a few times, then counted to five again. Rifle up, he led them into the third apartment. Billie was right behind him with her shotgun, and Ty brought up the rear after double-checking the hall-way was clear.

They looked around the corner to the kitchen. Billie banged on the bathroom door a few times, and Ty did the same with the bedroom.

Something thudded against the bedroom door.

"Got one," he called.

"I'm at the door," said David.

"Got your back," said Billie. She raised the shotgun.

Ty kicked the door hard and felt it slap the dead weight when the latch popped. He hit it again and it banged open. The ex was an older man with a Hawaiian shirt. Black pants and striped boxers gathered at its ankles. It stumbled back for a moment and then wiggled toward them.

"Oh, jeez," Billie said, biting back a laugh. She pointed to the nightstand where a pair of dentures sat in a glass of cloudy water. "It's toothless."

Ty put his rifle out at arm's length and braced the barrel against its forehead. The stocking feet shuffled out from under it and the ex tilted back to crash against the floor. As it twisted he walked over and put a round through its temple. The corpse went limp.

Cerberus barked from their walkies. "Who fired?"

"It's Ty. We had one ex. It's down."

"Copy that."

David's voice echoed from the living room. "We clear now?"

His partners nodded. "Clear," agreed Ty. He glanced from the ex to Billie. "Poor bastard died getting dressed."

"Bad enough being the living dead." She smirked and held her fist out to him. "If I come back, promise me you'll get my pants on."

He rapped her knuckles. "We'll see."

She yanked open the bathroom drawers with her free hand. Ty went back to the kitchen and pulled open the first set of cabinets. "Score!" he crowed. "First one opened, not even trying." He leaned from the kitchen and held out half a bottle of Captain Morgan rum.

"Nice."

"Whatcha got?" asked Billie from the bathroom.

"Booze," said David.

"Sweet. Epsom salts are medicine, right?"

"Yep," said David. "Grab it."

"Couple cans of soup," said Ty, "some ramen, half a box of Bisquick. Not much else." He held up the half-filled canvas bag.

David looked at the box. "Can Bisquick go bad?"

"I don't know. The date's still good."

× × ×

St. George twisted another bolt out of the concrete. The rust and paint made them slip a lot, but if he squeezed hard enough he could work them loose. It got high enough to get his fingers under and he yanked it free of the rooftop. The last solar panel shuddered for a moment as he tossed the bolt over by the air vent.

He paused for a quick glance down below. The street was still clear. Ilya was strapping down the panel that had come down ten minutes earlier. *Big Red* had seven of them so far, wedged in alongside scavenged bins and boxes.

The hero attacked the last bolt and a minute later the solar panel swung backward like a drunk. "Ready with the next one," he shouted. "You clear down there?"

"Ready and waiting," called Ilya. He pulled the ratchet strap he was working on tight, swung his rifle a little farther behind his back, and shot a thumbs-up toward the rooftop.

The hero hefted the panel in both hands and hopped off the rooftop. He soared down to the truck bed, Ilya grabbed the panel for balance, and they set it down. Barry shifted on his pile of blankets and muttered in their general direction.

"Two more up on the next roof," said St. George.

Ilya nodded. "Any idea who's getting these?"

He shook his head. "I think one of the East Central stages. I'm sure Stealth has it planned out."

"'Course she does." Ilya stretched another ratchet strap out and hooked it to a support.

St. George looked out at the street. "Still good?"

"Yeah. Nothing for four or five blocks."

Jarvis and Andy walked up to the truck, each holding a cardboard box packed with cans while Lee covered them. "Looks like somebody's granddad planned for World War Three," he said. "A bunch of Korean War stuff and there's at least two more loads of stuff like this in the duplex over there. A few cases of thirty-aught, too."

"You guys are just finding all the fun stuff today," said Ilya.

St. George flipped a can of turkey chili in his hand and slotted it back into the case. "Any sign of what happened to Grandpa?"

Andy shook his head while they slid the boxes to the back

of the truck. "Back door's off its hinges," he said, "some blood by the garage. No bodies. Either they ate every inch of him or he walked away."

"One way or another," added Lee.

"Get it all," said the hero, "but take your time. He might be wandering around there somewhere."

"Him and a couple thousand others," coughed Jarvis.

"All the more reason to be careful," said St. George. He glanced at his watch. "I'd love to finish this block today."

"We can do it," said Lee. The three men tossed out waves and salutes and marched back to the duplex.

The hero kicked off the lift gate and flew back up to the roof.

× × ×

"Last apartment on this floor," said Lady Bee. She set her swollen shopping bag down and banged on the door.

Lynne clutched her rifle. "So, that was them killing an ex?"

Mark nodded. "You find them stuck in bedrooms, bathrooms, stuff like that," he said. "They don't know how to work a doorknob, so they just get stuck in places. I've seen a lot in closets. Some people just crawled in there to hide and croaked."

"They don't feel anything," Bee said. "No brain activity, no feelings, no nothing. They're just walking corpses. Clear," she said to Mark.

He gave the door three hard kicks and the dead bolt ripped out of the frame. He stared into the dim apartment for three Mississippis and then moved in. It was packed with dusty IKEA furniture and pillows. "Avon calling," he yelled out.

"That stopped being funny before I was born," said Bee, adding a gentle kick to his ass as she slid past to the kitchen.

"That will *never* stop being funny," he assured her. "Lynne, watch her back. I've got the door."

They banged on the small closet and discovered a plastic garbage can filled with ooze and mold. "Kitchen's clear," said Bee. She looked at Lynne. "Bedrooms and bathroom next."

They tapped on doors. The bedroom was just as filled as the living room. The bathroom was barren, with faded black towels. A dark shower curtain fluttered near the open window and a swinging cord tapped out Morse code on the sill. "I think I remember this bathroom from a catalog," said Lynne.

Bee gave her a wink. "Now's your big chance to own it."

"Yeah, no thanks," Lynne said. She turned back to the medicine cabinet and an ex fell through the shower curtain.

It was a naked, swollen woman, Mexican or Indian, with folds of gray fat hanging off it. The dead thing stumbled over the edge of the tub, knocking Lynne down with its sheer mass and bouncing off the sink to fall on top of her. She screamed and got her arms up in time to block its neck and keep its mouth away from her. The teeth clacked together again and again, showering Lynne with flecks of ivory as its hair swept her face. The meaty hands reached down to paw her.

"Fucker!" Bee turned back. "Mark!!"

"Get it off me!! Help!!"

They'd fallen halfway through the door, and the ex's bulk blocked the entrance. Mark lunged in, leaping over the writhing corpse to the bathroom counter and down behind it. He wrapped his thick arm around the ex's neck and heaved. The ex lifted another few inches and Lynne thrashed and flailed and kicked her way out from under it into the hall.

"Bee!"

"Hold it still!"

The ex's neck popped as it twisted its head back. The jaws opened wide and it sank its teeth into Mark's forearm, gnawing at the heavy sleeve. The fabric darkened around its brittle lips. He howled and let it fall.

Lady Bee slammed her pistol into the back of its skull. She fired three rounds and it flopped on the carpet.

Mark fell over the corpse, clutching at his bloody arm. "I feel sick."

Six

NOW

ST. GEORGE LOOKED up from Vermont at the sound of shots. Ilya did the same from the back of the truck. Cerberus echoed on his earpiece, "Who fired?"

There was a long pause.

"Who fired?"

Lee, Andy, and Jarvis wheeled a cart full of supplies across the street. They stopped and looked around.

Above them a window smashed open. "Here!" Lynne shouted, waving an arm.

St. George threw himself into the air.

× × ×

The last shards of glass fell from the window as he soared through. "What happened?"

Lynne had pulled some hydrogen peroxide from her bag and emptied the brown bottle over his arm. "It was on her," Mark said through gritted teeth. "Broke its own neck to bite me."

"Stay calm," said Lady Bee. She slapped the side of his head. "If you work yourself up it'll spread faster."

Lynne tore the wet sleeve away from the bite. The shirt had taken a lot of it, but there were still bloody trenches gouged out of his forearm. The flesh was getting pale.

Mark saw the fading skin. "Oh shit," he muttered. "Shit shit sh—"

Lady Bee glanced at the hero. "We've got to do it."

St. George was already leaning out the remains of the window. "BARRY!"

× × ×

In the back of the truck, Barry's eyes snapped open, then clenched shut. He reached down into himself, found the trigger fused into his DNA, and flipped it.

Everything went white.

The blankets beneath him burst into flame as his clothing incinerated.

Arcs of raw power spat and twisted out to every metal surface. Ilya felt his skin burn and blister and threw himself off the lift gate. He blocked his eyes as *Big Red*'s paint seared off down to the metal and the wooden planks lining the truck bed scorched black. Two of the solar panels flared and burst.

A second sun shot into the air.

× × ×

The wall crumbled to ash as the blazing wraith passed through it. The shadows fled the room. "Bite," said St. George. "Left arm."

Zzzap nodded. *Understood. Do you have him?*

Lynne's eyes were wide and wet. "What are you doing?"

St. George grabbed Mark by the shoulders and pushed

him flat on the floor. Lady Bee grabbed his wrist and stretched the arm out straight.

"What are you doing?!" Lynne tried to pull St. George away. He shoved her back against the wall with one hand.

Sorry, man, buzzed Zzzap. *This is going to hurt like hell.*

Mark gritted his teeth, squeezed his eyes shut, and nodded.

The gleaming outline dropped its hand. The fingers swung down and passed through the man's biceps. There was a hiss, a puff of smoke, and Lady Bee fell back clutching the arm. Mark screamed while a scent like burnt barbeque filled the room.

Bee tossed the arm. One of her gloves came off and she crammed it in the amputated man's mouth. "Bite down," she told him. "Bite and try to calm down." She wrapped her arms around him.

There was a crackle of static as St. George keyed his walkie. "We've got a bite, everyone. Whatever you've got, get it to the truck. We're done and we're moving out in five minutes." He looked at Zzzap. "Get back to the Mount. Tell Connolly we've got wounded coming in."

On it.

× × ×

Big Red roared south on Vermont.

They stretched Mark out on the panel above the cab, strapping him down for safety. Lady Bee perched by his feet. Jarvis crouched next to him with a wet bandanna and tapped the man's cauterized stump. "Hey, stay awake."

"I'm awake," Mark hissed through gritted teeth. Sweat beaded across his face. "Give me another shot of the rum."

"Top five celebrity kills. Who were they?"

He held the bottle in his shaky left hand and took two awkward swallows. "Paula Abdul. Charlie Sheen. Frasier. Whatshername . . . the Asian cylon from *Battlestar Galactica*." His eyes fluttered.

"Hey!" Jarvis grabbed the bottle and shook him. "Come on, you got to stay with me. That's only four."

Mark blinked a few times. "Number one," he said. "I got Trebek."

"What? You're lying."

"Nah."

"You're delusional," said Jarvis. He wiped his friend's forehead.

Mark shook his head and coughed.

St. George swung up from the running boards. "How's he doing?"

"Serious shock," said Lady Bee. "Some blood loss. He's burning up. Not a hundred percent sure Zzzap took the arm in time."

"He's going to be fine," said St. George. "We'll be home in less than ten minutes. Barry's already there letting them know what happened."

Big Red swung hard at the intersection to add emphasis.

Lynne's knuckles were white on her rifle. "Why didn't she just shoot it?"

Cerberus looked down at her. "They're full of disease. You were under it. If she killed it and any of the fluids got on you, you'd be the one dying right now."

She winced. "Is he dying? Are you sure?"

The armored titan shrugged. "Probably."

"STOP!!"

Lady Bee pounded her hand on the cab's roof.

Luke slammed the brake to the floor and wrenched up the emergency brake. *Big Red* squealed on the pavement, leaving a trail of black rubber. Jarvis threw himself over Mark and pinned the wounded man down. Cerberus staggered. Bee pitched forward off the roof of the cab and St. George grabbed her as he lunged through the air.

Both front tires exploded. The truck dropped, stumbled forward, and the rear dually tires blew out. *Big Red* lurched a few more feet, limp wheels slapping the pavement, and came to rest just past the intersection of Melrose and New Hampshire.

"Son of a BITCH!" bellowed Luke. He pounded the steering wheel and threw open the door.

St. George set Bee down on the ground. "Thanks for the catch," she said.

He nodded. "Everyone okay? How's Mark?"

There were nods and thumbs-up.

Luke examined the tire. "Ruined," he muttered. "No patching these."

St. George poked the oversized wheel. "Don't suppose you've got six spares hidden away somewhere?"

"Yeah, just let me pull those out of my ass." Luke drove his boot into the sagging tire.

Cerberus glanced down the road. "How far are we from the Mount?"

"Little over a mile. Too far to walk before dark," said Lady Bee. "A bunch of blowouts and a nice, high-pitched brake squeal on a quiet evening. Every ex for six or seven blocks is going to be headed this way."

"Any guess how many that is?"

She shrugged and held her walkie up in the air. "Five, maybe six hundred. We're still too far to get a walkie signal."

"We're being jammed," boomed the titan. "There's something broadcasting wide-spectrum white noise nearby."

Andy and Lee were behind the truck, sweeping the road with their feet while the other riders covered them. Something on the ground clinked and Lee bent down. "Shit," he said. "Boss, come take a look at this."

"Good eyes, Bee," said Andy.

It was a thick chain, the size used for trailer hitches and fences. A pair of nails were welded across each link, a line of spikes stretched across the road. The chain was spray painted black, and a few old newspapers completed the camouflage.

"Jammed and crippled," muttered Andy. "That sounds like a trap to me."

"Worse," said Lee. "A trap someone set since we drove by earlier."

Ty looked around. "Seventeens?"

"Well, it ain't the exes," said Lee.

Lynne gripped her rifle. "So what the hell's the point of this?"

"We get left out here," said Luke with another glare at *Big Red*'s ruined tires. "Best-case scenario, from their point of view, we stay here, the exes kill us all, and they get half a truckload of supplies come morning. Worst case, we run away, the exes kill some of us, and they get half a truckload of supplies come morning."

"Why not kill us and take everything?"

St. George yanked the chain and ripped a post from the far side of the road. "I don't think they've got anything that can take out Cerberus," he said, "and I don't think there is anything that can hurt Barry once he's up. Better to just do the damage and let the world do the rest."

Lynne looked at the truck. "Won't they lose it all, then?"

Lee shook his head. "Exes won't eat supplies. Someone can just come by tomorrow, deal with whoever of us might survive the night, and help themselves to everything here."

"Everyone is surviving," snapped St. George. "We've got to get everyone out of here first. All the supplies second. Someone needs to go back and get one of the other trucks."

Cerberus shook the ground as she leaped from the back of the truck. "Someone meaning you," she growled. Her voice buzzed when she pitched it low.

"If you've got some jet boots you've been hiding from us, now's the time."

"I can hoof it with no risk."

"And I can fly it a hundred times faster."

"Why don't we wait for Zzzap?" asked Ty. "He's coming back, right? And he's faster than either of you."

"We don't know when he'll come back," said St. George. "He wasn't planning on it. As far as he knows, we'll be showing up at the gate in fifteen minutes. Maybe another five minutes of waiting before he'll come check. So he's here in twenty, back there by twenty-five, and the other truck doesn't get ready and get out here for another half hour after that. I can shave twenty minutes off that if I leave now."

Lynne coughed. "You mean . . . if you leave us? Out here?"

"It's the only way. I can get away from the jammer, use the radio, and be there to help them get another truck out. Cerberus will be with you."

The young woman shook. "But . . . but Lady Bee said there were hundreds of exes coming."

Bee rolled her eyes. "Maybe—"

"We can't fight that many. You're leaving us out here to die."

"You're not going to die. You'll be in the truck. They can't get you."

"Then why are you leaving? Let's all just wait in the truck!"

"You don't have anything to be scared of. They can't hurt you in the truck."

"They can't hurt YOU!" Lynne was breathing fast. "You're not scared because you can't be hurt, but they'll rip us apart."

"Honey," said Jarvis. "Relax for a minute."

She whirled on him. "How am I supposed to—"

He snapped his head forward, cracking her in the skull. She dropped into his arms.

"What the fuck!?" said Luke.

"There's a certain art to that," Jarvis said, rubbing his salt-and-pepper scalp with his free hand. "She'll be out for ten or fifteen minutes."

"What were you thinking?"

He nodded down the street. "I was thinking the sun's setting and I want to get home more'n I want to argue about how we do it. If all y'all want a piece of me once we're back, you're more'n welcome."

"I don't like it," muttered Cerberus, "but I agree with him."

St. George nodded. "You got anything?"

The armored titan panned her gaze around them. "Lots of movement. Nothing too close. Nothing warm. We're the only living people within two blocks. Can't find the damned jammer."

"Three coming up from the south," called Bee. "Two from the west." She cocked her rifle, and Andy echoed the sound with his own.

Jarvis hefted Lynne's limp form up to Lee and Ty. They climbed into *Big Red*'s back and the lift gate hissed up. St.

George stripped off his heavy leather jacket. "I'll be quick." He tossed the coat into *Big Red*'s cab.

"You'd better," said Cerberus.

"As soon as I'm there I can send Barry back out. He'll keep you charged until we get another truck here." His utility belt followed the coat into the backseat. He took a deep breath and a few running steps away from the truck.

The air hissed, the darkness fled, and Zzzap hovered above them.

Hey, he buzzed. *Not interrupting anything, am I?*

St. George staggered to a clumsy stop. "Bastard."

Saw this cloud when I was running to the Mount and thought I should head back to check it out.

Ty squinted at the gleaming outline. "What cloud?"

"He sees radio waves," said Cerberus.

Hey, did you guys know there's a signal jammer in that car over there?

Power to the People

THEN

FLYING WAS NEVER any different for me. Most people don't realize when I'm in the energy state I can't touch anything, so I'm just in the air all the time. That's my whole life. I'm either in a wheelchair or I can fly.

A woman called me this afternoon. She didn't say her name, but I was pretty sure then it was the one they call Stealth. I have no idea how she got my cell number. Hell, she called me Barry and knew I was at home. There was some sort of contagion in Los Angeles, and she needed me to help keep tabs on it. Being able to fly at just over Mach five was her main interest in me (despite what's been said in *Time*, *People*, and on that Learning Channel special, my top speed is nowhere near the speed of light). The fact that my energy state was immune to all diseases was an afterthought.

It took me half an hour to get to Los Angeles from Amherst. She was waiting on the roof of the Capitol Records building, a nice easy landmark, like she promised.

Apparently one thing she didn't know is what that outfit of hers does to men. Or if she did know she didn't care. If it was any tighter I could tell if she shaved her legs or not. Dear

God, I could actually see her nipples through that suit and I'd swear all the belts and straps were placed to accent her boobs and hips.

She gave me the lowdown on what I was looking for. People with pale skin, a lack of coordination and language skills, high resistance to damage, and a degree of aggression. Some of them might smell like rotted meat.

I have no sense of smell when I am Zzzap.

Sounds like you've got a zombie problem, I said, wondering what her curves would look like when she laughed.

She didn't laugh. I know sometimes people have trouble understanding me when I speak in the energy state. Jerry told me it sounds like I'm gargling a beehive. I didn't think that was the problem here, though.

So, how many have you seen so far?

Stealth unfolded a map. She pointed to three small crosses, scattered across the city.

Three? That's it?

"In a city with the population density of Los Angeles, an aggressive disease can spread to thousands of people within hours. I have seen three people who are infected. There is no telling how many are carriers that have not manifested symptoms yet."

Jesus.

"Do you know Los Angeles at all?"

Not really, but I'm good with landmarks.

She held the map out for me. "Study this. I need you to spend the next six hours scouring the city as many times as you can. Every street, every alley, every cul-de-sac." She pointed at one section. "Watch the Hollywood Hills. There are several canyons and hidden streets."

In the eight months since I became Zzzap I'd gotten very good at memorizing things. Not being able to hold a notepad or Post-it made it a necessity. I gave her a nod after studying the map for five minutes. *Why isn't the CDC involved in this?*

"At the moment, they believe this is a hoax. All three victims were inanimate by the time they were examined."

Dead?

Again, no answer. She was one stony bitch. She folded the map and it vanished into her cloak. "Can you do it?"

The first time might take me a few hours. I'll pick up speed as I learn the city.

"Proceed. I will meet you back here in six hours." She shook her cloak back around herself, doing a piss-poor job of hiding her curves, and walked away. God, if I didn't know better I'd swear all those urban-camo lines actually enhanced her ass somehow.

Moving low to the ground through a strange city, the best speed I could manage was around four hundred miles per hour. Much more than that causes serious weather problems, not to mention sonic booms (which can shatter windows, windshields, neon signs, and lots of other expensive things). I started circling the buildings, checking every person I passed for the signs of infection.

Alleys. Roads. Parking structures. Subways. Anywhere people could be. I peered in windows where I could, through walls where I couldn't. On my first pass, I'd say I saw three-fifths of the city's population. No sign of the mystery disease, although I did stop two muggings and halted a high-speed street race by melting the tires of both cars. I figured I could make at least one more pass before it was time to meet up with Stealth again, and hopefully I could catch a good chunk of the rest.

Street. Boulevard. Avenue. Drive. I was an hour into my second run when I saw him.

He was an old guy. His clothes were dark and a bit ragged. Probably homeless, staggering down an alley. His skin was the color of ash and his face was blank. Not emotionless, it just looked like he'd forgotten how to make any sort of expression. A quick check at either end of the street told me we were just north of Beverly between La Brea and Detroit.

I zipped back to hover over him, and a full minute passed before he twisted his head up to look at me. It usually doesn't take people long to notice the white-hot man-shape sizzling like a sparkler.

His eyes were cloudy. I thought he might be blind. He was staring right at me and not blinking. Something looked very wrong about him, and I couldn't figure out what.

Good evening, citizen, I said, careful to enunciate each word. *Are you okay?*

Still wide-eyed. Still no blink. Had I seen him blink once yet?

Sir? Are you feeling okay? Do you need any help?

His mouth opened, showing off an impressive collection of half-rotted teeth, and then he clacked them together again and again and again. It sounded like those little wooden things Mexican dancers wear on their hands.

A fun little trick the magazines and television shows never figured out. I can see all the electromagnetic energy in the air, including radio waves, television broadcasts, and satellite transmissions. I knew there were seventeen GPS devices within three blocks of me, and I could tell you the codes for each one. And if I had to, with a little concentration, I could duplicate them or override them.

Which is why it had been second nature to see the cell

phone built into Stealth's cowl and memorize the number. Focus on that and I could feel the signal a phone would translate into an audible ring.

"Who is this?"

"It's me, Zzzap."

"You do not sound like him."

"I'm transmitting to your phone. You're hearing my voice as I hear it, not how you do."

"Where did we first meet?"

"On top of the Capitol Records building a few hours ago. Listen, I think I've got one of your infected people here."

"Where are you?"

I described the alley and she said she'd be there in six minutes before hanging up. The old man was reaching up for me, his hands clawing at the air. It reminded me of a mission I'd visited in Brazil, and all the people who thought I was some kind of angel or something.

I settled down a few yards from him, inches above the ground. *Sir, there's a chance you may have a contagious disease*, I said. *Someone's coming to help you, but I need you to stay here.*

As soon as I landed he began to shuffle toward me, his arms still out. I flitted back and let off a gentle burst of light and heat, just enough to be felt. His teeth were still chattering.

It's dangerous to touch me, sir. You should keep your distance. Then I remembered what Stealth had said about language and damage. He probably hadn't felt the heat or understood me.

More clicking came from behind me. It was an older woman in tattered layers, showing all the infection signs. She was five yards away, also reaching for me. As I glanced at her I realized why she and the old man looked so wrong to my eyes.

Like I mentioned, I can see the whole spectrum. I try to limit myself so I don't get overwhelmed, but there's a bunch of stuff I just always notice, like infrared. Neither of them was warm. They looked weird because they were at room temperature—or alley temperature—blending into the surrounding brick and pavement. Also, normal people have an electromagnetic halo, and on both of them it was just a dim glow.

That's why I hadn't noticed the woman until she made a noise. I didn't see her because, in my eyes, she didn't look like a person. Hell, how many others had I missed while I was flying around the city? And how were these people still walking when they were corpse-cold?

Of course, it only took a few moments for all this to go through my mind, but it distracted me. Long enough that the man tried to grab my arm and sink his teeth into my biceps. Or what passed as a biceps.

A lot of my friends are physicists, which is how I got a handle on the Zzzap thing when it happened to me. When I'm in the energy state I have no physical form. I'm just a big ball of raging electromagnetic energy given shape and motion by my force of will and consciousness. In simpler terms, although it's not as accurate, I'm a very tiny G-class star that can think. Jerry thinks if it was possible for me to fall asleep in this state, I'd just lose cohesion and explode like a bomb.

End result, as I mentioned, I am dangerous to touch.

His hand charred to the bone in less than a second. There was a horrible crack as his teeth overheated, boiled inside, and shattered. A whole mouthful of teeth bursting apart at once—there's a sound you don't forget too soon. I leaped away from him, sent out a 911 signal, and tried to survey the damage.

The old man was burned. His mouth was ruined, just a burned-bacon hole in his face filled with bone shards and dark blood. And he didn't seem to notice. What was left of his jaw was still moving up and down. He and the woman had their arms up, reaching for me, as if neither of them had just seen the damage touching me could do.

What the fuck had Stealth pulled me into?

At the end of the alley a young guy in black yanked his Goth girlfriend in from the sidewalk and up against the wall. She swore at him and wrapped her legs over his hips. They didn't even notice me. Or the two infected people. Nothing like a quick dry hump between clubs.

The old woman was facing them. She lowered her arms away from me and started stumbling in their direction. As she passed the old man, he turned and shuffled after her. They were slow, great-grandmother slow, but I was between them and the couple in the blink of an eye.

I let the light and heat flare up around me, and heard the two kids gasp. The homeless people kept shuffling forward. The woman's teeth chattered like she was freezing to death.

Stay back, I said. *Medical help is on the way.*

Behind me I heard the Goth couple scamper away.

They kept lumbering toward me. I flew up and behind them. They followed, twisting their heads and arms so far they almost fell over. I'd seen this behavior before. Creature Double Feature out of Boston. Late-night movies on the Sci-Fi Channel.

Okay, enough's enough, I shouted. *I want you both down on the ground now!* I raised my hand and let the energy build. Sparks shot off my fingertips, and I knew looking at my palm was like looking at the sun. The shadows in the alley vanished. They didn't blink. I don't think I'd seen them blink yet.

Get down! This is your last warning.

The man banged his ruined teeth together with a noise like crunching glass.

In front of my hand the air superheated and did a trick everyone else on Earth needs a supercollider and a magnetic bottle to pull off. An arc of raw plasma scorched its way through the alley, a millimeter wide but igniting everything within four or five times that range. It could burn through concrete like the proverbial hot knife through butter, so searing the old man's thigh to the bone was no challenge at all. I lost it, and if this had been a normal man, I would've killed him, or crippled him for life at best.

As it was, he didn't notice. His stagger swung a little to the left, but he kept moving toward me. I don't know why I thought a leg burn would slow him down when having his teeth and tongue burnt out of his mouth hadn't.

They still hadn't blinked. Their eyes were dull and gray. I think they might've been blind. I still don't know to this day.

But right then, I knew what they were. I'd said it to Stealth as a joke, but here they were right in front of me. No joke, no gag, no doubt what these people had turned into. I didn't know how, but it was useless to deny it.

My fingers flexed again. The air boiled, night turned to day, and the man's head vanished in a cloud of fine ash. It was so fast his body stood there for a moment with nothing above the shoulders but a cauterized stump. And then it collapsed with steam drifting from the neck and leg.

The woman opened her jaws wide and brought her teeth together with a solid clack.

I heard the repeating bang, saw the heat spike, traced both bullets as they streaked down the alley and smashed their way into the old woman's head. Her face collapsed in on itself like a balloon. She dropped like a sack.

Stealth swung herself off her motorcycle and holstered the pistol. "Are these the only ones you have seen?"

What the hell is this?

She ignored me and checked both bodies. "We do not have time to waste. Are these the only ones you have seen?"

They were zombies! I shouted. *Real live zombies!*

"By definition," she said, "they are not alive."

But where did they—

"Are there any more?!"

I took a mental breath and tried to calm down. *I don't know.*

"You were looking, correct?"

I was looking for sick people, I snapped back. *I don't see things the way you do. To my eyes, they don't look alive, they look like furniture. So, yeah, there's a good chance I overlooked them if they weren't moving or making noise like these were.*

She mulled on this for a moment. "Can you identify them now?"

It's going to be a lot harder. It'll take more time.

"Proceed. Now that you know, kill any you find as quickly as possible. Destroying the brain appears to be the only sure way." She walked back to the bike. Her hips swaying under that cloak didn't seem quite as alluring.

There's nothing we can do for them?

She shook her head. "They are dead. It is a virus making muscles twitch in a corpse. Nothing more."

You're sure? What about Regenerator?

"He tried." She straddled the motorcycle and the engine growled. "You can reach me the same way if there are further problems."

She roared out of the alley. I shot into the sky and burned a path through the air back to square one.

Eight

NOW

ZZZAP CHARGED CERBERUS back up to full power while St. George crushed the jammer. Fifteen seconds after that Zzzap was back at the Mount telling the gate sentries to get a rescue mission together.

In the back of the truck, the scavengers lined the walls on either side, rifles ready. Lee and Ty stood on plastic milk crates, looking over the raised lift gate. St. George stood below them, a few feet out from Big Red's trailer hitch, his leather coat buckled tight. "We just need to last maybe half an hour until the other truck gets out here," said the hero. "Take your time and call your shots. It's not a contest and you don't want to waste ammo you'll need later. If anything gets within ten feet of *Big Red*, Cerberus and I'll take care of it, so no pistols."

The armored titan stood in front of the truck and flexed her fingers again and again while she stared at the setting sun. Lady Bee stayed on top of the cab as a spotter and to watch Mark.

Jarvis perched on the truck's hood. He looked down Melrose and called out "Military guy." He squeezed off a shot and a few yards out a buzz-cut ex in filthy digital camos spun, fell to its knees, and slapped its face against the sidewalk.

"Baldy," said Andy with a squeeze of his trigger. An ex threw its head back and dropped between the long shadows.

"Yellow shirt," called Ilya.

"Biker," added Ty.

They called off quick descriptions for a few minutes, and the exes dropped. "More from all directions," said Bee. "They're hearing the shots."

Lee turned to look at the sunset. He held up a hand and squinted at his fingers with one eye. "We've got maybe five minutes of sunlight left," he said. "Probably twenty until dark."

"They'll be here in twenty," said Cerberus.

Billie aimed her rifle. "Female cop."

Luke lifted his head from his scope. "Boss," he called to the back of the truck, "we got three, maybe four dead guys coming down from the north. Look like SWAT, maybe. Armored heads."

St. George glanced up at Lee and Ty. "You guys got the rear?"

They nodded, and the hero launched himself to the north.

A quartet of former cops. Ex-cops, he thought with a smile. Their eyes were pale behind dusty visors, and their dark uniforms almost hid the gore staining them. One was missing an arm, another had a twisted leg. They all had nametags, he realized as he dropped out of the sky and their black-gloved hands reached for him.

He wrenched the arm of the first one, Davis, and shoved it into a sergeant named Hale or Hall. The tag was too bloodstained to be sure. The impact sent both exes sprawling and

St. George turned to a dead man who had been named Webster. He grabbed the officer's helmet and twisted it halfway around. There was a crack, and he twisted it the rest of the way just to be sure. Webster fell to the pavement.

The last one grabbed him from behind and sank its teeth into his shoulder. He heard some of them crack. It gnawed on the leather while he reached up, grabbed the back of its neck, and flipped it over him onto the sprawled Davis and Hale-or-Hall.

He twisted their heads one by one. The last man had been named Carabas. St. George piled the bodies up in the center of the street and tried to ignore the chattering teeth. Did they know each other, he wondered, or work together? Or was it just coincidence to find them all here?

Luke shouted from the truck. "Nice work, boss."

The hero added two or three more bodies to the pile and then leaped back to the truck without another look. "How are we doing?"

"Peachy-keen," said Ty. "Schoolgirl." His rifle kicked and another ex fell.

A large mob stumbled toward the front of the truck, teeth chattering, and Bee and Jarvis took turns dropping them. "Hey," said the bearded man. He pointed at an ex shuffling out of the shadows toward them. "Is that Sandra Oh?"

Servos whined as Cerberus glanced at him. "Who?"

"That one there." He flicked his thumb against his rifle and a red dot appeared on one of the exes, an Asian woman with tangled hair. "Is that Sandra Oh?"

"I don't think so," said Bee, lining up another shot. "Denim shirt." Her rifle made a chopping noise as the ex stiffened and fell.

"Who the hell is Sandra Oh?"

"From *Grey's Anatomy*," said Jarvis. "The bitchy Asian woman."

The titan shook her head. "I never watched much television."

"Did you see *Sideways*?"

"I just said I don't watch television."

"It was a movie."

"Shoot the damned thing!"

"If it's a celebrity I want the points."

Cerberus thumped forward and drove her steel fist into the ex's face. The skull crumpled with a noise like a bag of chips and the creature cartwheeled back into the shadows. "Points are for the wall," she growled. The other fist backhanded a dead woman in an LAPD uniform, sending her flying into the side of a building across the street. "This is survival. Get back to shooting."

"Bitch in blue," he muttered.

She glared down at him and the ex fell as his round burst its head.

× × ×

In the back of the truck, Lynne groaned and pushed herself up onto her elbows. "What the fuck?" She touched her nose and the fingers came back spotted red. She flinched as another volley of rounds went off. "What's going on?"

"We didn't have time to argue," said Lee. "Still don't. Grab your rifle and get up here." He pulled the empty mag from his own weapon and slapped in a fresh one.

She wiped blood from her nose and grabbed the gleaming M-1 lying next to her. She checked the magazine and looked out at the dozens of exes stumbling toward *Big Red*. "I'm going to kick that jackass in the nuts when we get home."

"He offered to let you, if it makes you feel better. Black coveralls."

"Wifebeater," called Billie.

Something flared like the dawn far down Melrose Avenue. "I think I see Zzzap," said Bee. "He's on his way back."

The light pulsed twice and flared again. And then, echoing down the empty road, they heard reports over the endless clicking of teeth.

"Shit," said Jarvis. "Is that gunfire?"

"That's a *lot* of gunfire," corrected Ilya.

"Exes?"

Billie shook her head. "That's not just us. Somebody's shooting back."

St. George came bounding over the truck. He tapped the bead on his headset. "Melrose gate, you there?"

The radio hissed.

"Melrose gate, this is the Dragon at *Big Red*, do you copy?" More static.

Cerberus glanced at him as she lifted an ex by the neck. "Another jammer?"

"It'd make sense." He kicked an ex away and Jarvis put a round through its skull.

There was another surge of light and radios around the truck squawked. "*Big Red*, this is Melrose," a voice buzzed over the walkies. "You guys still out there?"

Cerberus hurled her ex through the windshield of a car as St. George keyed his mic. "Here. That you, Derek?"

"They're coming to you. ETA twelve minutes."

"Copy that," St. George said. He glanced over his shoulder and saw Lady Bee give a thumbs-up. "What's all the noise?"

"Seventeens. Got a little ahead of themselves. If the gate had been open all the way they'd've had us."

"Everything okay?"

There was a crackle of static. "Gorgon was waiting for them."

"Right at the gate?"

"Yep. He's feeling pretty amped right now."

"How?"

"Stealth told us it was a diversion, you getting stuck out there. We caught a half dozen. The others are on the run. Zzzap's keeping after them. How are you holding up?"

St. George planted his foot against another ex and sent it flying. He looked back at the truck again and the scavengers gave a variety of signals. He added up fists and fingers. "A third of our ammo's gone. Immediate threat of two hundred exes. We've still got one man down and he . . ."

He glanced up at Mark's slumped form and Lady Bee shook her head.

"He's not doing any better," finished the hero, "let's say that."

"Copy," said Derek's voice. "You should see their head-lights soon."

St. George took a breath and leaped back over the truck, coming down on top of an old Asian woman in a flowered blouse. He grabbed her by the hair and tossed her down the street into a chalk-skinned security guard.

The exes were a crowd now. A swarm of dozens on each side, all shuffling toward the crippled truck. The night echoed with countless clicking teeth and dragging limbs.

"Concert T-shirt," called Ilya.

"Hippie-girl," said Lee.

"Doctor," shouted Lynne. She had to reload and yelped when the M1's breech snapped on her thumb.

Cerberus grabbed two exes and smashed their skulls together. She let the headless corpses drop and brought her fist down like a sledgehammer on a man in a tattered business suit. She kicked the bodies away and they tripped another handful of exes as they spun across the pavement. Lady Bee and Jarvis made sure none of the fallen got back up.

"Boss!" shouted Luke. "A little help."

St. George stepped to the passenger side and a trio of exes fell on him. A teenage girl in a Jack in the Box uniform threw her arms on the hero and tried to sink her teeth into his neck. Another wrapped its arms around his shoulders as he twisted, tried to bite his scalp, and ended up gnawing a mouthful of hair it couldn't tear loose. The last one, a child, clung to his leg like a leech and chewed at the back of his knee.

He glanced up at Luke. "Watch the lift gate for me."

"Got it."

He waded a few yards away from the truck, dragging the exes with him. He worked his hands between himself and the teenager as she gnashed at his throat, felt a tooth drop from her mouth, felt her withered breasts under his palms, and shoved. She flew back and vanished into the night. Between gunshots he heard something in the distance hit the ground and crack.

His fingers closed on the child's neck. Two yanks shook the thing off his leg, and he held it at arm's length to look at it for a moment. It was caked in blood and gore. He hurled it at a shuffling dead man and watched them both fly back into a tree just off the road. They twitched for a moment, trying to move with shattered spines.

Another ex lumbered toward him, a heavy bald man with

a dark goatee. There were two bullet holes in his shirt. St. George tried to step forward and the ex swallowing his hair tugged him off balance.

"Son of a bitch," he muttered. He whipped his neck forward and felt his hair slide free to slap against his back.

The goateed ex raised its arms, clacked its teeth together twice, and its left eye vanished in a spray of black blood. It dropped to the ground.

"Thanks," St. George shouted.

"No worries," yelled Billie from the truck. "Priest."

St. George drove his hand into the hair-eater's throat and felt the bones shatter. He held the dead thing by its limp neck and swung it, knocking down two more exes. A backhand throw landed it on top of the wiggling pile under the tree.

"Headlights," bellowed Cerberus. She pointed at the faint glow past the overpass.

"About fucking time," growled Ty, lining up a shot. "Military-wannabe."

"Everyone get ready to move," said St. George as he walked back to *Big Red*. "All your gear, all the supplies we found, anything that rides in the truck. We leave nothing. Not a piece of rope, not a Band-Aid, nothing."

The rescue truck was *Big Blue*, a cobbled-together twin of their own vehicle. It surged up over the hill, engine growling, and crushed the exes beneath its tires. The men in its bed added their weapons to the hail of gunfire knocking down exes.

"Marines," howled Ilya, "we are leaving!"

Big Blue squealed to a halt a few yards away. "Somebody call for a lift?" shouted the driver. Johnny K leaned out the window and grinned at them. "Load up."

Luke bounded over the cab, sliding down next to Jarvis. "Gate to gate," he yelled. "We've got wounded and supplies. There're too many exes to walk it."

Johnny K nodded and threw his vehicle back into gear. *Big Blue* swung into position near St. George and the hero lowered both lift gates to create a walkway between the truck beds. The scavengers dragged bags and crates across. Lady Bee and Ty carried Mark.

Luke slid into *Big Red*'s cab through the window and started handing things out. Fire extinguishers. First aid. Ammo boxes. Flares. Jarvis and Lee ferried them to the other truck. Luke crawled out, clutching a police radio to his chest. "We're clear," he shouted to the armored titan.

Cerberus crushed a skull in her palm and nodded. She batted a few away and pushed through the swarm. They clawed at the armor and chipped their teeth on the metal plates. She trudged forward, dragging them with her as they filled her screens.

"Drop the gate," shouted St. George. He batted exes away, clearing a path for the battlesuit. Jarvis, Lee, and Lynne fired into the crowd while the others stabbed down with their pikes.

Cerberus swung her arms, shaking off the undead, and the pikes knocked them away. St. George peeled them from her, hurling them into the swarm. Bodies vanished beneath the shambling horde.

She stomped onto the metal lift gate and Luke flipped the switch, raising her up with a whine of hydraulics. "Hop on," he yelled to St. George.

The hero cracked an ex across the jaw and shook his head. "I'll slow the lift. Get her on board."

"Damn it, boss—"

"Give me a pike!"

Someone tossed the flagpole down to him and he swung it like a bat, cracking half a dozen exes in the skull. He pulled back and swung again, knocking down another handful before the shaft cracked. He rammed the broken pike through an ex's skull and kicked the corpse away.

Cerberus stepped up onto the bed of *Big Blue* and the lift gate gasped with relief. Luke toggled the switch and the metal plate swung up to block them in. "All aboard," he hollered.

Johnny K gunned his engine and brought the truck around, crushing exes as it made a wide turn.

Dozens of hands pawed at St. George, grabbed his clothes, his hair, his limbs. He lashed out, felt them fall even as new hands reached for him. They pinned him with sheer numbers and he felt a swarm of teeth across his body.

This would be a good end, he thought. Overwhelmed saving my team. A good way to be remembered.

There was a roar of automatic fire and skulls exploded around him. Bullets slapped his head and shoulders like hailstones. His sunglasses shattered and his headset twisted into plastic scrap. The weapons barked again and exes sprayed blood and meat over him as they slumped and fell.

In the back of *Big Blue*, Lady Bee stood with Jarvis, Luke, and Ilya. Their weapons coughed up smoke. Jarvis dropped his empty magazine and reloaded.

St. George wiped gore from his face. The rounds had cleared a wide arc around him. "What the fuck are you doing?!"

"You're bulletproof," shouted Bee with a grin. "Stop whining and get in the truck."

He landed next to the stripe-haired woman. "You just wasted a ton of ammo."

"Maybe we just wanted an excuse to shoot you," said Ilya with a smile.

"Thanks."

"No worries, boss."

Nine

NOW

THE PIPE CLANGED down across the gate, and the dead resumed their eternal grasping though the bars. The clatter of their teeth trembled in the air.

St. George stood and watched them. *Big Blue* was getting unloaded behind him. Lynne had just punched Jarvis hard in the back of the head. Mark was already halfway to the hospital.

"She wants to see you," said Gorgon. "First thing."

"I'm covered in shit," the other hero said without looking away. "Infected blood. Rotted meat. I think some actual shit."

"Yeah, I noticed."

St. George studied one ex, a rough-bearded man caked with as much dirt as blood. It had a gold tooth that flashed every time its jaw snapped shut. "What happened with the Seventeens?"

Gorgon shrugged. "About fifty. I just got up on the wall and dropped half of those imbeciles."

"So you're feeling pretty good."

"Better than I have in ages." He cracked his knuckles. "Tier five, easy. Want to go a few rounds?"

"I want to burn these clothes. And then get in the shower until sometime tomorrow."

"She said first thing," echoed Derek from the guard shack. He sighed and spat a stream of fire at the ground.

× × ×

It was a five-minute walk to "city hall." He could've made it in one good leap from Melrose, but he wasn't in the mood to rush. Instead he shrugged out of his jacket and tried to wipe some of the gore from it.

The building was named Roddenberry, after the man who created *Star Trek*. Like most of the newer structures in the Mount, it had been built without any consideration for what was around it. The lines and windows belonged on a college campus, not wedged between warehouselike workshops and the old water tower.

The elevators worked, but the stairs took more time and he could tell himself he was going easy on Barry. His boots echoed in the empty stairwell.

Stealth had claimed the entire executive fourth floor as her own. Most people in the Mount thought it was a status thing. St. George knew it was because it was central, had the best sight lines, and was already wired for mass communication. She wasn't the type who cared about status.

He rapped on a polished door and walked in. There was a large table people once sat at and discussed syndicated television shows and DVD box sets. Now all the chairs were gone and it was covered with maps and reports from across the lot. She'd moved over two dozen screens into the room, showing every street and every entrance into the Mount. She kept the curtains pulled, and the lights were dim if they were ever on.

Somewhere up here, past the low-profile door at the far end of the room, was a small suite where she lived. Or at least, where she slept, ate, and showered. The office of some high-end producer who just wanted his own full, private bathroom and a place to take a nap. St. George had never seen it, and only knew it was there because she'd let it slip once seven months ago. He knew it pissed her off to think she'd admitted to any sort of need or weakness.

"You smell horrible."

Stealth stood in the shadow of the open door behind him. As always, she wore her full uniform, even the mask. Her face was a tight, black surface of vague features, hidden even further by the shapeless charcoal hood shrouding her head. As far as St. George knew, no one had ever seen her face.

"You told Gorgon you wanted to see me first thing," he said. "So I'm here wearing four or five liquefied exes."

"You could have showered."

"That's not how they heard it."

She stood an inch or two shorter than him, but her cloak and hood made it hard to be sure how much. They wrapped her like a flimsy toga, barely disguising her figure. Her charcoal and gray uniform could've been body paint. "Would you prefer to clean up and speak later?"

"Are you actually offering me a choice?"

She stared at him for a long moment. "No," she said, "but I know you like to feel you have one."

He smirked. "What happened with the Seventeens?"

"You first, please. Mark Larsen. How was he attacked?"

"Just bad luck. An ex stuck in a shower. They didn't see it or hear it until it was on top of a rookie."

"Lynne Vines?"

"Yeah. Mark tried to pull it off her. It broke its own neck to bite him."

"Nothing they could have done differently?"

"Not as I understand it."

"Is he going to live?"

St. George looked at his boots. "I wouldn't put money on it, but anything's possible."

She nodded. "Now, the trap."

"Not much to tell. They knew we'd be heading back that way. They dropped a jammer and a spiked chain across the road." He described every detail he could remember about the road, the time, even the chain itself. She prodded him now and then. He talked about waiting for the ride and killing the exes.

"So you were protecting yourselves for twenty-five minutes and then your team fired several bursts on full auto to save you."

"I didn't need saving."

"They thought you did and acted accordingly, that is what matters. How much ammunition?"

"All together?" He ran some numbers through his head. "Three-fifty, maybe four hundred rounds."

"The truck?"

"It's a landmark right now. Needs all-new tires, possibly new wheels. If we can get a crew there in the morning before the Seventeens strip it, it should be salvageable."

Beneath the mask her face shifted. She pushed back the hood a few inches and pressed slim fingers against her temples, turning her eyes up to the ceiling and pushing her chest out ever so slightly. After a year and a half, St. George could talk to her without his eyes straying when she struck a pose. When they strayed now, it was a deliberate choice.

"Tell me it was worth it."

He leaned against the table. "We got around four hundred pounds of food. A third of that's a big bin of wheat flour. Some basic medicine and first-aid stuff. Lee and Andy found a shotgun with about thirty shells and a bunch of 30.08." His fingers did a quick drum roll on the table. "We only had two-thirds of our usual time."

"I understand."

"So what happened here?"

"They attempted to rush the gate. I counted twenty-three of them."

"Gorgon said fifty."

"Gorgon enjoys a degree of exaggeration where his own exploits are concerned."

St. George almost made the laugh sound like a cough. "What gave it away? That we were a decoy?"

"Your situation made no tactical sense," she said. She tapped her maps, running a finger down the same stretch of Vermont he'd been on earlier. "If they knew what was or was not in your truck, they either would have attacked when you were farther away from the Mount or not at all. If they did not know, it was foolish to set a trap at all since they know you go out with almost every mission, often with another hero. Since theft was not the motive, the next would have been just what they accomplished—leaving you, Cerberus, and Zzzap stranded."

"Getting us out of the way for an attack," he mused. "You are amazing, my dear Holmes."

Stealth pointed to a section of the map south of Century City, making a slow circle with her finger where she had marked several streets and blocks with green ink. "They are becoming more aggressive and frequent in their attacks. We may need to take offensive measures."

"You mean, go after them?"

"I mean locating and eliminating them."

He furrowed his brow. "In what sense?"

"In the sense of eliminating them."

"We're not killers," he said. "We sure as hell can't be saving mankind if we go out and murder a couple hundred of them."

"By my estimates the Seventeens have grown well into the thousands," she said. "And unlike our group, they are mostly fighters."

"That doesn't matter."

"It will."

He slammed his hand down on the map and felt the table crack. "We aren't going to stoop to that," he said. "We're the good guys. The idea is to save everyone, not just the people we like."

There was a flurry of movement on one of the monitors. Van Ness Gate. A small ex, a boy, had squeezed through the barricade of trucks, and was staggering toward the gate guards. They tripped it with a pole and pinned it down with their rifle stocks. A woman ran into frame with a sledge and crushed the little skull.

St. George and Stealth watched in silence as they wrapped the small figure in plastic and started hosing down the pavement.

"If that is your feeling on the matter," she said, "we can proceed in that direction for now. You know I value your opinions."

The hero let out a breath and twin trails of smoke curled up from his nose. "A year and a half ago I was doing maintenance at UCLA," he said. He stared at the map, at the dozens of green crosses and lines south of Wilshire. "You see movies where society collapses this quick and you just laugh it off. You figure there's the police, the military, the feds . . . I mean, they couldn't all lose it at once, right?"

Stealth looked at him. Even through the mask, he could feel her skeptical stare. "They did."

"But not everyone loses it at the same moment," he insisted. "You'd think people would've helped each other, tried to hold on to things."

"Do you remember Katrina?"

He tossed the name back and forth. "Which one? We've lost two or three, I think."

"Hurricane Katrina," said Stealth, "which decimated New Orleans in 2005. The levees collapsed, brought the floods, and what happened? No one came to help and the city fell into chaos in mere days. Looting. Gangs. Militias. There were hundreds of thousands of citizens who had spent years believing their government did not care about them and were now seeing the proof of it. Then the same government that left them to drown for a week came in, imposed martial law, and ordered them all into what were essentially concentration camps without food or water."

He shook his head. "Yeah, but that was—"

"And now the dead are walking," she said. "Exes, zombies, ghouls—whatever you wish to call them. There were epidemic warnings and hazmat teams everywhere, dead people getting up to attack their friends. The police could not stop them. The military could not stop them. We could not stop them." She ran a finger across the zip codes of Los Angeles.

"If people in one city reacted as they did to rising water, is it a surprise things collapsed during a worldwide crisis like this?"

He took a slow breath and set his jaw.

She turned back to the monitors. "Is there anything else to report?"

"No."

"Go take a shower."

He glanced across the room at the low-profile door. Her head tilted beneath her hood.

"Go *home* and take a shower," she said.

× × ×

St. George cleaned his hair, then scoured his body, then cleaned his hair again. Even through the steam and the soap, he could smell death. He scrubbed and shampooed and rinsed and repeated until the hot water ran out, and then stood in the cold for another ten minutes.

His apartment in the Mount was a penthouse compared to the place he'd had before, back when the world was alive and he was paying rent. Like most of the living quarters, it was a large office converted into a passable apartment. A living room with a couch and an overstuffed chair, a decent kitchen, and a separate bedroom. He even had some of his own clothes and belongings, not just stuff he'd scavenged since they all moved to the Mount. Being a superhero had a few perks, even after the Zombocalypse. He'd been able to fly home and loot his small studio.

He was half dressed when someone rapped on the door. He knew the knock.

"Hey," said Lady Bee. She held up a battered box of Cheez-Its. "Thought I'd stop by and check on you. And I brought food."

"Thanks."

"You looked like shit when we got back."

"Well," he said with a smirk, "there have been one or two missions when things went better."

She let her coat slide off her shoulders. She was still wearing the too-small shirt. He could see her bright red bra. "You going to invite me in?"

He examined his bare feet. "I don't think I'm in the mood, Bee."

"You know you say that almost every time, right?"

"I'm serious."

"I know."

"People trusted me to get them home safe."

"I know. I was holding his arm, remember?"

He sighed and stepped away from the door. She tossed her coat on the chair before flopping on the couch. "You want some crackers?"

"Not that hungry. Go ahead."

She unzipped her boots and kicked them at the door. "Nah. They're one of those weird flavors nobody ever liked." She stood up, two inches shorter without the heels. "Want to watch a movie or something?"

"I don't have anything new."

"So what? We never see more than the first half hour anyway." She pulled his face down and kissed him.

He pulled away. "How am I supposed to relax?"

"Well," Bee said, "usually we take off our clothes, find a handy piece of furniture, and spend half an hour or so thinking very naughty and improper thoughts." She tugged at the bottom of her shirt and two buttons popped open. She gave him a wink and pulled at another one.

"Seriously." He ran his fingers through his long hair. "This was a fucking disaster. What are people going to think?"

She sighed and let go of the shirt. "They're going to think you're human."

"I'm not human. I can't be."

"Trust me, I've checked. You match up. Just a lot more stamina."

"We're symbols. All of the heroes. People look at us and think we can still fix everything."

"You're a symbol, yes," she said. "But you're still a guy. A guy who just had a very shitty day and needs to remember there's more to life than that. If you want to mope all night, fine, that's your choice. We'll eat stale Cheez-Its and watch a movie and not talk. Personally, I'd like to get over today with a hard, fast fuck, maybe followed by a long, slow one."

"I'm still not sure I'm in the mood."

She yanked the shirt open the rest of the way. The red bra was low-cut and edged with little satin frills. "Give me five minutes and I can change your mind."

"Bee . . ."

"Two minutes if you let me take your pants off," she said and ran her tongue across the edge of her upper lip. "If you like, I could even wear a cape and a black pillowcase over my head."

"Cute."

"You're not saying no, though."

Bee pushed him back into the chair and climbed on top of him. He could feel things stirring in his pants, despite himself, and he pushed his palms up along her warm, smooth back. "You realize we'll be up all night," he said as she kissed his neck. "Exhausted all day tomorrow."

"We'd better be if you know what's good for you."

She pressed herself against him, he grabbed her, and they forgot the day.

Subtle Beauty

THEN

SWAT SERGEANT HALL considered telling me to leave, or perhaps something more emphatic. I could see it in his eyes. If he could see my face, I am sure he would have nodded and ignored everything I said, even though I had saved his life on two separate occasions. The mask over my face is a relief. It covers my eyes, nose, cheeks, and lips. It hides my curse and makes discussions such as this one easier.

I have become known as Stealth, although it is not a name of my choosing. I believe some people consider it a "sexy" name appropriate for a female hero. I am, in fact, a beautiful woman and have been all my life. It has never made a difference to me, and I have made no special efforts or arrangements to either preserve or enhance my looks, but I have been reminded of this fact by every man I have ever met and several women as well. In that sense, beauty has become like a rash I cannot rid myself of, but is not worth the effort of removing by some drastic measure.

"You cannot reason with them," I told Hall again. "They cannot be intimidated by displays of force or numbers. Your men must begin aggressive measures if you hope to hold them back."

"And by aggressive you mean killing them?" He glanced back at the wall of riot vehicles waiting to move out. In the distance we could hear the loudspeaker warnings and faint cries. "I can't order my men to fire on sick civilians."

"If it helps you and your men, by any possible definition the infected are already dead. As the president said in his address, they are ex-humans, no longer alive." I gave a slow nod from my position on the wall. A quick-release carabiner on a drainpipe created the illusion I was clinging to the bricks above him, yet another sleight of hand to give me power and authority. "Do not attempt shots to cripple or immobilize. They will have no effect. Only decapitation or destruction of the brain."

He shook his head. "I don't need to hear more of this zombie-movie bullshit."

"It is the most effective method."

"Great. Maybe next we can try fighting them with the Force."

One of the other SWAT officers shouted above the din. "Snipers have movement three blocks south. A group of infected coming this way." They looked to Hall for a decision.

I understood bad decisions. As a junior in high school I participated in three successive beauty pageants: Teen California, Teen USA, and Teen Universe. The Teen Universe was the one I was interested in because it came with a full scholarship to the college of my choice. Winning the other two were merely requirements in reaching that goal. In retrospect, this chain of decisions may have been the worst mistake of my life.

My eyes met his again. "I understand your frustration, Sergeant Hall, but we are running out of time. The chances of containing this outbreak are already low."

"Do you know what'll happen if we start shooting at civilians?"

"I have an excellent idea of what will happen if you do not."

He shook his head. "The CDC will be here in—"

"They will not come," I told him. "There have been major outbreaks on the East Coast around Washington. All resources are being focused there. It is up to you and your men to contain this here. I will give you all the help I can."

Another call came from the vehicles. As Hall turned, I reached back, released the carabiner, and swung to the left. The trick to moving swiftly while climbing is using your arms and minimizing your legs. I slid around the corner and up.

Sergeant Hall was right-handed, which meant he favored his right side overall. I had chosen my "crouching" position on the wall beforehand, and it allowed me a quick exit to his left. When he turned back from the armored barricades, his eyes first passed through all the space I had occupied. When something vanishes from sight, human nature is to look side to side first, then up. Since his head was already moving left, he would turn his eyes back to the right, giving me a few seconds to complete my "disappearance" and add to the illusion.

Not all my power is sleight of hand. I graduated class valedictorian with eight new school records in track and field. I had also broken most of the weightlifting records, but this was overlooked because my school did not have a women's weightlifting team. Despite being offered full scholarships to both MIT and Yale, my guidance counselor, Mr. Passili, suggested I might want to use my pageant prizes to attend one of the "easier" colleges "better suited to a young woman like yourself."

Neither he nor the school pressed assault charges, although I was told years later it was still apparent his nose had been broken. My first semester at MIT I made Dean's List with a perfect 4.0. I sent a copy of my grades to Mr. Passili, but never got a response.

There was a police sniper on the far corner of the rooftop, but he was too busy watching the streets to notice my arrival. I moved to the southeast corner and dropped to a lower building. Two more rooftops led me to the alley where my motorcycle waited. I landed on the seat, cut down Cahuenga, and headed across town on Sunset.

I passed eleven infected in three blocks and shot each of them in the forehead. At Sunset and Las Palmas I stopped to put another round in the ear of a gray-skinned boy with a bloody mouth.

I was revising my estimates. Perhaps things had spread too far. Most civilians were following instructions and staying indoors, although some went too late. Stories were already circulating of the unlucky people who locked themselves in with infected family members who turned hours later. There was also a bothersome number who insisted on going out to fight the infected on their own. The majority of them were being killed, and a fair number became carriers themselves. If it spread any farther, a safe zone would need to be established.

Several other "superheroes" had joined in the attempts to hold back the contagion. Regenerator, Banzai, and Gorgon were trying to keep order at the emergency shelters and field hospitals. Blockbuster, Midknight, and Cairax were holding the west side. Zzzap was attempting to fight on both coasts, but I knew the constant travel was taxing him. The armed forces had deployed a prototype exoskeleton, heavily armed and armored, in Washington, D.C., to help with containment, although I believed it was a publicity stunt to boost morale rather than a serious stratagem. The Dragon was, at my suggestion, fighting the exes directly since he was one of the few who could. I was worried he was beginning to develop some kind of feelings toward me.

In college I took several lovers, both male and female. It sprung from a desire for experimentation, although not in the way most college relationships are labeled. As I had suspected, sex turned out to be a fleeting diversion with no real rewards. Even more annoying, my skill as a partner was often judged on my appearance and not on any other abilities or aspects I brought to the arrangement. It was through these experiments I realized my beauty would always be my defining trait, no matter what a given situation required.

Over junior and senior year's winter and summer breaks I was offered jobs modeling for Victoria's Secret and Abercrombie & Fitch. I took them all and appeared in eleven different catalogs and two in-store ad campaigns. The money paid for two years of masters studies, where I wrote a groundbreaking thesis on DNA fragment tracking and identification. Despite complete faculty backing, no journal would publish a scientific paper written by a twenty-two-year-old underwear model. Twenty-two rejections. By sheer coincidence, that year I was also ranked number twenty-two on *Maxim*'s "Hot 100 List," between Elisha Cuthbert and Cameron Diaz.

I have double doctorates in biochemistry and biology, with further studies in psychology, anthropology, and structural engineering. I wrote a book on memory structures and mnemonic devices explaining how anyone could improve their recall by at least threefold. It sold fewer than four thousand copies and now can only be found in remaindered bookstores with a "70% Off" sticker. By contrast, a paparazzi photo of me posing on a runway at Cannes was downloaded over twenty-three million times because my top slipped and there is a clear view of my left nipple.

I knew I had the physical prowess and skills to have a direct, positive effect on the city of Los Angeles. If people were willing to see me only as an object, however, then I would oblige and operate outside the judicial system as an unnamed thing.

My last civilian appearance was on an episode of *Jeopardy!* at the age of twenty-six. I won seven episodes in a row by runaways before I became bored and stopped trying. I was the longest-running female contestant the show had ever had. That money, $570,400, financed my uniform and equipment.

A quartet of exes stumbled into view on Las Palmas drawn out by the noise of gunfire. Three women and a man. They had fresh blood on their mouths. I gunned the bike's engine, spun the rear around, and headed toward them. A fifth and sixth wandered out of the narrow space between buildings. I came to a halt a dozen yards from them. With both weapons firing, it took three seconds to eliminate all of them.

While I listened for signs of trouble, I reloaded. Both of my Glocks are the 18C military variant with the extended magazine, but it was not an evening to be caught low on ammunition. I carried four spare magazines in my harness, plus the two in the pistols. There were an additional two hundred rounds in the cycle's saddlebag. I had used a quarter of my ammunition in ninety minutes of patrolling.

Another ten minutes and twenty-three more kills brought me to La Cienega. A major intersection. A police car sat near the sidewalk, three of its four doors hanging open, the front crumpled against a Ford truck. Skid marks indicated the driver had hit the brakes, tried to swerve, and crashed.

There were fourteen bodies surrounding the vehicle. I could see one dead officer on the pavement by the driver's-side door. A Mossberg police shotgun lay a few feet from his left hand. The others had been exes. Besides the fatal head shots, they each had a collection of bullet wounds in their arms and chests. One had the curling wires of a Taser trailing from his stomach.

I heard a moan from the far side of the car.

The other officer, a woman, was bleeding. She had dark hair, the bulk of a bulletproof vest under her shirt, and a set of pins and tags identifying her as ten-year veteran Officer Altman. Her left arm had been bitten several times. Two fingers were missing from that hand, along with part of a third, and she had made a rough bandage from a bandanna. Her right ankle was soaked with blood. Her left cheek hung open. She was crying. She was still alive.

"How long since you were bitten?"

She jumped and tried to raise her gun before she saw me. "Oh, thank God," she said.

"How long? If it has been less than two hours there is a slim chance you can be saved." Even as I said this, though, I took note of the paleness of her skin by the wounds. She was sweating and her eyes were having trouble focusing.

Altman shook her head. "They overwhelmed us. We tried the Taser, warning shots. They just kept coming."

"You have been told not to waste time with such measures," I said. "The only way to stop them is to kill them."

Her eyes hardened for a moment and she glared at me. "They're still people."

"They are not. That is why your partner is dead and you have a day at best. Have you radioed for assistance?"

She shook her head. "One of them bit through my microphone cord. I can't reach the car radio."

I walked around the car and closed doors until I reached her partner. He twitched twice and I put a round through the base of his neck. Altman cried out at the sound. At this range, the vertebrae exploded. The twitches stopped.

"The car is still secure. I can leave you here until help arrives, or you can attempt to drive."

"You're not staying?"

"No." I lifted her to her feet.

"Fuck you."

"There are too many exes at large. The next twenty-four hours will decide if Los Angeles can be contained or if it will be lost. That outweighs the needs of one police officer who ignored the order to make kill shots."

Altman settled into the driver's seat and dragged her legs into the car. I pulled her partner's sidearm, his spare ammunition, and retrieved the Mossberg. "It may be several hours before help can reach you," I told her. "You will need to defend yourself until then. Do you have food and water?"

She snorted back a laugh. "What, like a box of donuts?"

"A first-aid kit?"

She nodded.

"Use whatever antibiotic agents you have in it. It may give you extra time."

"You really think I've got a chance?"

"It is difficult to say. There have been some cases of recovery, if the victim receives immediate medical care."

"How soon is immediate?"

I paused. "The attacks happened in a hospital."

"Yeah, that's what I thought."

I ordered her to lock the doors and left her. If she did die, she would be trapped in the vehicle. As I walked back to the motorcycle I shot two women, each wearing a House of Blues staff shirt. The bike roared back to life and I resumed my path across Sunset.

In one of the earlier Sherlock Holmes mysteries, Arthur Conan Doyle (not yet a Sir) made an observation on logical deduction. When you have eliminated the impossible, whatever remains, however improbable, must be the truth.

There is, however, a specific flaw in that maxim. It assumes people can recognize the difference between what is impossible and what they *believe* is impossible.

The ex-humans have been appearing for twelve weeks now. Three months since the first known sighting. They have been captured, studied, and killed. There are warning posters, public service announcements, and news reports. Yet people still cling to the impossibility of the living dead even as it looms over them, attacks their homes, and devours their neighbors. Soldiers, police, and private citizens force themselves to believe the exes are just infected with some curable disease, despite all the evidence, and will not take the necessary steps. They will not accept the truth. They will not act on it.

The outbreak will not be contained. It is too late.

The world as we know it is over.

Eleven
NOW

THE THIRD-FLOOR conference room in Zukor hadn't been touched when the building was refitted as a hospital. The table was a glossy black slab surrounded by overpriced, high-backed chairs. Stealth sat at the head of the table with a casually dressed St. George to her right, Gorgon to her left in his usual body armor and duster. A handful of civilians filled the other seats, residential leaders from across the Mount and their staffs. At the far end, Doctor Connolly stood by a large flatscreen TV, tapping her laptop while comparing last-minute notes with Josh.

Stealth leaned closer to St. George. "Who did you send out?"

"Luke with three mechanics, plus twelve guards," he said. "Cerberus is backing them up."

"They left at sunrise," added Gorgon. "The gate's staying in constant contact. They reached *Big Red* twenty minutes ago. No sign of the SS, no other traps. They'd just gotten the first tire done when I walked in."

Connolly nodded to Stealth and the room grew quiet. "I know you've gotten regular updates," she said, "so some of this may seem like old news to you. I just want to go over everything, because we need to change a lot of preconceived notions we've had until now.

"We know it's viral. A virus that mimics leukocytes—white blood cells—in appearance, so a visual check of the blood will miss it most of the time. We know it's highly infectious. It's not airborne, only passed by contact with bodily fluids, but it can survive a very long time outside a host while still in an active state. So a dead ex, stained clothes, even a dried blood smear on the wall—all of them can transmit the virus."

Gorgon leaned back. "That would imply almost everyone's been exposed to the virus at one time or another."

"Precisely," said Connolly with a nod. "This was the big discovery that made us look at everything again. The ex-virus is more aggressive and replicates faster than anything on record. We still haven't even figured out how it can multiply and spread so quickly. It blows Marburg and Ebola out of the water, to the point it should be a complete failure as a disease." She paused.

One of the civilians, a bitchy former LA city councilwoman named Christian Nguyen, clicked her fingernails on the table. The chattering sound made several people flinch. "Except . . . ?"

"Except it isn't lethal," said Josh without looking up.

Beneath her mask, Stealth's expression shifted. "I beg your pardon?"

"It's not lethal," repeated Connolly. "We've run hundreds of tests, infected our lab rats as fast as we can breed them. The ex-virus is not a fatal contagion."

A frumpy man with a gray beard, Richard-something, coughed. "I think there're about five million ex-people outside who'd disagree with you," he said, looking proud of himself.

The doctor nodded. "That's what's why it's taken so long

to isolate this. During the outbreaks, everyone was operating under the misconception the virus was lethal *and* somehow reanimated people. But it isn't. It's two separate things."

"Wait," said Gorgon. "How isn't it fatal? Everyone who gets bitten dies within two or three days."

"Yes, they do," she nodded. "Here's where it gets interesting. You've all heard of the Komodo dragon, yes?"

Most of the heads in the room nodded.

"Okay, for years people thought Komodos were poisonous because their bite was so lethal. Turns out their saliva is like the agar in a petri dish. It's a perfect growth medium, so it's just brimming with every bacteria and virus present in the tropics. They bite you, break the skin, and all that stuff gets shot straight into your bloodstream. Suddenly your body's dealing with thirty or forty major infections at once."

Stealth steepled her fingers. "And this is what exes do?"

Connolly nodded. "When a person dies, lividity sets in, and all the fluids in their body start heading down. Since they're still standing, exes have a lot of material build up in their jaws and cheeks. The brain gets heavy blood flow, so anything in the bloodstream ends up there. The salivary glands, sinuses, and tear ducts drain out, so anything in the lymph system is there, too. Plus you've got all the necrotic bacteria that manifest in a dead body. And, of course, the ex-virus itself. And then the ex bites you, and dumps all of that into your bloodstream."

"But people are dying so fast," said Christian. She spoke with the tone of a person determined to trip someone up. Her dislike of all superhumans was no secret. "How is it possible one person could have that many diseases in them?"

"One person, no. But this is a cumulative effect. A bites B. Between blood loss, the shock of the bite, and whatever germs or viruses A just pumped in, B weakens and dies. Now B becomes an ex and bites C, but C gets both A's and B's diseases. When C becomes an ex, the next victim gets A, B, and C's infections. It's like a reverse-pyramid scheme, where every iteration gets everything the previous ones had."

Stealth gave a faint nod. "Which is why the outbreak spread faster as it grew."

"Right. After five or six generations of exes they each had dozens, maybe even hundreds of diseases in them. Think of Los Angeles two years ago. Imagine how many different bacteria and viruses there were in that hundred or so square mile area. The common cold. Chicken pox. Measles. Mumps. A couple strains of influenza. A few dozen different STDs. Even some folks with typhoid, Lyme disease, or malaria. You couldn't come up with a disease that wasn't represented in LA somewhere. Two months in getting bitten by an ex was like getting injected with the CDC's wish list. Once you add an immunodeficiency disease like HIV into that mix, well . . ." She shrugged.

Richard-something and one of the women murmured. Gorgon swore out loud.

"If everyone in the Mount submitted to blood tests," Connolly continued, "we'd find out the majority of us are infected with the ex-virus. It just doesn't do anything until you die."

Stealth tapped her fingers together. "So the early cases of people being cured?"

The doctor shook her head. "They were cured or stabilized as far as whatever other diseases they'd contracted from their bites, but . . . no. If and when they did die, I'd guess they still became exes. There's no way to be sure until a bunch of people die under conventional circumstances. Our preliminary tests seem to confirm it, though." She took a moment, weighing a thought in her mind. "I need to say . . . this is the final nail as far any hopes for a cure go."

Christian tilted her head. "How so?"

"As I said, the ex-virus itself isn't fatal. It didn't kill anyone. Every ex out there died of influenza, measles, blood loss . . . something else. They were killed by the secondary effects of the bite. They're just as dead as anyone else you ever heard of who died from a disease."

Richard-something raised his hand. "Do you know yet why it brings them back to life?"

Josh cracked the knuckles of his good hand against his thumb. "While a person might be dead, many elements of their body remain alive for hours, even days. You've all heard of hair and fingernails growing on a corpse as the skin cells continue to function. Transplants involve taking the still-living organs from a dead individual. Even at the grocery store, the beef or chicken you bought from the meat case was fresh because, on a cellular level, it was still alive."

Doctor Connolly nodded. "The ex-virus toughens up cells, makes them hardier. So while the person dies, their individual cells don't break down as fast, and the dead body continues on as a gigantic aggregate of living cells joined by the virus."

"But how?"

"Still working on that one. There's a good chance we'll never know for sure. The ex-virus doesn't behave like anything else on record and we don't have the resources to study it more in depth than we are. It seems to involve the central nervous system as people have suspected from the start. That's why destroying the brain is the only thing that stops them—the virus is all through the body, but it primarily resides in the brain and sends impulses along the nerves. You'll still have the enhanced cells, but nothing stimulating them into action."

Doctor Connolly bent down and tapped her screen to advance her notes. "On top of that," she continued, "they're cold. It seems an active process of the infection is to lower a body's core temperature down into the fifties after death. This helps slow the decay rate even further."

"So," Stealth said, "can you estimate how long they last?"

"Off everything we've seen so far, I'm going to say the average ex can exist for twenty-eight months before decay progresses to a point where it can no longer remain active. Give or take two months, and not counting outside influences. Farther north, with seasonal changes, one could exist for four or five years. In the tropics, with the constant heat and humidity, a few months less. That cold snap we had back in February probably added a few weeks to all their lives here." She shrugged.

"It's hard to make any exact estimates without knowing the particulars of patient zero," said Josh. "Since we'll never know exactly when she or he changed, making those initial calculations is impossible."

Gorgon scratched his ear by the band of his goggles. "So, you're saying they should all be dead in another year or so."

"No," said Connolly. "All the ones created during the initial outbreak should be. The ones that turned during the fighting should be done a few months after that. The ones that turned while we were settling in the Mount should be a few months after that. Then there are all those odd kills here and there—the people who made it a few weeks or months past the end on their own before dying."

"And then there's all of us," said Stealth.

The doctor nodded. "Yes. We have to assume a good number of the Mount's population will change once they die. Especially any of you who have been in active contact with exes. So there's another thirty months."

"What can we do?"

Josh ran his fingers through his silver hair. "At the moment, nothing. There's no way to immunize against the ex-virus. We can't cure it once someone's infected, assuming we even spot the infection. All we can hope for is years of controlled deaths like we practice now. Someone dies, you put a bullet in their head before anything can happen."

"Best-case scenario," said Connolly, "no one who's alive today will ever see the end of this. We're looking at maybe three generations of controlled deaths before we can even be somewhat sure we've eliminated the virus. Six, maybe seven decades."

Another mutter made its way through the conference room.

"I'm sorry," she said. "I wish it was better news."

Christian rapped her nails on the table again. "Where does that leave all of us? Will we ever get to leave the Mount?"

"As I see it, we're damned if we do, damned if we don't," said the doctor. "Keeping everyone centralized lets us keep tabs on everyone, but it also means the virus could spread like wildfire if there's an outbreak. Let everyone spread out and we lose track. Someone dies in their sleep, has a bad fall and breaks their neck, and suddenly we're starting all over again."

"So we're all just sup—"

"Thank you for your time, doctor," said Stealth, cutting off further comments. "You may all leave now."

Christian furrowed her brow, but closed her mouth. She let her fingertips chatter on the tabletop for a few moments before getting up to leave.

"That was abrupt," said Gorgon. "Even for you."

"There is too much to do. I cannot waste our time on inconsequential questions."

St. George nodded. "So, now what, then?"

"Go meet up with the repair team. Your presence there will reassure them and speed the work."

"They've got Cerberus."

"You should go."

He sighed. "Fine. I'll radio ahead and tell them I'm half an hour out. Should get there just in time to drive back with them."

"Thank you."

He gave a nod to Josh as he walked out.

"You know," said Gorgon, "that felt a lot like you were getting rid of him for the afternoon."

"I was." She turned to him. He couldn't see her eyes, but somehow she could still project that cold stare. "We have prisoners. I want them interrogated."

His smile was grim beneath the goggles. "My pleasure."

Twelve

NOW

THE PAVEMENT SHIMMERED in the sun. *Mean Green* and *Big Red* were side by side. Ty, Billie, and the rest of the guards had spread out to deal with the occasional ex while Luke and the mechanics replaced the tires of the crippled truck. The front end was done and they had both wounded wheels off on the passenger side.

The guards had split into four teams of three, watching the road in all directions. Whatever exes got too close were dispatched by one guard with a pike while the other two spotted with their own spears and rifles. They tried to avoid noise.

Cerberus walked a slow perimeter around the two trucks, followed by Jarvis. She paused at each cardinal point to stare as far as she could down the road. Her radios scanned back and forth across the wavelengths, listening for any sort of traffic amid the static.

Jarvis sighed after their fourth circuit of the tandem trucks. "So Mark got Trebek?"

Cerberus looked down at him. "Yeah."

"Where?"

"Culver City, nine months ago," she said. "Someone said they filmed *Jeopardy!* over there. At Sony."

"And you're sure it was him?"

The armored shoulders shrugged and turned back to the street. "Looked like him. We didn't stop to check his wallet or anything."

"So you're not sure?"

Another massive shrug. "It looked like him to me. I mean, his mouth was all bloody and everything, but it still looked like him. The shape of his face and all."

"Damn." He kicked at a scrap of old newspaper. "Alex Trebek. That's tough to beat. Ty told me he got Sulu and Chekov from *Star Trek* and that seemed pretty big. The real ones, not the ones from that remake."

Across from them, Billie put her pike between the legs of a one-armed ex and levered them apart. The dead thing staggered, spun, and fell on its side. She drove the weapon down through its ear and the steel point clunked against the pavement.

"I got a bunch," continued Jarvis, "but no one really huge. Megan Fox. Chris Rock. Veronica Mars. Scott Bakula. The little blonde from *Smallville*. On the same day I got the bad guy from *Heroes* and the fat guy from *Seinfeld*. Oh, and that morning newswoman on Channel 11 who always shows too much cleavage. I'm pretty sure I saw Lindsay Lohan once, but we were driving and couldn't stop to get her."

"Too bad," said Cerberus. She toggled lenses and peered along New Hampshire Avenue past Ty. Almost six blocks up the street, an ex with dark hair and white clothes stumbled toward them.

"You got any big names?"

"I don't think so," she said without looking at him. "I never kept track of actors."

"How'd you live in LA and not keep track of actors?"

"I didn't live in LA. I lived in Virginia."

"So how do you visit LA and not look for celebrities? That's all anyone does."

She turned her head to the east and the armor focused its sensors down Melrose. "Most of the time I don't know if no one tells me. They're just exes."

Ty spun and cracked an ex in the head with his spear, then reversed his spin to sweep its legs while it staggered. He made a show of twirling the pike and driving it through the ex's mouth. A few teeth spun free when he yanked the weapon out.

"So, do you know anyone you got?"

Cerberus sighed. It was a raspy noise over her speakers. "A few television people," she said. "I don't remember any of their names. The lead actor from *House*. Apparently he was impressive. So was the woman from the assassins movie."

"Which one?"

"I don't know. The one with the husband and wife. They're both assassins but they don't know it. *The Smiths*?"

"*Mr. & Mrs. Smi*—holy fuck! You got Angelina Jolie?!"

"Yeah, that's her."

"No way!" He kicked the side of the truck. "No *fucking* way!"

"Hey!" Luke glared at him.

He threw a finger to the driver and glared up at the battle-suit. "How the fuck did you get Angelina Jolie?"

"I broke her neck. It was pretty straightforward."

"I got to get out of the Mount more," muttered Jarvis. "All y'all's got better celebrities than me."

× × ×

Gorgon marched across the lot to the holding cells by the Lansing Theater. In earlier years the little rooms had held reels of archive film. Now the solid doors kept things in instead of out.

The hero was a few yards away when he saw the puddles. Notches had been cut out of the bottom of each door, just high enough to let in air, some light, or a tray of food. Now something like cheap wine was spilling out from two of the slots.

He yanked open the nearest cell. The Seventeen had slit her wrists. Classic side-to-side, none of that new-age, up-and-down-the-arm nonsense. The left gash was clean and deep, the right a bit ragged. The floor was wet and red, and the red seeped up into her shirt. A single-edged razor blade rested in her hand, the type grocery clerks used in box-cutters. The type that was supposedly hard to get after 9-11, because they were so easy to hide.

Gorgon slammed the door and opened the next cell. The kid, a teenager, had started to cut his throat and chickened out. The razor was on his cot and his hands were pressed tight over the slash in his neck. "I need a doctor," he said as he squinted against the sunlight. "Please, I'm hurt bad." The blood on his hands was thinned with tears.

"You're not dead," snapped the hero. "You'll be fine for another half hour." He reached forward and grabbed the blade.

"No, please! Please, I need a doctor. I think I'm gonna die!"

Gorgon locked the cell and moved to the next. The third had done both wrists, too, but he was still standing. No, Gorgon thought. Not still standing. He's already back on his feet. Doc Connolly's right about people carrying the virus.

The ex turned at the waist in a smooth arc, its feet shuf-fling to follow. Its limbs were still fresh and flexible. It stared at him with gray eyes and pulled its lips back from its teeth. One of the front incisors had a pentagram engraved on it.

Thirty seconds passed before Gorgon leaped from the cell and slammed the door. He double-checked to make sure the ex was locked in while keying his walkie. "Stealth, I know you're always listening in," he announced. "I need you down at the cells. Now."

× × ×

"Cerberus," called Luke. "Another lift?"

She thudded over and gripped the lower edge of *Big Red*. Luke gave the steel fingers a few nudges and shot her a thumbs-up. The battlesuit's exoskeleton hummed and lifted the passenger side of the truck a foot into the air. Two of the mechanics slid the heavy stands across the pavement, tap-ping them with mallets. Luke talked her down and *Big Red* settled back onto the steel jacks. "Thanks," he said as the mechanics attacked the dually tires.

"Not a problem."

"We should be ready to go in about half an hour."

Cerberus nodded and looked over the truck. The ex in white was just over a block away, close enough to see without magnification. It was an Asian girl sporting a long braid and a bloodstained karate uniform with rainbow trim. "Ty," Cer-berus called, "heads up."

"I see her," he said. He saluted the titan, turned back to the street, and the ex was in front of him.

It lunged and he just got the pike up in time.

Andy dove in with the blunt end of his own spear, shoving

the Asian girl over. The ex spun, twisted, and was back on its feet reaching for Ty. His pike slammed up and the creature bit down on the shaft while it lashed out at him. He thought of horror movies and the twisted things that moved too fast.

"What the fuck is this?"

Ty gave a hard shove and knocked the ex back a few feet. It caught its balance again. He held out the pike to trip it as it stalked toward him. The wooden shaft slipped between the dead woman's knees and he gave the weapon a yank to the left.

The ex stumbled, caught its balance, and took another step toward him.

He took a few quick paces back and reached forward again to trip it, batting the woman's foot away as it took a step. The ex swayed for an instant before it swung the foot back and lunged again.

"Shit," muttered Ty. He heard his spotters shift their weapons, knew their rifles were coming up, and felt his heart thudding. "No firing," he told them. "I've got it."

The pike lined up with her slack mouth and he lunged forward, ready to break through teeth and palate. His hands slid up the immobile wooden shaft and caught three splinters. Cerberus's gauntlet was clamped on the rear of the pike. "Don't."

"Why not?"

She stepped forward and settled one hand on the ex's shoulder. It was enormous against the dead girl. "Because Gorgon would kill you if he found out."

The creature's fingers clawed at the steel digits as it tried to gnaw through the armor.

"Why would he . . ." Ty closed his eyes and sighed. "Shit, that's her, isn't it?"

"Yeah."

"Pretty damned nimble for a zombie," said Andy.

"You should've seen her when she was alive. It was like watching a superball bouncing in a closet." Cerberus shook her head. The ex flailed in her grasp like a scarecrow in the wind. "Last I heard she was wandering around Griffith Park somewhere. It sucks she made it back down here."

Andy shrugged. "So what do we do with it? I mean, if we can't kill it, are you just going to stand here until the truck's done?"

"Got an idea. Something I heard someone say once."

The battlesuit reached out and her hand wrapped around the ex's head like a spider. Just for a second she considered crushing the skull. She could still see one of its eyes staring out between the huge digits, and its teeth scraped on a metal fingertip. Then she picked the dead thing up and turned it around, pointing its eyes back up the street. "Keep quiet for a minute or so."

The ex thrashed a few times against the grip, becoming more and more lethargic each time. Its arms settled down and were limp at its sides.

"Out of sight, out of mind," whispered the titan. Her fingers opened with the faint hum of electronic motors and the Asian woman stumbled forward. Everyone stayed silent until it was halfway up the block, except for the crunch of Billie impaling another ex with her pike.

"So Mark got Trebek and you got Angelina Jolie." Jarvis spit on the pavement. "Now my only hope for a great one is Jessica Alba."

Cerberus shook her head. "That one's down. Cairax killed her. St. George told me the story."

"The demon guy? I thought he was an ex now."

"He is, but he wasn't then. She's the one who bit him. Killing her's one of the last things anyone saw him do."

"How'd she bite him, anyway? I thought he was all scaly or something. Lizardy."

"He's fireproof. And tough enough to shrug off Tasers and shotguns."

"So how'd she bite him?"

Cerberus pivoted her head, locking him in her sights. "He's not all scaly."

"What's that supposed to—No!"

"Yeah."

"You mean they . . . he . . . when she was *dead*?"

"I never met the guy, but Zzzap and St. George both say he was kind of messed up in the head, way past the whole magic-sorcerer thing. Multiple personalities or something. Didn't always make the best decisions."

"Fuck no, he—"

Her hand shot up, silencing him. Luke looked up from the side of the cab and stopped the two mechanics with their sockets. A moment passed as the steel skull panned to the south. "Can you hear that?"

Luke cupped his ears.

"Something big," said Cerberus. "Heading this way."

Jarvis shook his head and then froze. "Wait a sec."

They could all hear the engines now, and the low cries running alongside them. In the odd acoustics of the dead city, the sounds echoed and growled. Luke stood next to Cerberus, his ears still cupped. The mechanics were spinning the lugs on for the last set of tires. Ty, Billie, and the rest threw the pikes in the truck beds and swung their rifles into their arms.

Inside the battlesuit, she watched long-range sensors

begin to light up. Her arms itched with the lack of cannons. "This is Cerberus," she barked into her microphone. "We have incoming hostiles, request immediate reinforcements. Zzzap, Gorgon, Dragon." She looked at the mechanics. "Are we going to be done in time?"

"Just need another minute."

"Everyone mount up! Zzzap!" she shouted into the microphone. "Damn it, Barry, I know you can hear me!"

Luke pulled himself up into the cab and *Big Red* rumbled to life. "We got another jammer?"

"No."

"Is he supposed to be flesh?"

"No, of course not." She thudded back to the lift gate. *Mean Green*'s engine gunned as the mechanics threw their tools in the back. "You done?"

"It'll get us home."

Down Melrose the trucks swung around the corner. There were two oversized pickups and a garbage truck with steel bars across the wide windshield. Something large and purple was stretched across the massive grille. Seventeens swarmed and howled on each vehicle.

"Raise the gate," Cerberus said.

Billie's hand froze on the switch as Jarvis swung himself over the side of the truck. "How will you—"

"No time. Raise it and get out of here."

"You heard her," bellowed Harry, *Mean Green*'s overweight driver. "She'll hold 'em off. That's what she does, right?"

The Seventeen vehicles roared closer. The thing chained to the front of the garbage truck moved, thrashing against the bindings. The armor's lenses punched in, swelling the image in her view. "Shit," Cerberus hissed, recognizing it. "Go!"

Mean Green dropped into gear and lunged down the street. *Big Red* was a beat behind it. Bullets pinged off the steel lift gate. One of its new tires blew and the big truck kept going on the dually.

A few rounds bounced off the battlesuit as she thudded over to a phone pole. She grabbed it, yanked, and felt the wood splinter under the armor's fingers. The thick beam crashed down across the street. She scooped up an Accord near the sidewalk and flipped it out into the street, too.

Mean Green was out of sight. *Big Red* was just reaching the overpass. The Seventeens were a block away.

She threw her legs forward and ran.

× × ×

"Why do I need to see this?" asked Stealth.

Gorgon stood by the cell doors. "Because you won't believe me if I just tell you."

"What could be so impossible for me to believe?"

"Just come over here."

Her head tilted to the puddles of blood. "Suicide."

"Two of them. They smuggled in razors, but only two went through with it."

"Regrettable. Call a cleanup crew."

"That's not the problem." He gestured her to the last door.

"Did they rise? I am sure you can deal with them one at a time, and Doctor Connolly would probably like to see them. I have things to do."

"Not more important than this."

She glared at him. Gorgon unlocked the door and swung the cell open.

× × ×

The suit could run. It could hit forty-five miles an hour on pavement, less on dirt, gravel, or sand. She hated doing it because she could watch her power levels drop with every stride. It wasn't cheap to make twelve hundred pounds of armor and electronics move fast.

Behind her there was a crash she could feel. A quick blink shifted her screens to the armor's rear-view cam. The garbage truck had dropped the two huge arms that caught and flipped dumpsters, battering aside the phone pole. They speared the Acura like a pair of metal tusks, barely slowing the enormous truck at all.

She switched back to the main view. The battlesuit had caught up with *Big Red*. Forty percent of her power was already gone. She could see abandoned cars shake as she ran by. An ex stumbled into her path and she plowed over it, crushing it to a pulp.

"Turn," she bellowed to Luke. "North on Western. We can cut across Santa Monica and circle down Gower."

"What about Harry and *Mean Green*?"

"Fat bastard's probably back at the Mount already," she shouted. "They're fine."

Luke spun the wheel and *Big Red* lurched onto Western, weaving between dead cars. She stomped after them, cracking the blacktop with each footfall. The freeway ramp was up ahead and Sunset a few blocks past it.

"SHIT!!" Luke tensed and stood up in his seat. *Big Red* squealed, tires smoking as it slid forward another twenty feet. Shouts came from the back as the guards were thrown forward.

Cerberus tried to dodge and smashed her shoulder into the driver's-side corner of the truck. *Big Red* lurched, the fiberglass sides crumpled, and the battlesuit spun away, stumbling over a low sports car and crashing down on the sidewalk on top of a crawling ex. Her screens went gray for a second as the computers tried to keep up with the whirling images.

Inside Cerberus, Danielle tried to clear her head. Even with the armor it had been a hard hit. She blinked a few times and the suit tried to interpret the subtle commands, racing through half a dozen views and status reports as it tried to get the cameras back online. The flashing screens didn't help her throbbing skull.

"Chains," shouted Luke. "They've got the whole road trapped!"

Big Red's tires sent up white smoke as the truck reversed. Cerberus pulled herself up with a parking meter, crushing it in the process. "Where to?"

"Side street," shouted Luke.

She shook out her electronic limbs and ran past the truck. She could hear the Seventeens getting close. She glanced down Marathon and the targeters highlighted the line of spikes. "Wait!" She grabbed the chain and yanked it free of a bolt on the north side of the street.

The truck spun in a violent three-point turn behind her. "Clear?"

"Clear." There was a classic Volkswagen Bug parked in a driveway. She glanced at her power levels as *Big Red* raced past her and debated throwing it at the dump truck. Instead she whipped the chain out onto Western just as one of the pickups roared into view. The spiked links caught one of the

Seventeens in the head with a flash of red and yanked him from the back of the truck.

The pickup's engine roared and it shot forward. She lunged and drove her fist through the grille. The engine block crumpled beneath her knuckles as her punch pushed it up into the cab of the truck. The Ford twisted into scrap around the titan, carried onto her arm by its own momentum. Two red-centered spiderwebs blossomed across the windshield where the driver and passenger slammed forward. One of the bed passengers sailed over her shoulder.

The garbage truck shrieked to a halt out on Western and a few more rounds pinged off her armor. She kicked free of the ruined Ford and headed west after *Big Red*. Behind her she heard the steel tusks of the garbage truck hit the pickup.

Luke cut onto St. Andrews Place. In his side mirror he could see the blue and silver titan thundering down the road behind him.

Ahead of them the Dodge pickup squealed in, grinding an ex beneath its tires and blocking the end of the street. Luke hit the brakes and threw *Big Red* into reverse.

Cerberus skidded to a halt, sparks shooting off her feet. Her targeters locked onto the Dodge. A bullet clanged on her shoulder. The battlesuit tallied enemy weapons and manpower. She ached for her missing cannons and imagined the truck exploding into the air.

Behind them, the garbage truck rolled across the north end of the street. On its grille, the dead thing twisted and pulled, its eyes locked on Cerberus. She tried not to look at it.

A hail of shots rang out. Ty's neck flashed red and he fell back with a thud. Jarvis threw himself to the left just as a second shot sprayed part of his shoulder into the back of the truck. Billie and the rest dropped behind the steel lift gate. Cerberus could hear them cocking rifles.

She stomped forward and spread her arms. Behind her Luke gunned the engine, letting *Big Red* shudder.

A pale, bald man with a goatee crawled from the back of the garbage truck onto the cab. Half his face was tattoos, and he was dressed in the colors of the Seventeens, with a green shirt and a bandanna tied on one arm. His AK was held out away from his body. Around his feet, the other Seventeens kept their weapons aimed at Cerberus and *Big Red*.

"Hey, big girl," he shouted with a grin. He gave her a lazy salute from his sunglasses. "If you all done running, mind if we talk for a minute?"

× × ×

The ex with the engraved tooth was sprawled across the cot. As the midday sun blasted into the small space it twisted its head up to the door. It lay there with its blank eyes facing into the glare.

Gorgon stepped back and Stealth watched it for a moment. "Why isn't it attacking?" she asked the other hero. "Is there something wrong with it?"

"Are you Stealth? It's hard to see with the light. You're just a hot little blob of shadows."

For the first time since Gorgon met her, the woman in black froze. He'd done the same thing ten minutes ago.

The dead thing brushed itself off with slow, deliberate motions. Then it stood up from the cot and bowed with a grin. "I come bearing a message," croaked the ex, "from my chief, the Boss of Los Angeles."

The Luckiest Girl in the World
THEN

I HAVE TO ADMIT, it's a little creepy when their necks snap. Stealth says they don't feel any pain. It's like breaking a toy more than killing something. Gorgon agrees with her. But it's still such a creepy noise.

Kick. Back flip. Crouch. Sweep. Lunge. Springboard. Snap.

For the most part, it's like shooting fish in a barrel. I'm two or three times faster than a normal person. When you consider these things move at maybe quarter-speed, it's almost impossible for them to touch me. There was a scary minute a few days ago when I got surrounded by them, but once I calmed down I got out of it. Stealth was right—she's always right. You can get out of anything with your brain first, your fists second.

Spin kick. Spin kick. Roundhouse. Snap. Flip up to the fire escape.

Hands down, the worst part of this whole crisis was telling Mom and Dad the truth about my "part-time tutoring job." With martial law and a national quarantine, they weren't going to buy my usual "off to the library, back late" excuse. Still, the whole country's being overrun by zombies and I had to argue with them before they'd let me out of the house.

Swing. Launch. Bounce. Flip kick. Snap.

And what was the huge issue? Were they upset their oldest daughter was some kind of mutant? That I'd been risking my life and fighting crime since sophomore year of high school? That I'd lied to them?

"You can't be Banzai!" cried Mom. "Banzai is a boy. It was in the paper."

"Yeah, I know. It helps hide my identity."

"That name," shouted Dad. "How could you pick a Japanese name for yourself? You're Korean!"

"It's a word. It's just a word."

"Your grandfather died fighting the Japanese! He died at the hands of people who used that word as a battle cry, and now you use it like some sort of badge of honor."

"But how could anyone think you were a man? My beautiful girl."

"I wear a mask, Mom. And let's face it, Sarah got the . . . she got your figure. She's fourteen and she's bigger than me."

The discussion went on like that for an hour. I even had to prove it, showing them the costume, doing a couple jumps around the room. And then another hour convincing them I needed to go help out.

Vault. Flip. Split kick. Bounce. Snap. Bounce. Snap. Bounce. Snap.

God, it's sick, I know, but I am still loving this. After a lifetime of being the quiet girl who sat off to the side, becoming the fastest, wildest, most colorful hero in the city was the best thing that had ever happened to me.

Half a dozen exes down and I swung up the fire escape to the roof. I needed to find the rest of my team.

Stealth had me, Gorgon, and the Mighty Dragon covering Beverly Hills and West Hollywood. She was downtown with Midknight and Blockbuster. 'Genny was backing up cops in Hollywood proper. The demon-guy, Cairax, was over in Venice. I heard Zzzap had shot back to the East Coast to help the Awesome Ape.

It'd really gone crazy this past week. No way to hide it or deny it. Ex-humans started showing up all over Los Angeles, doing all the things zombies do. By Wednesday I was hearing reports about them in New Mexico and Las Vegas. That Sunday the president declared martial law, but they were already in New York, Boston, and Washington. And he thought all he was going to have to deal with first term was the economy and the last guy's screwups in the Middle East. This morning there were zombie outbreaks in Europe.

Gorgon—Nick—was waiting for me on the roof. No helmet for a change, just his goggles. I know this whole situation was making him feel useless. He hated not having his bike, but the rooftops were so much safer. And his eyes didn't work on exes. Guess they didn't have any life-energy for him to steal. Still, he knew how to fight, knew all our strengths and weaknesses, so he made a great field coordinator.

"Any problems?"

I grabbed him and kissed him hard. At least I didn't have to tell my folks that part of my secret life. By the way, Mom and Dad, I have random, stress-relieving sex with another hero. The one called Gorgon, with the goggles. He's twenty-nine, white, he took my virginity when I was seventeen, and we have to do it doggy-style most of the time to protect me from his eyes. I guess you could say we're dating.

He pulled back. "What's so funny?"

"Nothing. Just thinking of some of the things I could've told my parents when I confessed."

He smirked. "Dragon's cleaning around the Beverly Center again. We should head north, clean up anything we find, and meet up with him."

I took a running jump and cleared the alley with a double flip. "Waiting on you, slowpoke," I shouted.

Nick'd taken a hit off somebody. He was strong. Not full-strength strong, but definitely above normal human levels. What he called tier two. It took a little effort, but he leaped across to join me on the next rooftop. We headed north at a jog, watching the streets and alleys for movement.

People think alleys and streets would be the big worry running across rooftops, but really it's just shoddy mainte-nance. Loose bricks. Weak beams. I slipped on a sheet of tar paper once that wasn't even fastened down. Leaping from building to building is the easy part.

We'd gone six blocks, almost to Santa Monica Boulevard, when Nick stopped. His hearing's better than mine, and he waved me toward the cross-alley to the east. I bounced to the edge of the roof.

There were some homeless people cornered against a sag-ging chain-link fence. One ex-human on the far side was trying to bite them through the links, two were staggering down the alley toward them.

"Should just take a minute," I said.

"I'll take the one. Focus on saving those people."

"I can handle them—"

He was already sliding down an old metal drainpipe. I launched myself across the alley, did a Jackie Chan bounce from the brick wall to the fire escape, back, and into a zom-bie's head. The ex tumbled and I rode him to the pavement, letting my weight and momentum crush his skull. The force rolled me into a crouch that put me in a perfect place to sweep the other one. He hit the ground with a nice crack.

"Get out of here!" I waved the people away. "You're supposed to be in a shelter, so get going!"

They moved. One of them hugged his hand to his chest.

I grabbed his arm. "Let me see."

He shook his head, but held it out anyway. I could see the teeth marks, dark around flesh that was already turning pale. He was crying into his thick whiskers.

"Tie your arm off tight," I said. "Use your belt, a scarf, something. Make it hurt. Tell them you've been bitten as soon as you get to the shelter." I turned to his friends. "He's infected. Make sure the medics know."

"Big B!" shouted Nick. "A little help."

On the other side of the fence, Nick had dealt with his one zombie. We hadn't seen all the others in the shadows. Almost a dozen. And more flowing in from the far end of the alley.

A running start sent me over the fence. I hammer-kicked the closest one, dragged him to the ground, and felt his neck break under my heel. "Over the fence or up the pipe," I said. "Your choice."

"You can't fight this many."

"Not going to. I'm covering you. Move that sexy ass."

No time to think, just to move. Leap. Flip. Bounce. Snap. Back flip. Roll. Sweep. Spin kick.

A scream made me turn. I hadn't killed the last ex on the other side of the fence. It had grabbed the last of the homeless, a black woman, and sunk its teeth into her leg. She was shrieking and trying to kick it off.

Nick had just made it up the pipe and out of reach. He was moving so slow. His strength was gone, used up. Damn it. He saw the woman and swung himself over the fence. Even without any power, I knew he could deal with one.

Something brushed my shoulder.

Vault. Back thrust kick. Roll. Too many of them to get distracted. A few steps gave me the momentum to bounce off the alley wall, up to head height. Kick. Flip. Split kick. Snap-snap. Crouch. Sweep. Leap. Spin kick. Snap.

Nick was safe with his ex. Time to get away from all of mine. I just needed an opening. The fire escape was in front of me. Launch. Bounce. Flip kick. Snap. Bounce. Snap. Bottom rung of the ladder. Swing.

Slip.

The rung was coated with years of grime and oil and rust mixed into something that felt like slimy mud. It slipped out of my hand. I fell.

It wasn't the first time I'd fallen. Not even the first time with enemies around. Heck, I even managed to scissor my legs as I dropped, knocking two of them down and getting my feet under me. But they were too close. I needed room to move.

I panicked. Just two seconds of panic. Three, tops.

Arms wrapped around me from behind and grabbed my almost nonexistent boobs. It was the way guys copped a feel in school—a back-hug gone wrong. On top of falling on my ass in front of my sort-of boyfriend, I was getting felt up by a zombie.

And then it bit my shoulder. The teeth ground down through the heavy cotton of my costume, breaking the skin, tearing at the muscle. Blood gushed down my arm. My blood was very hot.

I twisted free. Like Nick and the Dragon and my self-defense teacher all said, I spun and used my momentum to drive the heel of my hand at the ex. It was an Indian woman. She was beautiful. I shattered her nose and drove the bone into her brain. She staggered back and dropped.

My balance was shot. Too much pain to bounce. I swept the three nearest exes and used their bodies for extra height, throwing myself at the fire escape's ladder again. I swung my legs up, wrapped my knees over the rungs, and pulled myself away from their clawing hands.

Nick met me halfway down the fire escape, helped me to the roof. Then he tore open the top of my costume. I didn't want to look, but he swore and I couldn't help it.

It was as bad as I thought. The ex had bitten through the shoulder of my sports bra. A chunk of skin—a chunk of *me*—the size of a half-dollar hung loose, floating on a river of blood that just kept flowing. My fingertips were sticky. I was babbling. Terrified. I knew what the bite meant. I didn't want to be dead at eighteen. I didn't want to be one of them.

I don't know what I was saying, but Nick kept shouting "You are *not* going to die!" until I stopped. His goggles hid a lot of his face. I wanted to see his eyes so bad right then. He poured something clear on the bite that sizzled, then some powder that burned. The bleeding stopped. He poured the last of the clear liquid and wiped away a lot of the blood. I could see my skin getting pale on the edges. "I'm going to get in touch with Regenerator," he said. He pulled my hand up and had me press down on it. "He can fix this, babe. He can heal you."

"He can't," I said. "Stealth said so."

Nick shook his head. "He can't help people who've changed. You've just got a bite. He can heal it. Remember when he healed your broken leg? My gunshot?"

"Do we have enough time?"

"We've got plenty, babe. Plenty of time. A couple hours, at least. And he's just over in Hollywood. Not even two miles from here." He slid a phone from his belt.

"You sure?"

"I am so sure." Then, to his phone, "It's Gorgon. Where are you? Banzai's been bitten."

He was listening when I heard the screams. Two voices. Man and a woman. West of us. It took my mind off my shoulder.

"No, it was just a minute ago. I cleaned it out."

"Nick," I said. "Did you hear that?" The male voice was shouting orders. A warning? I couldn't make out the words, but I could tell he was slipping into fear. I'd heard that edge on a lot of voices lately.

Nick nodded at the phone. "Hollywood and Cahuenga? We can meet you there in twenty minutes."

I swung my arm a few times. Not stiff, not too weak. The shoulder was already getting numb. I knew that was a bad sign, but it also meant I could start using it again. I pulled my top shut and retied the sash.

The cell vanished back into his belt. "He's waiting for us there. The National Guard has an emergency medical center set up. You're getting top priority."

I finished the knot and shook my head. "The people first." The bloody shoulder ruined the colors of my outfit, but I didn't think anyone we met was going to complain. I headed west. "You coming?"

"Damn it, Kathy!"

"We can't leave them. Plenty of time, remember?"

Down on Fairfax there were nine exes. Three people. Two girls and a guy. One of the women was already down. The exes were closing in, but still wide.

Plenty of room. Just the way I liked it.

Nick caught up with me. Without the helmet he looks so

hot in his Gorgon outfit. I kissed him on the cheek. "We help them," I said, "and then we go meet up with 'Genny."

I hurled myself off the rooftop. Spun on a lamppost. Double flip. Split kick. Snap. Crouch. Sweep. Hammer kick. Snap.

God, I love this.

Fourteen

NOW

CERBERUS CRANKED HER speakers and her voice boomed across the street. "You want to talk, be quick. That other truck'll be back in a few minutes with reinforcements."

The bald Seventeen barked a laugh and gestured to someone out of sight. Half the chains dropped from the front of the garbage truck.

The beast darted forward, its talons scraping on the pavement, and got yanked back by the remaining chains. Even dead, it was fast. When the ex moved, the silver pendant bounced on its bony neck, half bound by the collar they'd put on it.

"Is that what I think it is?" whispered Andy.

"Yeah," Cerberus said. There was a metallic hiss to her voice when she whispered. "That's Cairax."

"Shit."

It was hairless, and death hadn't changed its leathery skin much from the splotchy purple of a fresh bruise. It was still gaunt, and even with its curved spine it was as tall as Cerberus. Its head was like a monstrous deep-sea fish, with cloudy, saucerlike eyes bent in a permanent scowl by the thick brow ridge, and a forest of fangs and tusks jutting out past its lips. The long, spidery fingers each ended in a knifelike claw. Its tail dragged on the ground, the barbed end twitching now and then.

"You and I both know they didn't hear your radio," the bald man said. "So you've got about ten minutes for that truck to get home and another twenty to get back here." He pointed down at the beast. "How many people can he kill in that time?"

Cairax lunged again and the garbage truck shook as the chains went tight.

A quick blink shifted her screens and gave her picture-in-picture of the rearview cam. She could just see Andy's profile behind the lift gate. "Who's hurt?"

"Jarvis is bleeding pretty bad but I think we've got it. Ty . . . I think Ty's dead. Half his throat's gone." There was a pause. "We've got four guns on Cairax's forehead."

"He's bulletproof," hissed Cerberus. "He's mine. Get baldy."

The Seventeen banged on the roof of the garbage truck with the AK's stock. "You all done whispering over there?"

"You wanted to talk," she thundered. "Talk."

"Here's the deal," shouted the bald man. "They all drop their guns, you get out of the suit, we take everyone hostage, and you all get to live."

"Hostage?"

"Our chief wants one of your people. And all the guns you've got in your little film-studio fort. Your ninja-woman boss trades the man and the guns for all of you. Everyone goes home happy."

"And then we've got no weapons and you march in."

He barked out another laugh. "No weapons? You looked in the mirror, big girl? Your side has all the best weapons. You've got all the living weapons."

"And you've got some dead ones."

"A few," he said with a smile.

× × ×

"The Boss of Los Angeles," repeated Stealth.

Within the cell, the ex nodded. "You want to hear it all now or you need a minute? I know this messes with people the first time they see—"

"Speak."

"Game's changed. We're expanding and you've barely survived until now. You can keep your home here on one condition."

"Which is?"

The ex held up his arm and pointed a pale finger past her. "We want him."

Gorgon raised an eyebrow. "Me?"

"You've fucked with the SS since you first appeared," said the dead ganger. "We owe you big-time, all of us. We're going to torture you for a month, bleed you a drop at a time, and then choke you with your own balls. And after you die, you'll come back and we'll do it all again."

"I'm shaking," said Gorgon.

Stealth held up a hand. "Who is your leader?"

"He's the Boss of LA, head of the Seventeens. He rules this city except for one little fort here in Hollywood."

"That does not tell us who he is."

"Everyone called him Peasy on the news," grinned the dead thing, "so that's what he's been using."

A long moment passed before Stealth tipped her head. "Is there any more to this message?"

"Figured you'd send a team out for the truck we spiked

last night. Some of our people are taking them hostage right now. You get them when we get the eye-guy."

"I doubt that will happen."

It grinned, showing off the pentagram. "I don't. Got a few superpowers of our own these days."

× × ×

Cerberus shifted, her feet scraping on the pavement. "And if we don't feel like being hostages?"

The bald man looked down at the straining thing on the front of the truck. "I let the demon loose and take anyone it doesn't eat."

"It'll go after your people, too."

He shook his head. "No," he grinned, "it won't. Any other clever ideas?"

She heard a faint scrape and looked back again. Another rifle barrel had slid out, peeking over her shoulder. She switched back to main view and tried to see the bald man's eyes behind his sunglasses. "I'm thinking I could throw your big bad truck half a block once I tear the demon's head off," she growled.

"You got to get current, big girl," the Seventeen said. He slung his AK back over his shoulder and waved his arms at the buildings around them. "You're still thinking then, not now. We're the way things are, the way they're going to be from now on. We're the majority. You need to get out of this superhero-survivor mentality if you plan on seeing Christmas."

Her arms ached for the cannons. One burst would turn the bald man to mist. A cloud of red mist with boots.

"So, I see a lot of guns aimed this way," he said. "You want to drop 'em all, or are we going to do this the fun way?" Again with the stupid grin.

The titan flexed her fingers, wrapping them into armored fists the size of footballs. "It's not going to be fun."

"Matter of opinion. Any last words?"

"Yeah." She glanced up at the sky. "What took you so long?"

The bald man looked up and the air exploded into flames between them.

St. George landed in front of *Big Red*, inhaled, and spat a second cone of fire at the Dodge. He leaped back up, twisting in the air over the pickup, and threw more flames down on the people in the truck bed.

The Seventeens screamed. A few leaped from the Dodge, and as they did it blossomed into a ball of light and heat. The tree branches above caught fire.

Another leap carried the hero back to the garbage truck. The demon flailed at the air in his direction. Gunfire washed over the street. The rounds chimed as they struck Cerberus and wrinkled St. George's clothes. A few sparked off the pavement. His new sunglasses exploded into shards of black plastic.

Some spotty return fire came from *Big Red*. The Seventeens crawling from the burning Dodge winced and threw up their hands.

The bald man stood on top of the truck and grinned. He swung his AK down and emptied the magazine at St. George. The hero's leather jacket shredded apart.

"HOLD YOUR FIRE!" bellowed St. George. Smoke poured from his mouth as his voice echoed on the street over the gunshots, the sound of the burning truck, and the cries of the wounded Seventeens.

The bald man's AK ran out of ammo and locked. He shrugged and tossed it down into the truck. "Give it a rest," he called out to his people.

"So," said St. George, "let's review. You've just wasted a bunch of ammo, we did not. We're bulletproof, your people are not. We're near our base, you are not. Did I miss anything?"

"I've got the demon," said the bald man.

"Then set it loose," St. George said. "If you really think a zombie version of Cairax can take two heroes who were both better than him when he was alive, go for it."

The bald man's smile faltered.

"Just keep in mind, the minute you do, the kid gloves are off. Right now you can all walk away. You unleash that thing and we take it and you apart."

The two men stared each other down across the dusty street. A curl of smoke twisted from St. George's nostril. Cairax leaned forward again, snapping the chains tight.

The bald man nodded. "This one's yours, dragon man," he said. He stomped twice and the huge truck began to back away. "Just remember if Peasy doesn't get his man by—"

A crack echoed on the street and the Seventeen's glasses leaped from his head. The bald man tumbled back into the garbage truck and it came to a halt with a hiss of brakes.

Billie lifted her eye from the sights.

Fire flashed in St. George's mouth. "What the hell was that?!"

She shrugged. "Cerberus said to take him out."

"What?"

"Before you got here," explained the armored titan.

"Things changed. They were leaving!"

"So what?" said Billie. "They just killed Ty!"

One step put St. George at the truck. He yanked the rifle out of her hands, twisted it into scrap, and she flinched away. "They kill," he shouted at her. "We don't. Not unless there's no other choice. We're the good guys. We're supposed to be better than them."

"They killed Ty," she snarled. And then her eyes went wide.

"Hey, dragon man," called someone behind him.

The bald man.

He was back on top of the garbage truck. A gory hole spread across the side of his face. The eye hung low in the shattered socket, and the flesh had peeled back to reveal the ivory teeth set in his jaw. The slow blood was dark and clumpy.

His good eye leered at them from a sunken socket. Without the sunglasses, they could see the chalky irises and wide-open pupil. The eyes of the dead.

"As I was saying," he said, "Peasy gets his man by the end of the week, or we grind your home into the mud. You got me?"

St. George stared up at the dead thing. "What the hell are you?"

"New rules, dragon man," the ex said. "We've been playing by new rules for months and you're just finding out now."

The hero landed on top of the garbage truck next to the dead man. Down in the bin, a score of rifles leaped to cover him, but the bald man waved them away. Up close St. George could see the ragged flaps of flesh Billie's shot had made, the dark veins under the skin, smell the decay. The ex grinned at him through its mangled face.

"End of the week," it said. "The boss gets what he wants, or you all die." It reached up and gave its mangled face a prod. "You might want to get in a little target practice before then."

The ex stomped his foot again. The truck beeped as it backed up to Marathon. St. George stepped back, gliding down to the street. The bald man gave him a salute as the truck turned and rolled back out to Western.

Cerberus thudded up next to him. "He's an ex."

"Yeah."

"How?"

"I don't know." He glared up at her. "Where the hell do you get off telling them to kill people?"

"We were outnumbered and outgunned. We did what we had to."

"Do it again, Danielle, and I will peel you out of that suit and scrap it with my bare hands. Clear?"

"Don't get all high and migh—"

"Luke," he bellowed. "How many extinguishers are you carrying?"

"Just the one we brought with us. We stripped most of them out last night."

He pointed at the flaming Dodge. "Somebody get that fire under control. The rest of you, spread out. Standard watchdog. Try to raise the Mount again. Get *Mean Green* back out here with some more firefighting gear."

"*Road Warrior*'s already got two extra extinguishers on it," said the driver.

"Whoever can get out here first. Last thing we need is a major fire running loose in the city."

There was a single gunshot from the truck. Billie lifted her pistol from Ty's forehead and rammed it back into her holster.

Fifteen

NOW

GORGON POUNDED HIS FIST on the door as he entered the mill. "You here?" he called out. He shrugged out of his duster and walked into the huge room.

Cerberus had adopted one of the studio's workshops as her own. It was a large space, but the armor maintenance filled most of it. Film-set walls made a small private area for her bed and a few pieces of furniture. The plumbers had knocked one of the side-by-side bathrooms apart and re-placed it with a bare-bones shower.

The room was centered on four large worktables made from full-sized sheets of plywood. Carved shapes of foam were mounted on each one, cradles for specific pieces of equipment. One table had a laptop. Another had a small Honda generator mounted under it.

A four-step ladder stood between them. The metal titan stalked back and forth by it, fastened to the wall by a thick power cable that ran into the armor's waist. "Where've you been?"

"Domestic disturbance." He threw his coat over a chair and tugged at his gloves.

"We're going to be late."

"We'll be fine. Not like they can start without us."

"The wrenches are over there."

"Okay."

"You're not going to be able to get it all on your own. We should wait for St. George."

He shook his head and tapped his goggles. "I told you, I broke up a fight on the way over here. I'm good for an hour or so. I told him to just get Barry."

"Are you sure?" She stood in front of the ladder and held her arms out to either side.

"Stop putting it off and strip," he said with a smirk.

"Fuck you." She blinked a few commands to the suit's computer, whispered a passcode, and across the armor two dozen matchbook-sized panels popped open to expose bolts. The wide collar of armor slid apart to reveal another four sockets. "The head first."

"Yeah, I know." He stepped up the ladder and looked her in the eyes. "We've done this a couple dozen times now."

"Sorry."

Gorgon slid the Allen wrench into the collar and worked out each of the front bolts. A few minutes later he reached around the armored skull and loosened the two in the back. He pocketed the wrench and grabbed the helmet with both hands. "Ready?"

Cerberus nodded, the faint hum of the battle suit vanished, and its eyes went gray as it stiffened into a statue. He heaved and the armor's sixty-pound head came up. He heard a faint hiss as seals opened, half a dozen clicks as USB plugs popped out of sockets, and then a deep breath.

Danielle had pale skin that made her freckles stand out. Her strawberry-blond hair was damp and plastered in strings against her forehead. She winced at the sudden expanse of open space, blinked a couple times, and tried to peek over the armored collar. "Got it?"

"Yes, I've got it," he sighed. He stepped down the ladder and set the helmet down in one of the cradles near the laptop. "You reek, you know that? How long have you been in there?"

"Thirty-nine hours."

He climbed back up the ladder and attacked the bolts on her left shoulder. Fifteen minutes later the armored limb was in its own cradle and he was working on the next one.

She shook out her hand and squeezed the fingers into a fist two or three times. Her arm was sheathed in black Lycra. It looked skinny and frail compared to the rest of the battlesuit.

Gorgon moved the ladder behind her. Six bolts held the back half of the torso in place. He finished the last one and tapped her on the head. "Ready to get out?"

She wrapped her arms around the suit's chest and nodded.

The armor plates scraped apart and the torso split down the sides. The back half was the size of a car hood. Six interlocking plates attached to a titanium spine weighing three hundred pounds. Gorgon tipped the section toward himself, took a step down the ladder, and let it drop into his arms. He took a few steps back and set it down on one of the tables.

Danielle twisted her head back. "Good?"

He stepped up the ladder and put a hand on the small of her back just below a harness strap. The Lycra was damp with sweat. "Got you."

She let go of the chest plate and dropped back. He got his arms around her, took another step up, and lifted. She wiggled her hips and her legs slid free of the armor.

"Jesus," he said. "You stink like a locker room."

"Shut up and put me down. And watch your hands for once."

He let her legs drop and she put weight on her feet. Her knees buckled and she grabbed at him.

"Sure you're good?"

Her skintight suit let him see every tremble and quiver. "I'm fine," she said. "It just takes a minute." She took a few wobbly steps until she was used to being human again and stumbled to the nearest table.

"We've still got about forty minutes if you want to shower."

Danielle stretched a pair of cables from the laptop to the helmet. "You're not exactly springtime fresh yourself," she said.

He glanced down at the wet spot she'd left on his chest. "Yeah, well, that's why I always bring a spare." He peeled off his T-shirt and tossed it on the table near the armor's right arm.

A longer cable unspooled to the back section on the next table. She seated it and accessed the main processors along the armor's spine. Her attention went to the laptop and made it clear she had no interest in seeing his very broad and naked torso. A few strokes on the mousepad activated a set of diagnostic programs and she glanced over the screen to watch him pull the fresh shirt across his chest.

"I'm going to hit the shower," she said. "Are you going to wait?"

He shrugged. "If you want."

She nodded at the flimsy curtain separating the bathroom from the workspace. "I'm trusting you to at least act like a gentleman."

"I'll be working on my goggles with my back to you."

Danielle rolled her eyes and wondered if he was ever going

to take the hint. A minute later she was surrounded by the comfort of the tiny shower stall. She left the curtain open just enough so it didn't look deliberate. Not enough she felt exposed. Ten minutes later she walked from the shower to her bedroom in a wet towel and bared her teeth at his back.

"Set," she said a few minutes later.

"Wait there." He gave one of the tiny screwdrivers a half turn and tapped the trigger a few times. On the workbench, his goggles flashed open and shut. Another slight adjustment, another test, and he lifted the lenses back to his face.

"You good?" She'd walked up right behind him.

He turned. "Yeah. Thanks for the tools."

"No problem. Let's get this over with."

She killed the overheads at the door, leaving a circle of light at the center of the room. The last sections of the armor still stood between the workbenches, headless, armless, and backless. The power cable ran off into the darkness.

Only a few hours and she could have it back on.

× × ×

Gorgon scowled across the table. "What's he doing here?"

Josh sighed and turned to St. George. "I told you this would be a waste of time."

"He is here because I asked him to be," said Stealth.

"Why?" asked Danielle. "Connolly's our senior doctor. If anyone should be here it's her."

"Because he understands the virus," said Stealth. "And he understands us."

"And Doctor Connolly's setting a broken arm right now," said Josh. "Nice to see you, too, Danielle."

Barry placed his palms on the table and hefted himself

up out of the wheelchair. He swung his butt onto the table-top. There were half a dozen pictures of the prisoner scattered across Stealth's usual collection of maps.

"You are all aware of this new development. The Seventeens have found a means of keeping their intellect and awareness when they transform into exes. It would appear they still pose a threat to us." She held up one of the photographs. "Eduardo, last name unknown. He claims to be here under the orders of the gang's boss, an individual by the name of Peasy. According to Gorgon, the number and style of Eduardo's tattoos indicate he has been with the Seventeens for only a few months at best, which would be the proper rank for such an assignment."

Danielle blinked. "They're still initiating people?"

Gorgon nodded. "It's what they do. The gang just exists to grow, build up prestige, grab territory. There's no outside system left, but they still want the power."

"Next question," said St. George. "Have many of the Seventeens changed? Are most of them exes?"

"I dropped over a dozen of them when they attacked the other night. They're still alive. The majority of them, at least. And all five prisoners were alive when they were brought in."

"Are you sure your power doesn't work on the . . ." St. George shrugged. "On the smart ones? Maybe they're different somehow."

"I tried Eduardo in the cell. No effect. He's dead."

"About that," asked Barry, "did all the prisoners change?"

Stealth set her fist on the table and rested on her knuckles. "The two who committed suicide both became exes. So far only Eduardo has shown signs of intelligence."

"And we're sure he's intelligent? Not just spitting out words like a parrot or something?"

"As of yesterday he has taken part in three conversations. He is making definite, deliberate responses."

"Just playing devil's advocate," said Barry, "but we're usually fighting with the Seventeens over food and resources. From what I've heard so far, it sounds like these smart ones don't go chasing after people. I mean, none of them actually need to eat to survive, right?"

Josh nodded. "Eating seems to slow down decomposition somehow, on a minimal level, but it doesn't sustain them. We think it's just some sort of basic, primal urge from the reptilian part of the brain, one of the only things that still works."

"Good thing that's the only primal urge they act on," murmured Barry. It got a few chuckles.

"So this could be a good thing," tossed out St. George. "A new breed of exes that don't need to kill people."

"They might still do it for fun," said Gorgon.

"Of course, if they do decide to go after people, we're their main resource," said Danielle. "The Mount's just become a big grocery store."

"Open twenty-four hours," said Barry. "Thank you for shopping."

"So what is causing it?" Stealth glanced at Josh. "Some mutation in the virus?"

He shook his head. "The ex-virus doesn't mutate. We've grown thousands of cultures. No variation at all. If I had to guess, I'd say these smart exes have some quirk in their own cells that's making the virus react differently to them."

"So this is something new."

"You know what I'm wondering?" said Barry. "Why are the only ones we've seen Seventeens?"

St. George shrugged. "If you woke up as a smart ex, would

you come running up to the Melrose gate? There may be hundreds of them who are hiding from us."

"Doubtful," said Josh. "If it's a cellular mutation in the victim it has to be extremely rare. Last numbers I heard said there were over three hundred million exes in North America alone and there's never been a report of anything like this before."

"Out of three hundred million," argued Gorgon, "a few hundred is still pretty rare."

"Maybe the people are all just starting to mutate now," said Barry. "It could be some sort of evolutionary response to the virus, a survival-of-the-fittest thing."

Stealth shook her head.

"Maybe the virus just started to mutate now," added Gorgon. "There could be some new influence we don't know about."

Josh glared at him. "The virus doesn't mutate!"

"How can you be so sure?"

"How? Have you forgotten who I am?" He pulled his withered hand out from his pocket and thrust it at the goggled man. The parchment fingers trembled in the air. "I've been living with this damned thing hanging over my head for two years now. It doesn't change or *I'd know*!"

"Oh, that's right," said Gorgon. "I forgot, you're the fucking expert when it comes to dealing with the ex-virus."

"Shut the hell up."

"That's how Kathy died, wasn't it? Because of your expertise?"

"Yeah, you know what?" Josh straightened up and reminded them all how big he was. "Your teenage girlfriend's dead."

"Fuck you!"

"She died and I couldn't save her. She's dead, so's Meredith, so are millions of other people. Millions! You don't have any sort of special pass on grief, so just deal with it."

Danielle didn't lift her eyes from the map. "Like you have?"

He stabbed a finger at her. "You're the last one to be pointing out damaged people."

"*Quiet!*"

Stealth turned her head to each of them. "The next person who interrupts," she said, "I will break their right ring finger. Is that clear?"

They looked at her with raised eyebrows and slack jaws. Then, one by one, they shifted their gazes to St. George.

The Mighty Dragon shook his head and crossed his arms.

"Whipped," murmured Gorgon.

Josh and Danielle bit back their laughs. Barry tried and failed.

Stealth and St. George glared at him.

"May we continue?"

They nodded.

"We are all making wild guesses and assumptions. Without information there is nothing else we can do." She gestured at the map. "Therefore, we need to go make an assessment. The Seventeens' exact location, numbers, resources. If we can, determine how many of them have become exes. We know most of their activity has been centered here in Beverly Hills, between La Cienega and Century City. The last time Zzzap made a pass, three months ago, this seemed to be their base of operations."

Barry nodded. "They've used cars and a lot of the old National Guard barricades to block off roads and make walls.

Gregory, Maple, Pico, Century Park East. They're all just one massive pileup, three cars high at places. Decent amount of barbed wire and stakes, too. Pretty much impassable by anything that can't think and climb." His finger made a set of slashes across the map.

Gorgon shook his head. "That's a hell of a lot of space. How many people are we talking about?"

Barry shifted on the table. The dark woman traced the outline he had described. "We are estimating about twenty-two thousand," she said.

St. George's palms hit the tabletop. "What!?"

"That was three months ago. A population of that size has had several births and deaths since then."

"They've got twenty-two thousand people living there," repeated Gorgon. "They're doing *better* than us?"

"It's like the Dark Ages," Barry said. "They don't have electricity past a few generators. Barely any working vehicles that I've seen. Most of their people are using torches and cooking over bonfires. Half their guards are armed with baseball bats and spears."

"They have raw numbers," said Stealth. "We have everything else."

St. George cast his eyes between the woman and the dark-skinned man. "Why didn't you tell us this?"

"I decided it would be demoralizing to the populace of the Mount. The more people who knew, the better the chance it would slip out."

Gorgon shook his head. "So this asswipe gang we've been telling everyone is no real threat is actually ruling their own kingdom with almost five times the manpower we've got?"

"Assuming they recruit children and the elderly into their ranks," said Stealth, "yes, they are. I believe less than twenty percent of that number are actual members of the Seven-teens. To continue the medieval analogy, the rest are living as serfs in exchange for protection."

Josh pointed with his good hand. "Is that Roxbury Park?"

"It was," said Stealth. "They are using it as their own farm now."

He nodded and twisted his lip. "I proposed to Meredith there."

Gorgon sighed. Barry looked up to examine a ceiling panel.

"Question," said Danielle to fill the silence. "What about this Peasy, their big boss?" She looked at Gorgon. "You dealt with the Seventeens all the time. Who is he?"

The goggles swept back and forth over the map. "No idea. None of the guys I knew who were near the top before things fell apart. Might be a new player."

"Are you sure?"

He shrugged. "There were a dozen or so men in their upper circle. The only ones with similar names were two Pedros and one idiot who called himself Painkiller, real name Fernando."

Stealth tilted her head under the hood. "Painkiller?"

"He was a fucking idiot, trust me. Convinced he had some kind of superpower. Tried to fight me twice with his eyes closed, once while wearing a welding mask."

Danielle tilted her head. "Did that work?"

"No."

"Did he have any kind of power?"

"Besides a superhuman ability not to learn from his mistakes? No. Neither of the Pedros struck me as ruthless enough to run the gang, either. Good lieutenants, not real leaders."

Stealth looked at the map. "Is there anyone in the next level who might fit?"

"The next level is a hundred guys. Probably twice that if they've gotten as big as you're saying. Without a real description it could be anyone. Hell, Peasy could be someone who just moved in and took over." He swiped at the map and knotted his fists once or twice.

"What?"

"It pisses me off," he said. "I used to know the SS backwards and forwards. We've downgraded them as a problem for so long we don't know a fucking thing about them anymore."

"Thus, the recon," said Stealth. "A small team. Two at most."

"Just us?" asked Gorgon. "Or were you thinking of civilians?"

She shook her head. "After Zzzap, St. George and I are the fastest. We are also the best suited to operating without support."

St. George raised an eyebrow. "How tough do you think this is going to be?"

Stealth ran her finger across the map. "Four and a half miles each way. Keeping a low profile, that is a full day of travel with no backup. With actual reconnaissance time, we will be gone for almost two days."

Danielle tapped the map. "Why not just have Barry do another flyover? Faster and easier."

"Since he cannot hold anything," said Stealth, "we cannot get images. Everything would come down to his memory, descriptive ability, and how long it would take to debrief him."

"Plus, I'm not exactly subtle," he said with a wink. "Hard to do covert ops when you're brighter than the sun."

"We need to see what they are doing when they believe we are not observing, get a solid idea of their forces, and perhaps discover who this Peasy is."

The pen Josh was twirling between his fingers clicked on the table. "Oh, hell."

"What?"

"Not Peasy," he said. He looked up at them. "Pee-Zee."

Barry tilted his head. "What?"

"I was thinking about the virus and how it doesn't mutate, and that got me thinking about the contagion and all the news announcements they kept making to keep people updated, and then it just hit me—"

"Pee-Zee," repeated Stealth.

St. George glanced at their faces. "Am I the only slow one?"

"Patient zero," said Josh.

It's What's Inside That Counts

THEN

EVEN WITH THE SHORTAGE of pilots these days, we rated air travel. The rest of the team was in a passenger plane, sitting in real padded seats. I was on a bench, leaning against the interior wall of a C-130J Hercules, strapped into a five-point harness. Cerberus was broken down into over a dozen components and stored for transport. The crates were strapped to the sides of the plane, heavy Anvil cases mounted on solid wheels. With the way things were collapsing across the country, I wasn't about to let it out of my sight.

The Cerberus Battle Armor System took five months to design and another four to build. At least six weeks of that was waiting for parts. Plenty of people had been working on exoskeletons before me. There was the Hardiman stuff the Navy tried in the sixties. Just before everything fell apart, Hugo Herr at MIT had one. UC Berkeley had their Bleex rig and the Hulc. Sarcos Incorporated had a great one. And all I had to do was flash my DARPA card and say "national security," and I got to look at the blueprints and software for all of them, whether they liked it or not.

Then you can add in all the optional extras. The Army's Future Force Warrior system. Interceptor body armor. The latest Taser designs. Motion-sensor targeting programs. All this technology was just sitting around, waiting for one clever woman to put it all together.

Yes, I stole from the best.

New York's been lost. No one wants to say it, but there it is. The entire city's gone. Boston, too. And Chicago. Washington, DC's hanging on by a thread, but I understand the president and his cabinet were evacuated to NORAD over a week ago. The West Coast cities seem to have fared a little better, probably because they've got more sprawl and less concentration. One of the last decisions made by the DOD was to ship me and the suit out west. I was supposed to team up with some of the "superheroes" out there and be a visible symbol of government power, action, and safety in Los Angeles.

The rest of the Hercules was taken up by a platoon's worth of Marines. I say "worth" because they were a patched-together group, a few surviving squads, individuals, and raw recruits out of basic that had been reorganized to make a functioning unit. I knew soldiers tended to be younger than most people thought, but seeing a bunch of kids all still in their teens drove it home. They were loud and boastful and bragging. And they were white-knuckle scared. Almost two-thirds of the current enlisted US military servicemen were dead. Half of them were still walking.

Our plane tilted and everyone shifted their feet. One of the flight crew spoke for a few minutes to the platoon sergeant, a tall, heavyset man who spent the flight checking his troops. He nodded to the airman and walked back to me.

"Little course correction," he said. His voice was loud and brash over the roar of the engines. He was ten years older than most of the men and women following him.

"Is there a problem?"

"No, ma'am, there's been a development at Burbank. We're diverting to Van Nuys."

"That's farther into the Valley, isn't it? We're going deeper into held territory?"

"Technically, yes, but the airport is a safe zone. Approximately two hundred civilians and staff there."

"How much longer?"

"Thirty minutes." He held out his hand. "Staff Sergeant Jeffrey Wallen."

I nodded at his nametag. "I know."

"I've been meaning to compliment you on your outfit."

I'd been issued a flak jacket with no tags and a helmet. I wore them over my street clothes. "Well, nothing says military consultant like the Red Sox and digital camos."

"You a fan?"

"An ex-boyfriend left it in my apartment. It's got long sleeves and I don't care what happens to it."

"No love lost?"

"None."

"When'd he dump you?"

"How do you know I didn't dump him?"

The staff sergeant shook his head and sat down next to me. "Nobody dumps somebody back home. It's always the other way around."

I smiled. "Seven months ago."

"That's cool," he nodded.

"Go for it, Wall!" A few yards back in the plane, one of the Marines sent a double thumbs-up our way and the others hooted and cackled. It was the happiest, the most normal they'd looked for the whole flight.

Wallen stared him down, but it was a friendly stare. "Sorry about that."

I shrugged it off. "They're just blowing off steam."

"So, you're on the Cerberus team, huh?"

"You could say that, yeah."

He nodded. "You been with them a long time?"

"Why do you ask?"

"I'm just wondering about this guy," he said with a shrug. "What do you know about him?"

"Who?"

He jerked his thumb over at the crates. "Danny Morris," he said. "The guy in the suit."

"I'm sorry . . . ?"

"A bunch of the guys are just kind of wondering why a lab professor suddenly decides to be a government-sponsored superhero, y'know? Especially someone with no service history."

I bit my tongue and nodded. "Makes sense."

"So how much do you know about him?"

I toyed with a couple crude answers, but settled on "Quite a bit."

"Like?"

"Genius IQ. Confident. The only person who completely understands how the suit works and can use it with any degree of competence."

"Arrogant cocksucker, then? You can say it, I won't tell."

I smirked. "I think all of you need to keep in mind that suit can flip a Humvee with one hand."

"For real?"

I nodded. "It threw a three-ton test weight fifty-five meters in one of the early trials, and we've made improvements since then."

"Shit," he grinned. "That's bitchin'."

"Yeah. Also, never say Danny."

"No?"

"No. It's always Danielle. Or Dr. Morris."

"Danielle?" He struggled with it for a few seconds and then his eyes went wide. "Oh, shit. Sorry, ma'am. Dr. Morris. All of us just heard the name on the radio and—"

"Staff Sergeant, sir!?" The airman was snapping his fingers again. Wallen gave me a quick glance and swayed across the deck. They talked for a moment and his shoulders sagged. He gave a sharp nod to the Marines as he made his way back to me. They weren't buying it, either.

"What's going on?"

"Van Nuys has been compromised. One of their fences fell fifteen minutes ago. We're landing in a hot zone."

"Can't we go back to Burbank?"

He shook his head and leaned closer. "Burbank's gone. Completely overrun. Right now our best bet is to land at Van Nuys and come out fighting."

"Aren't there other airports in Long Beach and San Diego?"

"Way too far out of the way."

"Where's my team? Are they meeting us there?"

He looked me in the eyes. "Your team landed at Burbank forty-five minutes ago."

"They—"

"We don't know anything for sure. The tower there's gone silent. But we have to assume they're gone."

"So we're fighting?"

He nodded and set his jaw. "Don't worry, ma'am. We're Marines."

"I'm not worried." I undid the buckles on my flight harness and stood up. "Let's get the crates open."

Wallen blinked. "What?"

"We're going to fight," I said. "That's what I'm here to do. I'll need ten men for some heavy lifting."

He looked at the crates and back at me. His military brain was jamming up in an unexpected, noncombat situation. I'd seen it happen before.

I shrugged out of my flak jacket, swayed over to the cases, and yanked on the first ratchet strap. "With my four-person team it takes me ninety minutes to put the suit on. Give me enough men, Staff Sergeant, especially if they've got some basic electronics knowledge, and we can cut that in half. You can circle the airport once and I'll be ready."

I thumbed the combination locks, released the clasps, and opened the first crate. It was the helmet. The head. Cerberus glared out of the case at me with wide eyes and a fierce mouth.

It was what Wallen needed to see. "Little," he snapped, "Netzley, Carter, Berk. You and six other volunteers get over here and help the lady get ready to kick some ass." Then he reached past me and pried open the second ratchet.

I tried not to think too much about stripping in front of them, but to their credit only two of the male Marines and one woman stared as I dropped my clothes and pulled on the skintight undersuit. Cerberus doesn't have a spare millimeter for excess clothing. From an ideal, technical point of view, I should be naked, but there are limits to what I'll do, even during the apocalypse.

Just over forty minutes later Wallen connected the last USB cables while Carter and Netzley held the battlesuit's head over mine. He met my eyes. "Is that everything?"

I nodded. "Good work, Staff Sergeant."

"Just show me it was worth it." He nodded to the two Marines and the helmet dropped down over me. I was plunged into claustrophobic darkness and the tight space of the dead suit pressed in. I had twenty-three seconds while they locked the bolts and the mainframe booted.

Not all my work was stolen. I'd come up with the two elements that had been hindering everyone else.

First was a reactive sensor system with no delay. Most exoskeletons were clumsy because every one of the wearer's movements had to be fed back to the mainframe, which then made calculations and fed instructions back out to the individual joints and limbs. The whole process could take as much as half a second when someone was making complex movements like, say, walking, and half seconds start to pile up faster than you'd think they could. It slowed reaction time and forced people to move and act differently wearing the suits, against their reflexes.

In all fairness, this idea was somewhat borrowed as well, but I don't think I'm going to get sued by a brontosaurus. My grad-school roommate was a budding paleontologist who once mentioned the bigger dinosaurs had what amounted to a backup brain, a large nerve cluster that served no purpose but to keep their legs coordinated while impulses traveled up and down their spine. I stole the idea and created the idea of subprocessors built into every joint. Piezoelectric sensors fed to the minicomputers, which would relay back to the main processor while triggering the servos. Cut the reaction time to less than one-sixtieth of a second.

The power source was original. I'd love to say it's something amazing that would've changed the world and been installed everywhere, but it isn't. It's kind of exoskeleton specific. In very, very simple terms, it uses the negative movements of the suit to recharge in the same way hybrid cars use retrograde braking to recharge their batteries. Not a great analogy, but the best I can do that doesn't take six pages. And it means a forty-minute battery array can last over two hours of full use on one charge. Those two courses in anatomy and biometrics actually paid off in the long run.

The battlesuit's mainframe hummed to life and the darkness vanished. Staff Sergeant Jeff Wallen appeared in front of me with his men behind him. Power ran through my limbs and one hundred and thirty-seven tingling sensors lit up across my body. Targeting matrixes. Power levels. Ammo counters. Integrity seals.

I was strong again.

The Marines looked even younger and smaller as I gazed down at them. The tallest was three feet beneath me. "How long until we land?"

"Six minutes," said Wallen. "We're on final approach. Are you as badass as you look in that thing?"

My grim smile was wasted on them. "So much more than you can guess. Ready, Staff Sergeant?"

"Born ready, ma'am."

"Not ma'am," I said, and my voice growled over the speakers. "From here on in, it's just Cerberus."

He nodded and gave an evil grin. "Let's look alive, Marines," he bellowed. "We're on the ground and fighting in five." They leaped away and hid their nervousness with hollers and ammo checks.

The Hercules shook as the landing gear hit the tarmac. Inertia yanked us all in two or three directions. The suit's gyroscopic systems kicked in, made me a statue. I took a deep breath and rolled my shoulders. Cerberus did the same on a much larger scale and half a dozen armor plates shifted across the suit's back and shoulders.

The ramp dropped with a whine of motors and a hiss of

pistons. It wasn't halfway down before we could see the dead things staggering across the runway toward our plane. I raised my arm and three hundred and ninety-five thousand dollars' worth of targeting software kicked in. Crosshairs blossomed in my sight, ballistic information scrolled by in my peripheral vision, and the cannons thundered. Four exes exploded into dark puddles before the ramp hit the tarmac.

By technical definition, the Browning M2 was a massive, one-hundred-forty-pound semi-automatic rifle, but it was hard to think of it as anything except a cannon. Normally they were mounted on Humvees, helicopters, or aircraft carriers. The Cerberus suit had one of them mounted on each arm, their barrels reaching a good foot past its three-fingered fists. Twin ammo belts swung back to the file cabinet–sized hopper mounted on the armor's back. They could fire nonstop for three and a half minutes, with an effective range just shy of two miles.

I stomped down to solid ground flanked on either side by half a dozen Marines. Gunfire echoed across the landing strip and another ten exes fell. They were young and nervous, but they knew how to kill. I heard two screams as the dead fell on them. Having a three-hundred-ton aircraft hit the ground a few feet away hadn't stunned any of them. They were right on top of us.

I moved out from under the plane's tail. The suit identified dozens of targets. The cannons roared again and another handful of exes vanished in dark red clouds.

Another scream came from behind us and I switched views inside the helmet. There were two or three exes crawling on the ground. The engines drowned out their chattering teeth. Their legs and spines had been crushed when the Hercules rolled over them during its landing, but that didn't stop exes. One of them had Tran by the leg, gnawing through his camos and drawing blood. He beat its head in with his rifle stock and then fell over, clutching his calf and screaming. Netzley and Sibal stalked the other crawlers, and their skulls shattered with loud, harsh claps of gunfire.

"Dose him," shouted Wallen with a gesture at the wounded Marine. Carter ran forward and stabbed hypos into Tran one after another. There was a common rumor massive doses of antibiotics could save you from the ex-virus. It wasn't true. Officials have tried to stomp it out to conserve supplies.

The ramp hissed closed and I targeted another four exes. Their heads popped into red mist. O'Neill was next to me, and the empty brass smacked against his shoulder and scorched his uniform.

I glared down at Wallen. "This was the better landing zone?"

He scowled back at me. "Yeah," he barked. "What's that tell you?" His rifle banged and a dead Mexican man flew back, arms flailing.

"We've got radio," shouted Wallen. "Survivors are in the main building." He pointed across the tarmac, and a distant figure on a rooftop hopped and waved its arms.

As I turned my head, the targeting software haloed several dozen exes between the runway and the building. "Watch your step," I bellowed over the speaker. "Let me take point." I pushed past them and grabbed the closest dead thing, crushing its skull in my fist. Not efficient, but it was the kind of morale boost they needed.

I marched forward with the Marines flanking me. It took a month of fighting before officers realized the standard fire team didn't serve much use against the exes. There were no grenade launchers or M240s here. Just your basic M-16 for everyone, bayonets mounted, all set on single shot—no bursts allowed.

The walking dead continued to flail at us as we marched across the airfield. A quarter mile to the south the armor magnified the remains of a chain-link fence. It had been bent and twisted and pressed flat to the ground for a length of twenty yards, and dozens of exes were staggering through the opening every moment. No additional barriers or watch-towers. The people hiding here had trusted a chain-link fence with some barbed wire to protect them from hundreds, maybe thousands of massed undead.

"The perimeter's compromised," I told Wallen.

He gave a sharp nod. "We can't stay here."

My cannons lined up and fired a few dozen rounds at the distant fence. I watched a line of headless exes drop. The next wave tripped over their bodies, and so did the next. It wasn't much, but it was a space. "Suggestions?"

"The main resistance is in Hollywood," he said as we continued toward the terminal. "It's eleven miles east-southeast of here. We hole up with these folks for a minute, get some transport together, and then get moving."

Wallen's Marines cleared a path for us. By the time we'd reached the building they'd put down almost a hundred exes. We made it into the private terminal and I swore inside the armor. Not one defensive structure set up. These people hadn't prepared for anything. I wondered how long they'd been here, or planned to be here? Once that fence went down they were exposed and defenseless.

We could hear screams up ahead. And under the screams, hundreds of teeth clicking.

There were over thirty bodies in the hall. Only a handful had been exes. A few dead things were gnawing on limbs and clawing their way into torsos. The Marines made short work of them. One of the younger ones, Mao, threw up.

We passed a handful of offices before we entered the main section of the terminal. It was like the lobby of an office building. Maybe fifty people were scattered across the room as they tried to hold off twice as many exes. They were fighting with fire axes, shovels, and two-by-fours. Barely any firepower among them.

One fat idiot had a shotgun and kept blasting exes in the stomach. He didn't seem to notice when he took down one of his own people with his wild aim. "Fucking hell," he hollered, "the goddamned Army finally showed up!" He grinned, threw a loose salute at the Marines, and a teenage girl with a bloody, ragged torso wrapped her arms around him and took a chunk out of his neck. The fat man turned to throw her off and an old Chinese ex grabbed his arm and sank its teeth into his biceps. His shotgun went off one last time and he went down screaming.

Another dozen people had died just since we walked into the room. I stomped forward and began crushing skulls. Wallen was right behind me, driving his bayonet through eye sockets. The Marines were damned good. In five minutes every ex in the room was dead. Seven civilians had died, and one more Marine.

"Who's in charge here?" shouted Wallen.

A bulky man with a hunting rifle stepped forward. "That'd be me. Mark Larsen."

"How many people do you have here, Mr. Larsen?"

He looked at the bodies. "I think we're down to about thirty of us down here. I've got fourteen families upstairs."

"Any transport?"

"A couple trucks, including a diesel fueler. We've been waiting for someone to tell us where to go."

"Good man," said Wallen, clenching his fist. "Have someone get them warmed up and get your people. We're moving out as soon as possible." He looked at the crowd of Marines. "Alpha team, you're with the trucks. Beta, keep the families safe."

"Wall," shouted someone. "Another wave of exes coming from the south. Lots of them."

"How many is lots?" he shouted back.

O'Neill leaned in from the hall. "Maybe four digits, sir. We've got ten minutes, tops."

"I'm going out," I said. "I can get in deep and hold them off." He nodded and I followed O'Neill back up the hall.

The Marines were smart and well trained. They hadn't wasted time with a solid barricade, just knocked over a ton of stuff for exes to trip and fumble with. They'd settled back and were letting off controlled, aimed shots, like a shooting range.

There were just too many, though. The Marines were making a dent, but they weren't slowing the tide.

I marched toward the shambling crowd, cannons blazing. At this range, a round from the M-2s could go through four or five skulls before slowing down. I thundered through a hundred rounds in a few bursts and dropped twice as many exes. Then they were around me and I fired up the stunners.

Exes don't have any sense of pain, but they still have nervous systems, and those systems are still linked to their muscles. Which means a 200,000-volt blast will still drop one. The key thing to remember is it won't stop them. The second the juice is off, they're good to go again.

One pass of my hands and a dozen exes collapsed. I brought my arms back and watched ten more drop. Rounds splattered off the concrete as O'Neill, Laigaie, and Mao kept them down.

All around me. Ten, twenty, thirty of them. I swung my arms, swept a group of them together with a crunch of bones. They were hanging on my arms, on my legs, clutching at my waist. The sound of chattering teeth filled the battlesuit. I thrashed. I pounded. Warning lights flashed to remind me of the unexpected extra weight on each limb. I kept my eyes shut and crushed anything I got my hands on. My arms swung and I felt bodies slam against them.

I normally don't suffer from claustrophobia. Even when I first started wearing and testing the armor there weren't any panic attacks or nervous moments. It wasn't until the first time I waded into a horde of exes that I started feeling trapped in the suit.

Someone shouted my name. It came again and I opened my eyes. Dozens of corpses surrounded me. The Marines had fallen back another thirty or forty feet. And a fresh wave of ex-humans was closing on me.

Ma Deuce and her twin sister had a shouting match that left fifty or sixty exes sprayed across the tarmac. The armor thudded back while O'Neill and Mao dropped a few dead things. We moved out around the terminal toward a row of hangars. The lenses switched and I saw the row of families running alongside them.

Wallen turned to check our flank and a tall ex fell on him. It was like the cheap-shot scare in a movie. A brunette woman, so close he didn't have a chance. The walking corpse snapped its jaw and bit off most of his right cheek. The flesh peeled away and his nose stretched up with it for a moment.

He yelled out and froze. Just for a second. Long enough for the ex to get a second mouthful. There was a crack as his nose broke and was pulled off his face.

The Marines brought their guns up to shoot, but Wallen was flailing. A second ex latched onto his torso and sank its jaws in just above his collar. Dry fingers pulled at his arms, teeth pulled at his fatigues, and he fell back into the growing crowd of the dead. He never made another sound.

"Go!" shouted O'Neill. "We need to get to the trucks now!"

The M-2s turned the hangar wall behind us into confetti and I smashed through whatever was left. The Cessna inside got thrown out of the way as I cut through the next wall and into the hangar past that. The Marines flowed through the bottleneck. The exes bunched up.

Five minutes and another couple dozen dead exes later, we were at the trucks. Families were packed in the back and into the cabs. A third of the rifle platoon was missing. Netzley kept trying her radio with no response.

"Move out," I shouted. "I've got point, everyone falls in behind me. Anything gets within ten feet of the trucks, you put it down. Clear?"

There was a shout from the Marines, my optics flared to white, and I heard a dozen screams. The computer struggled to compensate and the airport reappeared on the screens. The light was all wrong. Everything was bright and washed-out. The civilians were looking up, their mouths open in awe, and two old Latina women were crossing themselves again and again.

Hanging above us was the shape of a man. It sizzled in the air, like high-tension lines on a damp morning. The white outline gave a friendly salute to Carter and tipped its head at me.

Howdy. The voice buzzed like someone talking with a kazoo, except you could understand him. *I heard you were coming. Would've been here sooner but a lot of people thought you were still landing at Burbank.*

The suit's sensors were still going wild. "What about the other team? Did the other plane make it?"

The burning wraith seemed to slump a bit. *They didn't. I'm sorry.*

O'Neill fired at a distant ex and looked back up. "You're Zzzap, right?"

Here to guide you to relative safety. The figure nodded at me again. *Doctor Danielle Morris, I presume?*

"No," said Carter before I could speak. "That's Cerberus."

Seventeen

NOW

IT WAS ELEVEN when they left. St. George sailed through the air, watching the streets below for any movement past the slow drift of exes. A few caught glimpses of him and tilted their heads to follow his path. One fell over backward.

He couldn't glide as well as he normally did. The backpack was filled with water bottles and a small first-aid kit. It was slim and light, but it sat wrong. His balance was off and he just couldn't find the sweet spot on the air currents.

On the rooftops below, Stealth flitted like a shadow. She darted between pools of darkness and leaped from building to building. When they got to an intersection she would throw herself out into space, grab his outstretched hands like a trapeze artist, and flip herself across four lanes of open road. Her cloak never made a sound as it billowed in the air.

The two heroes cut across the Wilshire Country Club, the upper-class neighborhoods of Highland, and the wide swath of LaBrea. Stealth killed eleven exes in that first hour, their necks snapped with blinding kicks. St. George just twisted their heads around.

They paused to rest on the roof of a deserted diner. "You doing okay?"

"I am fine. We do not need to stop."

"You look like you're slowing down."

The cloaked woman shook her head. "I am fine."

"Drink some water."

She held the bottle and paused. He felt her eyes on him.

"What?"

"Turn around, please."

"I'm sorry, what?"

She gave a slight tip of her head. "I do not want you to see me drink."

"You're kidding."

"No."

"You've known me for over two years, I'm probably the closest thing you have to a friend, and you're worried I might see your mouth?"

"Please, St. George. Turn around."

He sighed, shook his head, and went to look over the edge of the roof. There were over two hundred exes scattered over the broad intersection. Every few yards on the sidewalk a squat wooden stump reached up between iron grates. A few of them were wide remains of huge palms, but most were as thick as his arm.

There was a deliberate crunch of gravel. She handed him the backpack. "Thank you."

"I know you're not scarred or disfigured or something, so why are you so obsessed with hiding?"

"How can you know I am not scarred?"

He smirked. "There are dozens of horribly injured people at the Mount. Half your face would have to be missing to be worse off than them, and I can see enough to know it's all still there."

"It could be a small scar. Perhaps I am vain."

He nodded. "That would fit with the rest of the outfit, but I still don't buy it."

"You are still making suppositions. You have no evidence."

"Two questions, then. When's the last time someone called you by your real name?"

"I will not answer questions regarding my true identity."

"Didn't ask one. I just asked how long it's been since someone called you by your real name."

She tilted her head.

"I know 'Stealth' wasn't your choice for a name. Wasn't it someone in the *LA Weekly* or one of those that came up with it? You didn't use any code name or secret identity or anything. So Stealth isn't a name you picked. When was the last time someone used the name you were born with?"

Even in the dim light beneath the hood, he could see her expression shift under the mask. "Twenty-eight months ago."

St. George blinked. "You know just like that?"

She gave a single, sharp nod.

"Okay then, question two. When was the last time someone saw you without the mask?"

"Someone who knew me?"

"Anyone. When was the last time anyone saw you without the mask?"

"Thirteen months. When we were getting settled in the Mount, I spent an evening walking the streets in civilian clothes to judge the mood of the population. October 31, 2009."

"Halloween? The last time you didn't wear a mask was Halloween?"

"The irony is not lost on me. However, it struck me amid the many costumes one unfamiliar adult would be less likely to stand out."

"So the costume says you have no problem with people looking at you. Staying masked and never having a name means you're bothered by who you were and you're trying to hide it. I'm going to go out on a limb and guess you were objectified a lot."

She bowed her head. "Your deductive powers have grown considerably since we first met."

"It's all been your fine instruction, Mr. Holmes," he said, toasting her with a plastic bottle. He took another sip and pointed at one of the nearby remains of a tree. "D'you notice the stumps?"

She nodded. "Firewood. As Zzzap reported, they are using fires for heat, light, and food preparation. I would guess most bookstores, newsstands, and office suppliers in this area have suffered a similar fate."

"They've got the country club, too, don't they? And Century City."

"And telephone poles. And several hundred thousand tires, I would guess." She nodded at a row of wheel-less cars. "They would be unusable for cooking, but could still provide light and heat. Are you in love with me?"

He spit out a mouthful of water. "What?"

"You have regular sexual relations with Beatrice Strutton, but you remain emotionally obsessed with me. I believe she is aware of this as well."

"Okay, how do you know—"

"There is nothing that goes on in the Mount I am not aware of, St. George. You know this. And you have not answered the question."

"You're so smart, you tell me."

She turned her head to the exes below. "I believe you have

allowed what began as a physical attraction and fascination with my superior confidence to develop into emotions you hope I will recipro—"

"I was being rhetorical, y'know."

Stealth knelt against the edge of the roof.

"What?"

She stared down at the street below. "They are not moving."

"Because we're not."

The crowd of exes stood frozen on the street. Their mouths were still. Dozens of hands hung limp at their sides. They locked eyes with the two heroes.

Her head shook inside the hood. "Not at all. Not reaching for us. Not even moving their jaws."

The silent crowd stared up at them. White eyes. Cloudy eyes. Single eyes. Empty sockets.

"Okay," murmured St. George. "Just when you thought the walking dead couldn't get any creepier."

The dead things and the heroes stared at each other for another moment. Then the exes nearest the diner trembled, and the subtle shift rippled though the crowd. Dozens of feet shuffled on the ground. Their teeth snapped together. Their arms rose up as they clutched again and again for the people they could not reach.

"Well," he said, "that didn't seem at all suspicious."

She stood up from the ledge. "It is apparent something is altering the behavior of exes across the city," she said. "Are you ready to move on? We need to reach the Seventeens' territory at least two hours before dawn."

He tugged the backpack over his shoulders. "We'll be fine."

Stealth nodded and hurled herself across the rooftop,

leaping up onto the next building. St. George threw himself into the air after her.

The exes watched them go.

× × ×

Gorgon walked up Avenue C into the North-by-Northwest area. The name had started as a joke and stuck. Now the residents used it with pride.

He cast a long, fuzzy shadow in the streetlights. As it always did, the mental image of an old western flashed through his mind, the sheriff's shadow stretching up Main Street to some gunslinger's boots.

Near the edges of New York Street a figure waved to him from a small group. The bearded man, Richard-something. North-by-Northwest was his area. He stepped away from his group and toward Gorgon.

"What's up?"

"Do you have a moment?"

"Sure."

The bearded man gave a faint nod and took another half step away from the other conversation. The men kept talking, but their eyes followed the district leader and the hero. "There were a lot of rumors flying over dinner," Richard said. He twisted the big ring he wore on his middle finger. "I was hoping you could put them to rest."

"I guess that depends on what they are," said the hero.

The older man nodded. "Is it true you found some exes who can talk?"

Behind his wide goggles, Gorgon rolled his eyes and gave a silent sigh. The news hadn't taken long to get out at all. "Where did you hear that?"

"It's been floating around since *Big Red* got back yesterday. One of the men said it was a talking ex that killed Tyler O'Neill."

"Yeah, see . . . that's how rumors go crazy and why you shouldn't talk about stuff you don't know anything about." He swung the duster back and set his fists against his hips. The sheriff pose. "Ty was killed by the Seventeens. Regular punks using regular weapons. Doctor Connolly could confirm that if anyone bothered to ask her."

"We tried. She and Doctor Garcetti said Stealth asked them not to discuss it."

Gorgon closed his eyes and thought of a few choice profanities. "Well, I can. He died of a gunshot wound to the throat. He bled out in under two minutes. You can look in the back of *Big Red* for the stains."

The bearded man shivered and one of the ones lurking in the background stepped forward. "But there was an ex there. I've heard from a couple people there was."

Another silent swear or three. "Yes. Yes, there was. You're . . . Mr. Diamond?"

"Daimint. I run the leatherworks."

"Right, of course. Sorry."

"So the exes can talk now? Is that new?"

"We don't think they can all talk. Just some of them."

"Did you say exes can talk now?" echoed a woman. She dragged her husband over with her. Another couple followed them.

"They found a talking ex last night."

"You mean they're intelligent?"

"If they can talk, I'd guess so."

"Holy shit," said a newcomer, "what if we've been murdering them?"

"Hey, if it's us or them, I say—"

"PEOPLE!" Gorgon punctuated the bellow with a quick snap of his lenses. He saw half a dozen people tremble and felt the faint kick of borrowed strength. The scattered conversation vanished.

"Here are the facts, to the best of my knowledge." He threw a victory sign up for them all to see. "We have found two exes that appear to be intelligent. That's it. Two, out of *five million* here in Los Angeles alone. We're not even sure they're real exes. It may be a trick. All of us standing here know this has never been seen before. It's something new we're all trying to figure out."

A few of them looked at him but most of them examined their feet or the pavement.

"The medical team's going to examine our prisoner tomorrow. Once they get any answers, you know we'll get them to you. The safety of everyone here is always the priority. There's no point getting worked up over this, okay?"

There were a few halfhearted nods and grunts. The woman who had spoken before cleared her throat. "So there really are smart exes?"

"Yes," he said. "And here's something else—neither of them tried to bite anyone. I've talked to the one here in the cell. So has Stealth. It just stood there and talked with us. St. George, Cerberus, a bunch of the team that was out the other day, they all talked to the one out there. No attacks."

"St. George got shot by the one out there. I'm trying to repair his coat." This from Daimint.

"It shot him, yeah," agreed Gorgon. "It didn't bite him. The two we've seen don't act like smart exes, they just act like people. Unfortunately the people they're acting like are Seventeens. So get the word out, okay? All of you."

He let the coat swing closed and crossed his arms across his chest, just below the silver star. The all-done gunslinger pose. They took the hint and began to scatter.

"Thank you," said Richard-something.

"No problem. Let's try to keep this sort of thing down, okay? That's why we've got district leaders. Last thing we need is for people to think there's some army of genius exes out there trying to kill us all."

Eighteen
NOW

THEY STOPPED ON the roof of a large house at the corner of Gregory and El Camino. St. George hid between the twin plaster chimneys while Stealth crouched in plain sight, her cloak blending into the tile shingles and shadows.

A line of tire-less cars stretched down Gregory Way, stacked two high along the southern sidewalk. A Hummer filled both levels at one point, as did a small orange U-Haul truck. A few yards apart, concrete road barriers were wedged up against the vehicles, pinning them in place. Chain-link fence stretched out along the cars. Jagged spears of metal stood like trench spikes, and it took St. George a moment to recognize them as street-sign posts. Large patches of green were spray painted across the wall of vehicles in two or three different shades.

Every fifty feet or so, a tall torch lit the night and spewed oily smoke. Men and boys clomped back and forth across the car roofs, weapons resting on their shoulders or slung under their arms. The two heroes watched them patrol and make small talk. Several of them sported bare arms or shaved heads. Even in the flickering light they could see green bandannas and patches on every one of them.

The crude wall reached off four or five blocks in either direction before fading into patchy darkness.

"I count twenty-three sentries patrolling the wall," Stealth said. "Thirteen have firearms, only four of which are automatic weapons. The rest are armed with spears and clubs."

St. George let his eyes drift off the wall and up and down the street. Dozens of stumps dotted the sidewalk and lawns where trees and bushes once stood. This had been a cozy neighborhood back in the day. He swept the road again. "There're barely any exes here."

Stealth's head panned back and forth inside the hood. "I count at least forty along this street."

"Forty's nothing," he said. "We've got twice that, minimum, at each gate every day." St. George gestured at the Seventeens walking the wall. "People in plain sight, in a clear eye line, there should be hundreds of them swarming this place. That wall should be mobbed."

"And yet the exes hardly seem to notice the humans."

"Strange things are afoot at the Circle K," he murmured.

"What?"

"Never mind. Do you hear music?"

She nodded. "We can cross there." Her arm was out and pointing west, another long shadow in the night. "Midpoint between two torches. In another three minutes, if the guards follow the same pattern, none of them should be along that section of wall."

He nodded and counted off the time in his head. They raced across the tiered rooftop and threw themselves into the night. Stealth grabbed a streetlight, spun once around the arm, and flipped across the street. She grabbed St. George's waiting hand above the wall, kicked her legs, and sailed across to another rooftop.

He landed next to her, freezing in the shadow of a large dish antenna. She had spread her cloak and half vanished into the darkness again. They watched the wall behind them. More concrete barriers lined this side, along with tables and patio chairs the guards had pulled from nearby houses.

The guards continued to pace and yawn. One stopped to light a cigarette on a torch. Another swung his arms back and forth to fight off the faint chill.

Stealth gave St. George a quick nod and headed south across the rooftops. He took a single leap and sailed after her, looking down on the deforested neighborhood as he went. Here and there they saw chimney smoke, and a few of the quasi-mansions were lit with flickering candles. Twice they stopped as torch-wielding patrols passed on the street or between buildings.

A long block later they were crouched on top of a Pavilions grocery store. Stealth gave him a quick nod, gestured out at the broad intersection, and vanished into the rooftop shadows. An ex's head sat in the corner of the roof, left over from some earlier purge. It was shriveled from the sun and its jaw trembled up and down, still animated by the virus. The skull's cloudy eyes stared at St. George and he rolled it away across the roof.

Olympic Boulevard was six lanes across, although the number of turn lanes and medians made it hard to be sure. The southbound road split just north of the east-west boulevard and created a complex double-intersection with a triangular island in the middle of it. Music he didn't recognize jangled back and forth between the buildings.

All the office buildings and stores he could see had their windows smashed out. Bullet holes filled the huge orange globe of the 76 gas station across the street, and someone had set all the prices to $6.66. There was a pile of machinery in the station's parking lot and in the dim light it took St. George a moment to realize they were dozens of smashed stoplights.

The one exception was the large brick building south of the intersection. The entrance sank below street level and thick ivy grew wild and untrimmed from the balconies. There were silver letters under the green plants, but something about the structure said law firm to him. The building was untouched and illumination poured out of the doors and windows. It was a beacon of clarity in the flickering firelight. He could hear the low purr of generators under the music that blared through a half-dozen speakers.

Most of the upper windows along Beverly had lamps or candles flickering in them. Dozens of tall torches lit the road, each one using a set of wheel rims as a weighted base. A huge fire pit had been built on the top level of a nearby parking garage, and he counted close to fifty people gathered around the pungent tire-fire. They laughed and joked and passed bottles back and forth. Down the road behind him he could see another bonfire with its own crowd. There were a few hundred people out wandering, partying, or making half hearted attempts at guard duty.

A large, single-story structure stood just southeast of the intersection of Olympic and Beverly Drive, right in the middle of a turn lane. A handful of guards circled it and yawned. In the shifting light of the torches, St. George could see the chain link and the supports and the slow, swaying figures packed inside.

Stealth reappeared next to him. "There are no rooftop guards anywhere," she whispered, "and no evidence the sentries include them as part of regular patrols." She sounded annoyed. She pointed across the street at a tall building bearing the letters FI ST PROPER. "I believe that will give us the best vantage point, and the added height decreases the chance of random searches."

Hidden by the night, they circled around, crossed the street, and scaled the building. The two heroes settled down and St. George shrugged off the backpack. They peered over the short rooftop ledge.

Beneath their last position, a single torch in the lower parking lot threw random shadows across the front of the building. In the flickering light, something large was crouched before the grocery store. Its arms were unnaturally long and spread wide. The figure shifted and steel chimed and clanked.

Stealth pulled a small, squat monocular from her belt and held it to her eye. She cursed a moment later and slid it back into its pouch. "Too bright for the starlight scope," she said, "and it does not register on infrared."

"So it's big, inhuman, and dead. Narrows the choices a bit."

She nodded. "Its lack of movement implies it is bound. I believe we can rest until sunrise."

They settled down behind the rooftop ledge.

He shrugged out of the leather jacket. "How long do we have?"

The hooded head turned to the east. "Two and a half hours. I will take the first watch. Get an hour of sleep."

St. George balled his jacket and tested his head against it. "You're not going to burst into flame come sunup or anything, are you?"

She stared at him. "This is neither the time nor the place for humor."

"Sorry." He threw a last glance across the intersection. "Windows are all good and it's got working generators. That says town hall to me."

"Something of importance," she agreed, "but I would prefer not to guess until we have more evidence."

"Care to guess on their lack of exes?" He settled back down on the makeshift pillow. "They must be a hell of a lot more aggressive about cleaning them out than we are."

"Except we rarely hear gunfire," she said, "and there are no bodies."

THEN

SON OF A BITCH this hurts. No chance of getting a ... what is it, a morphine drip? A couple Vicodin? Novocain? Something?

Where was I ... ?

Magic, right. Magic gets a bum rap these days.

When you say magic, people immediately assume one of two things. One is you're an entertainer. You're someone like Houdini or Copperfield who does a lot of work with handcuffs, scarves, and playing cards. Not a magician so much as a conjurer, a sleight-of-hand artist. Someone who excels at distraction and misdirection to get a laugh, some applause, and maybe a contract in Las Vegas.

That's the positive assumption.

The negative assumption, the one I'd been living with since college, is you're a nut. You're someone who wears too much eyeliner, memorizes episodes of *Buffy the Vampire Slayer*, and grew up in a strict Catholic home where Dad was a deacon and made you be an altar boy and now you're trying to rebel. You went out and bought all the books by Aleister Crowley, Edgar Cayce, and Nostradamus. Probably have bookshelves full of crystals and star charts and sage hanging over the windows and all that other new-age bullshit.

Here's the thing, though. Amid all that bullshit there are grains of truth. Really, there are. If you put any serious effort into it and dig through all the shit, you'll find the seeds of real magic. It's like . . . It's like if you want to be a successful writer, but you need to wade through a thousand books written by hacks and wannabes to glean a few useful hints and tips. And then you use those to improve your actual craft, which makes it easier to find the real stuff the next time you go digging. Crowley, Nostradamus, all those guys—they were like the Internet idiots who manage to get one thing right for every ninety-nine things they get wrong.

No, not Edgar Cayce. He was a complete charlatan. Hell, Houdini proved him to be a fake twice while he was alive and once after he died—Houdini, not Cayce. Yeah, Cayce was such a predictable fraud Houdini exposed him from beyond the grave.

But I digress.

So, yeah, there's real magic in the world. Just like you read about when you were little. Fireball-casting, demon-summoning, mystic-warding magic. Most of it isn't that flashy computer-game stuff, but it's real. And it's like any other art. You have to practice a lot, even if you've got some innate talent for it. You keep researching the craft and you keep digging for those seeds of wisdom. Eventually you feel good and give yourself a title, and then if you're lucky someone who *really* knows how things are done beats you down and reminds you you're still just a novice. If you're unlucky, you end up dead. But I'll get to that in a minute.

The other thing is, like any art, all the artists are being

challenged to do something new. Yeah, you can learn all the basics and do the same things everyone before you did. Nothing wrong with that. But if you want to stand out, if you want to be remembered, you've got to do something new.

Jesus, doc, can't I get something? At least an Advil or two? Some kind of anti-itch cream? No, antibiotics wouldn't do a damn thing and we both know it. I've been fighting these things for five months, where the hell have you been? For that matter, why am I off in a trailer and not the field hospital? Where the hell is Regenerator? Isn't he supposed to be dealing with all of us, to get us back in the field as quickly as possible?

Bitten? When? Jesus. Is he . . . I mean, hell, what did it do to him? I'd think if anyone was safe from all this beside the Dragon it would be—Seriously? A full-on coma, not just knocked out? Jesus.

Not that well. He's sort of like any coworker, y'know? But you say it's not spreading much past the actual bite? That must look creepy as hell.

Okay, fine. Where was I?

Still on magic, right. Doing something new. No, this is all going somewhere. If you're not going to give me any good drugs you can at least humor me in my final days.

So, just like there's real magic, there's real evil. Not Enron-Exxon-Halliburton incidents that disgust you with their greed or callousness. I mean real evil. The stuff that burns your eyes to look at. The stuff that makes you taste metal and dog shit when you hear it speak. The kind of evil so many people have conditioned themselves to ignore at all costs. It can be standing right in front of you and you can't acknowledge it, because it'd be like sticking a red-hot weed whacker in your brain.

Yeah, you can call it the Devil if you like. Satan. Chaos. Entropy. The Beast. There's an infinite number of names and titles and personalities. No, seriously. Infinite.

Anyway, that's the downside to magic, see? Once you start learning it, you have to go one way or another. With the evil or against it. And if you're against it, well . . . real evil doesn't know mercy or pity or gloating. It'll just erase you. So learning magic is a real sink-or-swim situation.

And that brings me back to doing something new, see? Ever hear the phrase "fight fire with fire"? Well, that's what I decided to do.

Y'see, there's a ton of low-level control spells and enchantments and glamours. No, not low-level like *Dungeons and Dragons*, you dipshit. As in basic, introductory stuff. Mental nudges, persuasion, that sort of thing. The glamour lasts for maybe a day or two if you focus. If you're good, you can make the edges blur and people won't even notice they're doing something they don't want to. It's good for making cash, getting girls in bed, that sort of stuff. Your targets do all the rationalizing for you.

Anyway, higher-level stuff is farseeing, telepathy, possession. Yes, possession is very real. So is exorcism, for that matter. I'd done three before I was twenty-five. Second one almost killed me. No, trust me, you don't want to know. No, it was so much worse than that. Look, seriously, I'd rather not talk about it, okay?

Is it getting hot in here or is it me? It is me? Shit, fever's setting in already? Is it always this fast? I thought it took a day or two. No? Seven hours is the average? Holy shit, since when? That long?

Y'know, if you'd just let me put on my . . . okay, okay, I'm lying down again. Everyone stay calm.

So, yeah, possession is real, which got me thinking about demons. There are hundreds of types, dozens of magnitudes, but one thing they all have in common is trying to influence people.

So they can ruin your life, that's why. Didn't you ever go to Sunday school? Shit. If they can corrupt you, ruin someone else, fuck over somebody—that emotional chaos is like food to them. It's the whole point of their existence.

Anyway, it struck me demons are so eager to jump in and influence us, but it's kind of a two-way street. They can't open that path without opening it both ways. And I decided to take advantage of that.

It took a bit of work. Combining summoning spells and possession spells. And they had to be damned specific. I'm talking ten times past space shuttle reentry math specific. And then I had to forge a set of control glyphs around the enchantments.

Look at it this way. You know computers? RAM and ROM? That's what I was doing. Taking flexible, mutable spells—the random memory—and, what would you call it, hard-wiring them into a solid, single-purpose device—the read-only-memory. Make sense?

That's how I ended up just outside Novosibirsk, Russia, on the afternoon of August 1, 2008. I had a darkness lens I'd carved from volcanic obsidian with a piece of bone, and I used it to focus a total solar eclipse into the platinum medallion I'd spent three years preparing.

Yes, that one right there in the lockbox. No, not onto it. *Into* it. It contains the light of a black sun. When I put it on a very specific kind of portal called a Sativus opens to a realm those of us in the know call the Abyss, and that's when I exchange bodies with a reaver—a demon—that calls itself

Cairax Murrain. It's sort of a reverse-possession that links us through the medallion. Rather than the demon's mind coming into our world and stealing control of my body, I'm transposing its body to our world through mine and possessing that.

Well, then you explain it, dipstick. Did they call you a jarhead before you signed up or was that just a fortunate career choice for you? Well, if that's so why don't you give me the medallion and we'll see just how fucked in the head I am?

Ahhh. You've seen him, then, doctor? Me, that is. Yeah, I know, it's confusing. It's such an odd perspective shift. I'd guess it's kind of like role-playing. Well, I was thinking about all those online games my friends played in college, but I guess it would hold for that kind of role-playing, too. When you're pretending you're someone else and getting absorbed in that world, but you're still aware you're you. That's what being Cairax is like. It's still me, I'm still making all the choices, but there's this very thick filter over everything.

You know what it's like? It's like Jekyll and Hyde. I've got the same mind and the same personality, just a slightly different set of morals. Different ethics. But it's still me. He won't do anything I don't want him to do.

Me. Not he. I don't do anything I don't want to.

Look, just let me put it on. You're barely doing anything, and what you are doing isn't even slowing this down. I'm burning up, my head is killing me, and the only reason I'm not throwing up is because I haven't kept anything down for twelve hours now.

Well, that's not really my fault. I mean, yes, I knew what I was doing. Just . . . remember the filter I told you about? It didn't seem any more out of line than jerking off or something.

Hey! I think rape is a little strong. She'd been dead for at least two days. No, I was very aware of that. It just . . . it didn't matter as much when I was Cairax. Yeah, you could call it that, I guess. No, hard as it may be to believe, when I changed back my first thought was intense pain. Yeah, go figure.

No, it's not the first time I've heard that, either. Split personality's a nice, easy label for people who don't want to dwell on the reality of what I can do. One of my fellow "heroes" has tried to explain away my abilities with a lot of scientific terminology, too. Suggestion. Psychokinesis. Mass hypnosis. All from a man who converts his body into pure energy at will.

Look, why can't I just get an aspirin? Is that really so much to ask? I mean, they think I'm important enough for a private room, why can't I actually get any treatment?

Conservation of resources? What the hell is that supposed to . . . oh. Oh, I see. Things have gotten that bad, eh? And here I thought these fine gentlemen were here just in case I died and turned a little faster than expected.

Well, then. That makes all this a bit easier.

Here's the thing, doc. You can choose to believe in magic or not. You can trust everything I've been telling you or you can say I'm some latent psychic if it makes you feel better. It doesn't matter. I don't care what you believe in. The Loch Ness Monster, Bigfoot, faked moon landings, the 2000 election results—you can believe in whatever fairy tale you want.

Let's be honest about what you know, though. You've seen me fighting out there. You know if I put on that medallion I'll change. I'll change into something bigger, stronger, and tougher. You can call it whatever you like. Demon. Polymorph. Lycanthrope. Again, I don't care. But it's my only chance.

Yeah, I see them, guys. They're not much of a threat at this point, are they? We all know I'm a dead man.

What do you mean, you don't know? This is kind of a no-brainer. If I don't put the medallion on, there's no question I'm going to die. If I put it on, there's a chance I'll live. Even I can see that. Hell, Cairax heals faster than me. There's a good chance he's recovered by now, which means I'll be recovered as soon as I change back.

Thank you, doctor.

This might be alarming for all of you. It only takes a few seconds, but it's big and scary and loud all at once. No, it's not anything like that. You'd just be amazed at how much pain a demon can fit into just a few secaaaa—

—aaahhhhh, yes.

Much better. Back in my favorite skin.

Now, now, my dear little doctor. Don't be scared. I may be a bit hard on the eyes and the sanity now, but it is still me. Just remember that filter I told you about.

The fear makes you smell delicious, by the way. Yes, just like food. Absolutely delicious. I just thought you should know.

Please be careful with the rifles, gentlemen. My reflexes are so much faster now, and the tail does have a mind of its own sometimes. No, it really does. I would hate for you to make a threatening gesture with a bayonet and be eviscerated before I knew what I was doing. What it was doing, that is.

What? Oh. Very observant of you, my little doctor. It doesn't seem to have healed at all, does it? I feel better, but the sensations in this body are always so muddled. No . . . no, there they are. The tiny things are still there, chewing away, weaving themselves into my blood and muscle.

Oh, perhaps. However, in retrospect, I think I shall remain in this skin. If there is any chance for me to survive, it will be in this form, yes? As Maxwell I had an hour or so left, less if you decided to conserve any more resources. No, I believe Cairax has a far better chance of fighting off the infection . . . or any of the dangers that apparently come with it.

Gentlemen, I asked you to please keep—ahhh, there. See what has happened? I did warn you about the tail. Doctor, please, please, do not waste your time. You and I both know there is no chance he survived that. My dear friend, perhaps you should place your rifle down on the floor and lie facedown. That will be a safer place for you to avoid your companion's fate. Thank you. Doctor dearest, if you could get next to him. I would hate for you to be hit by any loose metal when I go through the wall.

Where? Back to the shore, back to the sand. While we fritter away time here the contagion continues to spread. We need every hand fighting it for as long as they can and I have, if you will pardon the phrase, an appetite for destruction. If we are all lucky, being in this skin may give me several days, perhaps weeks, to rip and shred.

No, no, my dear little doctor. You are perfectly safe. I may look like a monster, but I am still Maxwell Hale inside this skin. I would never harm another human being.

Very well. I would never *deliberately* harm another human being. Is that better?

The ingratitude of some people . . .

Twenty

NOW

MIKE AND JOHN stood in the small parking lot across from the cells and debated what to do with the prisoner. "Does he need to eat?"

John shrugged his lanky shoulders. "Of course he needs to eat."

"Yeah, but he's . . ." Mike shrugged back and scratched his beard. "He's an ex. Does that mean he only eats people or meat or what? What do we give him?"

"Good point."

"I mean, I haven't had any meat in two months. Remember when they found that case of tuna?"

"Yeah."

He mulled it over. "They've gotta have some canned meat stored away in the food bank. You think they'd free up some Spam or something for a prisoner?"

"I don't know if Spam counts as meat either."

"Well, fuck him. If we get him something and he doesn't want it, we can eat it."

"Good point," nodded John with a grin.

They banged on the door. "Hey," called Mike. "You hungry? What do you want for breakfast?"

A thump and some scuffling came from inside.

"What's his name?"

John's narrow shoulders bounced again. "I don't know. Everyone just said the dead guy."

They unlocked the door. The ex-Seventeen had fallen off his cot and was struggling to his feet. The cell stank and the blood had dried in a wide scab across the floor.

John peered around his partner's bulk and cleared his throat. "Hey, dead guy, what's your name?"

The ex's skin had gone chalky gray. He stared at Mike and displayed his engraved tooth. His jaws clacked together once.

Mike glared back at the ex. "Don't give me any of that gang attitude, dipshit," he said. "We're trying to be decent people. You play nice, we'll get you some breakfast, maybe something to read, whatever. You want to be a dick, we can just leave you in here."

The ex took a shaky step forward, then another. It raised its hands.

John took a step back. "Mike . . ."

The dead thing snapped its teeth together again. And again and again. It made an awkward grab at Mike's beefy arm and opened its mouth wide.

He took a quick step back just as John grabbed him by the shoulders and pulled. They stumbled through the narrow door, tripped over each other's legs, and fell. The ex shuffled out after them and tripped over a swollen crack in the pavement. It dropped onto John's leg with its mouth open and began to chew.

"SHIT!" Blood blossomed through his jeans, as John tried to shake the zombie off.

Mike rolled to the side and drove three hard kicks into the ex's skull. His sneaker slapped and bent on its head, but knocked it off his friend. The jaws flung a few red drops as they clacked together.

John dragged himself back and Mike fired one last kick at the dead thing. He tried to scamper away and the ex followed him. It crawled on all fours and bits of fresh calf dropped from its mouth.

"HELP!" screamed John. He tried to hold his hand over the wound as he pulled his skinny frame back. "EX! Ex inside the wall!"

Mike threw another kick and caught the dead thing across the jaw. Its teeth snapped on the sole of his Converse and gnawed at the slab of rubber. He shook his foot, but the ex hung on like a pit bull. It reached up and wrapped its arms around his leg. The hands didn't grab so much as press together on his knee.

The jaws snapped open and shut and now the teeth were on the ball of his foot. His little toe was in the Seventeen's mouth. He could feel the incisors through the canvas, like a chisel pressing down hard. A bone snapped and Mike screamed as his eyes watered up.

He heard the drumroll of boots on pavement. A blue and gold blur landed on the ex and pushed it flat against the ground. The figure wiggled, bent down, and the ex's head jerked back. Mike felt his foot slip just a bit free of the teeth. The blurry shape yanked again as the jaws tried to swallow more sneaker. The dead man's skull twisted back and Mike's heel banged against the pavement. He dragged himself away and wiped his eyes clear.

Lady Bee rode the ex like a horse, her heels on its spine and her studded belt circling its throat. She held an end in either hand, steering the jaws away from her. "Put it down!"

Derek, the Melrose guard, leaped across John with a sledge.

The handle slid through his grip and he brought the weight up and over in a high arc. The ex's skull collapsed and dark blood spurted from its ears and nose.

The belt slithered around the limp neck. Bee looked at the splatters of gore on it, sighed, and dropped it by the corpse.

John shuddered. His pant leg was balled at his knee and his wide eyes were stuck on the ragged bite in his calf.

"You people," Derek shouted at an approaching group. The guard pointed at John while he reached for his walkie. "He's been bitten. Get him over to Zukor. Carry him. Melrose gate?"

"Go for Melrose," buzzed his headset.

"Ex down over by the Lansing Theater cells. Need a cleanup crew."

"Got it."

Bee pulled off Mike's gummy shoe and sock. His arch and half his toes were bruised and twisted, but there was no blood. She whistled.

"You're shit-lucky," said Derek. "Broke your foot but it didn't break the skin."

"Oh thank God," cried Mike. "Thank God."

"What the hell were you thinking?" said Bee.

"It was a prisoner. They said he was a smart one, that he could talk and everything. We were trying to find out if he wanted anything for breakfast."

She and Derek each got an arm under him and lifted him to his feet. "And he attacked you?"

"Yeah, he attacked," Mike said. Bee was too short on one side, Derek too tall on the other. His foot swung and he winced. "It was just another fucking ex. It came at us, tried to bite me in the cell, and we tripped."

"Did he say anything? Did you piss him off?"

"It's an ex," said the hobbled man. He shifted to put his arm across her shoulders. "No talking, no thinking, just eating."

Derek looked at the corpse. "You sure?"

"Why don't you go ask John? I think he got a better look."

"Come on, smart guy," said Bee. "Let's get you to the hospital. I know you've been dying to get your hands on me."

"Dream on, slut."

"See, that's what a woman loves to hear." She gave the broken foot a light tap with her boot and he bit back a moan. "Why's it so hard for most of you guys to figure that out? You got this?"

Derek nodded, and Bee and Mike limped away.

× × ×

They'd found a comfortable spot on a rooftop that gave them a view. The elevator tower made a bit of shade from the late morning sun. Stealth had slid out of her cloak just before sunrise, making a sniper's nest for herself on the gravelly roof. St. George tried very hard not to look at her painted-on bodysuit and think about how easy it was to picture her naked.

She peered over the edge of the roof and down at Olympic Boulevard. From here they could see the triangular intersection that seemed to be a central plaza. People walked the streets in large groups that looked like work gangs. Her fingers produced the monocular from her utility belt, and she aimed the lens at the bound thing across from them. St. George pulled one of his own from a side pouch of the backpack.

The dead thing that had been Cairax was chained to the front railing of the Pavilions grocery store. It was a two-inch pipe, sunk deep in the concrete, and the bright, chipped paint clashed with the demon's bruise-colored hide. Its arms were stretched wide, and St. George guessed there were over fifty feet of thick steel links keeping those limbs tight against the rail, with maybe another fifty crossing back and forth over its chest and neck. The spiked tip of the long tail was bound to another pipe. Its head leaned forward, and the oversized fangs gnashed together like a slow-moving kitchen appliance. A pair of Seventeens stood a lazy watch at a small table.

Without looking up, Stealth asked, "Is that enough to hold it?"

"Probably." St. George had teamed up with Cairax a few times in the old days. He knew the monster was at least as strong as he was before becoming one of the tireless undead. "If he still had a brain, and some leverage, he could get out, but I'd say he's pretty safe like that. His tongue's been cut out, too."

"Or bitten off."

At the triangular center of Beverly and Olympic dozens of thick plastic pallets had been piled together into stacks a yard tall. Particle-board sheets crossed back and forth on top to make a platform fifteen feet square. A dirty section of carpet had been thrown across the center. It was backed up against a tall, spiraling monument of some kind. A severed head was speared on top of the metal center pole.

"Could be a stage," offered St. George. "Maybe they do live concerts."

He felt her eyes shift to him from her monocular even though her head didn't move. "There are bloodstains on the rug. I do not think it is from a musical performance."

"Depends on the band."

Another group walked by, this one armed with farm implements.

"All in all, it doesn't seem too different from how we're living."

"Except our guards watch the exes," she said, "not the civilians."

The cage measured thirty feet on a side and took up the short turning lane. It was made of the portable fence sections used for concerts and county fairs. Each panel was bolted together, plus extra chains had been wrapped around each connection. Braces reached down to buttress each section, and shiny white sandbags weighted each leg. A dozen sheets of fraying plywood were bolted against the walls. A similar structure could be seen a few blocks west on Olympic, past El Camino.

"I count approximately three hundred exes in the closest pen," murmured Stealth, "but I have yet to see one walking about."

"Sunlight speeds up decay." He gave an awkward shrug. "Maybe the smart ones stay inside until dark."

Stealth pulled a slim black panel from her belt and lifted it over the edge of the roof. The camera took three silent pictures. "Does that strike you as a very solid structure?"

"The pen? I was just thinking about that. It looks flimsy as . . . Wait a second." He squinted into his monocular. "See the door with the plywood crossbar? Look three bodies over from that, to the right."

"Yes?"

"The bald ex with tattoos. That's the one that chased *Big Red* and Cerberus. The one the Seventeens were taking orders from."

She adjusted the camera lens and brought the dead man into sharp focus. "Are you certain?"

"I was face-to-face with him. I'm sure. You can see where Billie shot him."

The hooded woman lowered the camera. "If he is intelligent, why is he penned in with the others?"

"He looks kind of mindless now, doesn't he? A regression of some kind?"

She nodded. "Or progression. Perhaps the intelligence is a temporary condition."

"Would explain why none of them are walking around free. Can't risk having one turn."

"Still . . ." Her face shifted beneath the mask, and he recognized the frown. "Why keep the pens within their safe perimeter?"

"You mean why not keep them two or three blocks away outside their wall? Good question." They studied the cage and St. George watched the sentries pace back and forth and light a pair of cigarettes. "They don't follow the guards," he said.

"Some of them do," she corrected him, "but they seem listless."

"Drugged?"

"Without an active cardiovascular system, toxins and sedatives will not circulate throughout their bodies."

"As far as we know. Still . . . same question. Why keep hundreds of exes within your safe zone, locked up in flimsy cages with minimal guards?"

× × ×

Gorgon was just past the Hart building when Richard called out to him. The older man had Christian with him. They took a few quick steps to catch up with him and tried to keep pace. "What's going on?" Richard asked. "I heard there was an attack this morning. Inside the walls."

The hero nodded. "John Willis. They've got him in Zukor, but it doesn't look good."

"People say the prisoner, the smart ex, got loose and attacked him."

Gorgon shook his head. "It didn't get loose. They let it out by accident. And according to at least three witnesses, it wasn't smart anymore. It'd gone . . . I don't know, feral, I guess? Mindless?"

Christian fell in step on his other side. "Are you sure?" It was the first time he'd heard her voice close to civil.

"It was dead by the time I got there. Bee and Derek Burke put it down. She seems pretty sure it was a regular ex at that point."

She raised a pencil-thin eyebrow. "Pretty sure?"

"I trust her judgment."

"I see," said Christian.

Gorgon stopped in the plaza. His knuckles went on his hips. Sheriff pose. He had two inches on Richard, but it was just enough to look down at him. Christian looked him in the eye. A few people walked by and ran their eyes across the impromptu meeting.

Richard twisted his big ring. "It's just . . . last night you were saying the smart exes weren't attacking anyone, then this morning one did."

"Well, yeah, but it was just a regular ex again."

"So you think," said Christian.

"What's the problem?"

"People are scared and we don't know what to tell them."

"Tell them to stay calm. It's still safe inside the Mount.

The walls are solid. The fences are solid. The guards are there. We're all here."

"So there's nothing going on? No need to worry?"

Behind his goggles Gorgon shut his eyes and counted to three. When he opened them, a few people were standing nearby, casually eavesdropping while they looked at a years-old display of photos on the plinth. "These little meetings would go so much faster if you didn't beat around the bush."

Richard nodded. "Sorry. It's just . . ." He twisted the ring again. "Two of the wall guards say they saw St. George and Stealth leave last night."

"Leave?"

"Leave the Mount," Christian said. Her voice had found its cold edge again. "Katie O'Hare was on wall duty and she said she saw them leaving over the physical plant."

Gorgon tilted his head.

"They didn't check out. They left between two guard posts. So no one would see them. And no one's seen St. George today." She gestured up to the sky with her chin.

"Yeah," said the hero. "I figured people would notice eventually."

Richard's eyes went wide. "So they did leave? They left the Mount?"

"They had a job to do. It's not that big a deal. He leaves the Mount all the time. Usually at least twice a week on some kind of mission."

"But she doesn't," said Christian. "Why did she leave?"

"Because they had a job to do."

"That needed both of them?"

"It's just a mission. They should be back late tonight. Maybe tomorrow morning."

Christian tilted her head. "Will they?"

He counted to three again and told himself not to open the goggles. When he looked again, four more people had stopped to listen. "What's that supposed to mean?"

"It's a simple question," she said. "Will they be back?"

"Of course they will."

"You know what I think?"

"I'm breathless to know."

"I think they left us. I don't think they're coming back."

Gorgon laughed. "Where the fuck do you get this stuff?"

"I think they discovered the exes were getting smarter and realized we were doomed here. And they decided to take off and find somewhere better."

Gorgon opened his mouth, stopped, and then tried again. "Honestly, I don't even know what to say to that."

"How about the truth?"

"I told you the truth. They're off on a mission. They'll be back tonight or tomorrow."

"A mission about the smart exes?"

"Sort of."

"Sort of?" She shook her head. "You know, it was bad enough before when you were all just vigilantes. Now we're all completely dependent on your kind."

"My kind?"

Richard's eyes bugged. "Christian, that's—"

"Invulnerable, strong, fast—the world's still pretty safe for all of you."

Gorgon's fingernails bit into his palms. "Plenty of my friends are dead, too."

"We need you to survive, but you don't need us. Why wouldn't you all just leave when things get bad?"

He leaned in close. "Because we're all better people than you."

Someone let out a quick cough of laughter.

Christian glared at him.

He stepped back and turned to Richard. The older man had tried to sink into the crowd. "Richard, you may want to take Mrs. Nguyen away before I put her in a coma for two or three weeks."

"I can walk myself," she spat. The crowd recoiled as she marched through them.

The older man twisted his ring. "I'm sorry. We just wanted answers. I didn't expect her to just pounce on you like that."

The hero looked at him. "Oh, come on. How long have you known her?"

"You know what she's like. It's like a game to her. She just says thing to piss people off."

"Yeah," said Gorgon. He sighed and watched the crowd. Most of them were following Christian as she spewed angry rants. "The things everyone's thinking."

"No, no," insisted Richard. "You know how much we—"

"I know how everyone here feels," said the hero. He tapped his goggles. "People think because of these I don't see things. Stealth doesn't, hiding in her little batcave. St. George doesn't, flying up in the air. But I see it all, every day. They're glad I'm here, but don't try to tell me people love me."

× × ×

They slid across the roof. St. George pushed ever so slightly against gravity and skimmed across the bleached-white tar paper. He walked on his fingertips, his toes dipping down to drag every few yards. Another severed head sat there, bobbing up and down as it worked its jaws. He gave it a slap with the back of his hand and it rolled a few feet away.

It took Stealth a minute to catch up to him. She moved silently on her palms like a black spider. As she reached him she shifted her shoulders and let her cloak slide back to the roof. The camera hummed as she photographed the structures from the new vantage point.

A murmur of discontent echoed up and they looked to the street.

Two Seventeens were dragging an older man with tanned skin and silver hair across the intersection from the ivy-covered brick building. He'd been stripped to the waist, his flabby torso was bruised, and one of his eyes was swollen shut. A few civilians followed them, and a crowd began to gather. One of the followers, an older woman, wailed and sobbed. She grabbed at one of the Seventeens, a man with a skinheadlike buzzcut. He shook her off and shouted at her in Spanish.

"What are they saying?"

"The woman is begging for mercy," Stealth translated. "The man said it is too late, he has been sentenced. Now she is saying if they let him go they will both leave."

From the rooftop they could see Buzzcut's grin as they dragged the man away behind the pen of exes. A moment later he reappeared, and both heroes realized what they'd missed on the far side of the pen the night before.

Buzzcut dragged the older man to the top of the stairs. They stood on the small platform above the cage and the Seventeen yelled to the crowd. There were three or four hundred people in the street and still more drifting from the buildings.

"You know how this goes," repeated Stealth. "Sentence has been passed. If the boss wants, he will still be spared."

St. George took a breath and shifted on the gritty roof.

The old man shouted something and Buzzcut clubbed his head.

"He is a monster," echoed Stealth.

The Seventeen turned the old man toward the cage. The exes were clawing at the air. Their clicking teeth were like a speed typist gone mad.

St. George went to stand up and Stealth slammed her hand onto his arm. It would've broken bones in a normal person. "No," she snapped.

"They're going to—"

"You cannot save him."

"I have to try." He shrugged off her grip, rolled to his feet, and saw Buzzcut push the old man.

She was a blur, spinning, sweeping his legs, knocking him back down. His head cracked into the rooftop and she was on top of him, straddling him, her forearm pressed into his throat.

He heard the screams and the gasp of the crowd.

"He is too far," she hissed. "He is already dead and you will reveal us for nothing!"

He grabbed her arms. She weighed nothing and he knew he could throw her clear across the roof and there was nothing she could do to stop him.

"The old man will still be dead and you will fail the Mount. Everyone there is depending on you."

The screams broke into a wet cough. All they could hear was the murmur of the crowd and the wailing of the man's wife. Beneath it were clicks and the sound of tearing meat. Someone, Buzzcut, was laughing.

"Get off me," St. George said.

She slid to the side. "We had no choice."

"I know." He stared up at the sky. "Just . . . don't talk to me for a while."

"It is always unfortunate when sacrifices must—"

"Don't," he said.

The old man's wife kept sobbing until someone led her away.

Twenty-One

NOW

"SOMETHING'S GOING ON."

It was almost three in the afternoon, and a crowd gathered at the wooden stage. Die-hard Seventeens were closest to the platform, sporting weapons and showing their tattoos. Others drifted in behind them, forming a loose outer ring. Within an hour the broad intersection was filled with thousands of people.

"Cairax," he whispered with a nod. The demon ex had stopped its slow struggle against the chains. It grew still and sat. Its tail fell limp.

Even from here he could hear the low thuds echo from within the ivy-covered building. It was a sound he knew from armored battlesuits and movie dinosaurs. The footsteps came closer, and something moved in the darkness of the building.

The hunched figure stepped through the double doorway with its head bowed low. Once the sunlight hit its skin it straightened up and added another three feet to its size. Then it stepped out of the sunken entrance and added another two. A quartet of Seventeens flanked it, three men and a woman, each with a rifle slung over their shoulders and a ma-chete tucked into their belt. The crowd howled and cheered and the giant threw two gang signs over its head with long fingers. A green bandanna crisscrossed each wrist and palm.

Its whole body was distorted. The arms were too long and thick, the chest and shoulders too broad beneath the tight wifebeater. It was bigger than Cerberus by at least two feet. St. George checked it against the man standing next to it.

"Eleven-and-a-half-feet tall," whispered Stealth. "I would estimate seven hundred twenty-five pounds." Her finger danced on the camera's button.

And it was dead. After all this time, St. George knew that skin tone at a glance. He spun the dial of his monocular, pushing the lens as tight as it could go.

A tattoo of a cross decorated its right temple running into the black buzzcut. On the opposite side of its head were a few flaps of inked flesh where the ear had been ripped away to show sinew and ivory. Beneath the dark eyebrows the bone had swollen and bulged, like some museum-exhibit caveman. The thick brow made the sunken eyes look even deeper, pearls of cloudy white in skull sockets. It had enor-mous teeth, the size of matchbooks, and its jaw pushed out to hold them all.

"It looks like a gorilla," he muttered. "Zombie Mighty Joe Young."

It lumbered across the street and onto the makeshift stage. Applause, cheers, and hollers echoed back and forth across the street. The ex held its monstrous arms up to the crowd like so many rulers before it.

"Look," she murmured. "The ones in the pen."

Across from the platform, three hundred exes had

stopped milling in the cage. Now withered salutes rose over their heads. A few blocks away, the exes in the second pen did the same.

"Jesus," he said. "What the hell is going on?"

Mighty Joe leered at the crowd and pumped his fists in the air. The exes thrust gaunt hands upward again. He brought his palms down to quiet the crowd and hundreds of dead arms flopped to their sides.

"They're responding to him," Stealth said.

"*DIECISIETE!*" shouted the monstrous ex. His voice echoed out of the swollen chest and down the block. "Forever and always!"

Most of the crowd echoed the cheer and howled. The exes opened their mouths in a silent shout.

"Eight more youngbloods," he roared. "They done their duty, shown their loyalty to the SS. They're in!"

A small line formed at the edge of the stage. Three Latinos, two Asians, two African-Americans, and a white girl. They were bare-chested except for the woman in her bra.

The first one walked onto the stage, very small next to Mighty Joe. The ex unwound one of his bandannas as a bodyguard grabbed the young man's forearm. Beneath the green cloth, the huge palm was pitted and slashed. He made a fist, shook his hand a few times, and the wounds glistened wet.

The female bodyguard pulled out her machete, cleaned the edge between two fingers, and pulled it across the fledgling Seventeen's hand. The man gritted his teeth as blood swelled up. The monstrous ex reached down and the bleeding limb vanished within his huge fingers. "One of us," he rumbled. He took the hand away and slapped his palm down on each of the man's shoulders.

The youngblood's legs trembled under the impact and he

nodded his head. They guided him past the giant to an old woman who washed out the wound and sponged the gore from his shoulders. Her peroxide foamed on his skin. The bodyguard was already slashing the next palm.

"Deliberate infection," mused Stealth. She lowered the camera.

"Followed by immediate disinfection. If this is patient zero, maybe he's got some purer strain of the ex-virus. Could be why some come back smart. He obviously is."

"Perhaps. I do not believe it is an ex," she said. The infrared monocular was pressed up to her eye again. "Its body temperature is seventy-one degrees. Twenty degrees higher than the average ex."

"And almost thirty lower than the average human," said St. George. "What the hell is he, then?"

"I am not sure."

"Doesn't look like he's got universal appeal, either." Half the mob shifted on their feet, not cheering with the hardcore Seventeens near the stage. The crowd members toward the back studied the ground or cast wary eyes at the ritual the huge ex was conducting.

"I would guess many of them did not realize they were sheltering with a street gang, let alone one led by a monster. They were looking for safety."

The ex turned to the group that had crossed the stage. Each of them had tied their hand in a swatch of green even as he rewrapped his own. "You're in forever now," he bellowed. "All of you. Even if you die, even if you come back, you're always a Seventeen."

He slammed his hands together once, twice, three times. The crowd picked up the applause. The youngbloods caught dozens of backslaps, head rubs, and arm punches.

"Getting close to two years since I got this," Mighty Joe continued. "Two years since I became the biggest boss in the city. Getting bigger and badder every day." He flexed arms like beer kegs and the crowd whistled and shouted.

"Everybody went down except us. The Bloods, the Crips, the XV3s. The police caved, the Army caved, even the fucking Marines went down. And we're still here and we're deep!"

He punched the air again. The Seventeens in the crowd howled and raised their weapons. A few shot at the sky. The exes threw up their arms. A low chant worked its way through the crowd and faded just as quick.

St. George tilted his head. "What are they saying? Ammo?"

"I believe they were calling him master of Mary. I am not sure of the refer . . ." She paused and her body stiffened. "That is not patient zero."

"How do you know?"

"A connection I should have seen earlier." Her words were almost lost in Mighty Joe's next bellow.

"We're the best, the strongest, the fucking chosen of God," the ex told the crowd. "It's why we lived, they died, and now they're with us."

He threw an arm out to the caged exes. They returned the salute.

"We're the rulers of the new world. This whole city is going to be our turf. There's only one thing keeping the SS from being absolute kings of Southern California—that fucking fortress of freaks holding down Hollywood."

St. George shifted.

"You all know I've got business with one of them. A lot of you do, too. I'm gonna carve my name in his chest, gouge out his fucking vampire eyes, and wear his skull as a necklace for my two-year anniversary." He pounded his chest with a fist like a gallon milk jug. Hundreds of dead hands slapped their rib cages in solidarity.

Stealth's eyes went from the stage to the exes and back.

"This is it. I want everybody gunned up and good to go. Tonight our army marches north. We're throwing down and wiping out the last of the old world."

"What army?" muttered St. George. "Most of these people are kids and grandparents."

Mighty Joe threw up one last salute and stepped down from the stage. He drifted through the crowd, giving knuckle punches and backslaps as he went.

In the cage, the walking dead performed an odd dance. Their legs shifted like a massive, macabre chorus line. Their arms raised, swung, and shifted. Three hundred moved as one.

"The exes are not copying him," Stealth said.

"What?"

"They are in perfect synchronization. All of them. They are not copying him, he is controlling them. He is exerting some level of control over every ex here. At least a two-block radius."

St. George watched as Mighty Joe turned his head to speak to one of his bodyguards and the cageful of exes did the same. Three hundred heads shifted to the right.

"That is why they do not need strong cages." She nodded at the dispersing crowd as she slid the camera back into her utility belt. "*Amo de la marioneta.*"

"What is that?"

"What they were saying. Puppet master. He is controlling all of them."

"Damn straight I am," bellowed the dead giant.

The clatter of rifles filled the air. Stealth and St. George dropped below the ledge.

"Who is that up there, anyway?" he shouted. "The hot bitch is Stealth, I'm thinking. That you, Gorgon? You finally grow some stones and come to give yourself up?"

St. George glanced at her. "When did he spot us?"

Stealth shook her head. "More importantly, how did he *hear* us?"

"I knew you'd show up sooner or later," Mighty Joe yelled. "Once I told you two about the Boss of LA, it was only a matter of time."

St. George furrowed his brow. "What the heck is he talking about?"

"The puppet master. He was speaking to us in the cell." Stealth looked across the rooftop. The severed skull had stopped moving its jaw and stared back at her. "He sees through all of them."

"He knew we were coming," said St. George. "Remember the exes last night?"

She slid across the tar paper, threw her leg into the air, and brought her heel down. The dried skull shattered under her boot. "Suggestions?"

"Get ready to run," he said.

"And you?"

"I'll catch up."

The hooded woman nodded and skittered across the rooftop. Once she was a few yards away she rolled and came up in a crouch with her cloak on. She gave him a nod and vanished behind an air-conditioning vent.

St. George counted to five and pushed down against gravity. His boots scraped on the roof ledge as he swung up.

Hundreds of searching eyes locked on him. Shoulder slings rustled, gunmetal scraped on holsters, and rounds slid home. He couldn't guess how many weapons were aimed his way.

"The Mighty Dragon," said the ex. "Not who I wanted but still cool."

"Always glad to please a fan," he called back. "You should reconsider this."

"Why?"

He waved at the crowd. "These folks don't want to get hurt."

"There'll be plenty of hurt. Not for us, though."

"You people," St. George shouted to the crowd. "You know who I am. You know what I can do. You know how foolish attacking me or my friends would be."

"Oh, yeah," bellowed the giant. "You're strong and invulnerable. But your friends aren't. You've got a fearsome rep and that's it. We've got an army and a plan."

"Is part of your great plan to announce strategy with the other side listening in?"

"I wanted you to hear," yelled the giant. "I wanted you to know and be scared."

"You don't scare me, big guy."

"You're not the only one hiding in there, though, are you? If your people hadn't killed my man, I would've had him tell them." The giant's face split in a toothy grin. "You know what, though? You've always got all those exes piled up at your gates, right? Time to start thinking big."

The enormous ex took in a breath, and all the dead things around him did the same.

× × ×

Derek checked his watch and looked at the crowd of exes pushing on the bars. Three more hours until his shift ended and he went to Mark Larsen's funeral.

The dead things reached and groped. He'd counted one hundred and sixteen of them earlier. Their jaws opened and closed as they stretched hands and bloody stumps through the gate. There were shiny patches where constant flailing had scoured paint down to metal.

Elena nodded at the watch. "What time is it?"

"Almost five o'clock," he said.

"Damn."

"What are you up to tonight after the funeral?"

"Some new DVDs from the library," she said. "Think I might stay in and finish off a bottle of Matt Russell's moonshine."

Makana, the other guard, looked up from his book. "Is that crap any good?"

She smirked. "Christ, no. But it makes me forget the day."

He mulled it over. "You want company?"

"Depends."

The rustle of dry skin on metal, the endless clack of jaws, it all stopped. The exes froze in the sinking sunlight. Their collective arms dropped to their collective sides.

Derek straightened up and raised his rifle. "What the fuck," he murmured.

The eerie silence stretched over five seconds. Then ten.

"TONIGHT."

Hundreds and hundreds of them spoke with one leathery voice that echoed across all thirty acres of the Mount. Some of it was clear. Some was just hissed air. Everyone understood it.

"TONIGHT THE SEVENTEENS ARE COMING TO KILL YOU ALL."

× × ×

The exes in the cage stared up at him. Their announcement echoed off the buildings. Even some of the Seventeens looked shaken.

St. George let a long breath of black smoke curl out of his nostrils. "We don't have to fight."

"Pussy." The giant ex chuckled.

"What's the point of all this?"

"The point?"

"Why fight? Why aren't we working together? With your power we could've had Los Angeles cleaned out months ago. Why didn't you join us?"

"Join you?" Mighty Joe furrowed his thick brow and glared up at the hero. "Motherfucker, you just don't get it. Why didn't *you* join *us*?"

St. George blinked.

A huge finger stabbed up at him. "Why you think we all wanted to kneel down and be your bitches? Life is good as long as you're in charge, huh? We don't kneel to no one, *pinche*. We're *Diecisiete*! SS always and forever!"

The Seventeens roared.

They opened fire.

Rifles. Pistols. Machine guns. Hundreds of firearms all aimed at him.

St. George closed his eyes and let one leg settle off the ledge to brace himself. The bullets were heavy rain beating on his body. They hit every inch of him. His skin rippled.

His muscles stung. His third leather jacket in a week became tatters, torn away in the high-caliber wind that tried to drive him back.

Under the percussion of gunfire he could hear the screams. Civilians pelted with hot casings as they tried to plug their ears. There were elderly people and children in the crowd. They were terrified.

It was going to get worse for them.

The hero ignored the bullets slapping him and sucked in air. Short, quick breaths filled every inch of his lungs. His chest swelled and he felt the warm sizzle in the back of his throat.

It took a few moments for the rain to stop. St. George opened his eyes and looked down. Saw their fear of the man who stood through all their bullets. The Seventeens were pulling magazines from belts and pockets while empty ones rattled on the ground in drifts of spent brass.

St. George sucked in a last mouthful of air and sent a cone of fire down onto the street. The tongues of flame lashed down and spun in the air. He swung his head and let it wash across the mob.

He couldn't actually reach them. The burning chemicals went a few yards from the rooftop and sputtered out a dozen feet above the ground. He didn't have the lung power for anything more. But it got their heads down and let him leap across the street to the top of the ivy-covered building. He sent another curtain of fire over the intersection and the crowd scattered a bit. Some of them fired into the air.

The flames died and their eyes found him. His bare chest gleamed in the sun above the dark, bullet-scarred jeans. The wind spread his hair behind him like a mane. "If you come to the Mount," St. George roared, "we will fight."

He reached down, never taking his eyes from the crowd, and tore a basketball-sized chunk of brickwork from the edge of the building with one hand. He held it up for them to see and then brought his fist around to shatter it.

"All of us will fight you. And we will not hold back."

The hero let the red dust run through his fingers before he hurled himself up into the air.

Twenty-Two
NOW

CERBERUS STOMPED ACROSS the streets of the Mount and
keyed her microphone. "Sun's going down. People are panicking."

"And this surprises you?" Zzzap's voice was crystal clear
over her helmet speakers.

"Just the level of it. We've kept them safe for over a year—"

"And now they think they're not safe. What have you done
for me lately, eh?"

"Nothing, apparently."

"I could come out and brighten things up."

"No," cut in Gorgon's voice. "The last thing we need right
now is for the power to go out and everyone see you flying off
into the air."

"Fair point."

"I'm trying to get generator crews out, but until they're up
and running you stay put. Got it?"

Cerberus keyed her mic. "Who put you in charge, anyway?"

"I did. One of you guys want it instead?"

A long silence filled the airwaves.

"Yeah, that's what I figured."

She tried to come up with something clever and the motion sensors went mad. "Hang on a minute. Got a big crowd."

A crowd of a dozen families, couples, and individuals was jostling its way up through the long shadows of Third Street. Their bodies were wrapped in backpacks and duffel bags. Their arms were filled with bundles and suitcases. One little boy clutched a cat carrier that shifted and yowled.

In public-address mode, the voice of Cerberus echoed down the street. "Everyone stay calm," she thundered. "There is no need to panic, no need to rush. Calm down."

She switched back to standard volume and singled out one man, fortysomething with a dark ring of hair. A special-effects expert who'd become a repairman inside the Mount. "Where do you think you're going, Henry?"

The nearby crowd stopped to see who she was talking to, and he glared up at her. "Are we prisoners here? Do I have to answer to you?"

She shook her armored head. "Of course not. You're free to go where you want."

"Damn right I am." He pulled his wife and son in tight. "And we want out of here. We all do."

The crowd murmured and barked in agreement.

"I understand," Cerberus said. "I just think you need to step back and think for a minute."

"Don't tell us what to do!"

"I'm just telling you to stop and think, that's all," the titan said. A few blinks raised the suit's volume by three decibels. "Everyone calm down, stop for a minute, and think. Yeah, what happened a little while ago was scary as hell. I don't understand it either and I'm scared, too. The Seventeens are coming and there's going to be a fight. A big one."

"All the more reason not to be here," the repairman

snapped. He tried to shove past her and she blocked him with a hand twice the size of a hubcap.

"Oh, please," she scoffed. "How can you be safer outside the Mount, Henry? In here you've got guards, lights, and walls. Out there the sun's going down and there are five million exes waiting to eat you."

A few people near her flinched. Half the crowd had stopped to listen.

"That's right. They're going to eat you," she repeated. She kept the suit's unblinking gaze on Henry and ignored the dozens of families around them. "The second you're through that gate they will tear the flesh from your bones with their teeth and fingers. They will rip you, your wife, and your son apart in a matter of minutes."

The crowd shuddered as a whole. Henry turned away and met his wife's eyes.

"That's if you're lucky," she continued. "If not, you might survive and get to watch them change one by one. And then you'll have to smash their skulls or put a bullet in their brains or just let them kill—"

"Shut up!!" a woman screamed. "Just shut up." Nervous talk rippled back and forth across the crowd.

Another few decibels. "I don't like it either, but we all know it's true. It's easy to forget because we've got a life in here, but out there it's still hell." The battlesuit took a few steps back, thudding on the cobblestones. She upped the volume again, almost back to PA levels. "If anyone wants to leave, I'll walk with you to Melrose right now. I'll try to protect who I can when you go through the gate, but my priority has to be the people inside the walls. You all know this."

Some of them glanced at the gate. They could all see it from here. None of them moved.

Henry figured out he was the example, and she felt a wave of sympathy for him. He hated her and he knew she was right. It would take him months to live this down. If he was alive months from now. "What should we do, then?" he growled.

"Get home," Cerberus said. "Seal the stages, just like we've always planned. Anyone who can fight, I'm pretty sure we'll need it and we can use you, but it's more important to stay and protect your families."

She stomped back a few steps and the last rays of sunlight gleamed on her armor. "And for God's sake, everyone try to stay calm," she added. "Tonight's going to be bad enough without a riot inside the walls, okay?"

× × ×

Stealth had covered half a mile. She raced across rooftops, hurled herself over alleys, and dispatched any ex in her way with a savage blow. When St. George caught up, she was charging down Doheny Drive, her hood draped back over her shoulders. He dropped down, grabbed her by the shoulders, and bounded back up to the rooftops.

"You okay?"

"I am fine," she panted. She took three deep breaths, stilled the gasping, and pulled her hood back into place. "You are bruised."

He looked at himself. Red and purple spots blossomed across his skin. And most of his pants had crumbled away. "You notice I'm bruised before you notice I'm almost naked?"

"I have seen naked men before. I have never seen you bruised."

"Yeah, well, it takes a hell of a lot. For the bruising."

"Are you all right?"

"Yeah, I think so." He looked at her, hidden in the shadows of the hood. "Since when do you actually care?"

"Of course I care," she said. "You are a valuable asset."

"Flattery will get you everywhere."

She glanced at the sky. "We have less than half an hour until darkness."

St. George shook his head and gestured for her to rest. "Don't worry. We've got a good lead. Even if they were ready to march, they can't make it across the city that fast."

She glared at him. "If he was controlling the ex in our cells from Century City, what kind of range does that indicate?"

A map of Los Angeles blossomed in his mind, covered by a wide red circle. "Hell."

She pointed at the street below them. The milling exes were all still shuffling and stumbling, but there was a rhythm to their movements. They were wandering north. "His army is already at the Mount," she said. "You should go on ahead of me."

"No way. We go together."

"I can manage without you."

"Maybe. But the Mount can't afford to lose you, either." He held out his hand. "You're a pretty valuable asset, too."

She looked at him for just a moment with the faint tilt of her head that meant she was thinking. Then she grabbed his hand with both of hers.

St. George leaped into the air, dragging her up behind him. He swung his arm and Stealth flew through the air to land on the rooftops across the street. She took off running and he soared after her.

× × ×

Gorgon stood between Christian Nguyen and the trucks. Christian stood between him and the crowd. Harry the driver stood near her left shoulder, Diamint by her right, and almost two hundred people behind her.

"You can't tell us what to do," she snapped. "No one elected you. No one voted for you. If we want to leave, you have no authority to stop us."

"I don't," he agreed, "but I've got a responsibility to keep you safe. Even when you don't want me to."

She laughed. "We've all seen your idea of safe," she sneered. "We're surrounded by monsters and someone dies every week."

"And you think there's somewhere better out there? You think Burbank is fine and we're just keeping it secret?"

"That's for us to find out," said Diamint. "None of us came here to die."

"No one is going to die!"

"The Seventeens are all exes now!"

"We're supposed to be safe," yelled a woman. "St. George said it would be safe here."

"You are safe," Gorgon shouted.

"The Mount's already surrounded!"

"You're not fooling anyone," yelled Christian. "We're just cannon fodder to you. You're going to use us to cover your own escape! You're going to leave us here to die!"

The crowd tilted and became a mob.

"We're taking the trucks. That's that." The heavyset driver stepped forward with his fists clenched.

Gorgon lifted a warning finger. "Don't try it, Harry."

Harry tried it and ended up on his back with a bleeding nose. A blond man made a run for the trucks and Gorgon backhanded him into the mob. Someone deeper in raised a pistol.

"You can't stop us all," Christian shrieked, and her face dropped as the words left her mouth.

His goggles irised open and he left them open. He felt dozens and dozens of eyes lock onto his. The strength crashed over him like a wave, every muscle in his body spasmed, and his nerves buzzed with pins and needles like they'd been asleep for days.

Tier six, he thought. A solid tier six.

Over seventy people dropped. Their legs folded, their necks lolled, and they fell with their eyes still locked on his. He was pleased to see Christian was one of them. She was going to have a great bruise on the side of her head.

"There's too much going on to deal with this right now," he bellowed. The lenses snapped shut. "You all need to go back to your homes and make sure the buildings are secure. Those of you who can still walk need to help those who can't."

Their eyes went skyward and a murmur passed through the crowd.

St. George dropped down to the pavement. Except for a pair of shredded jeans he was mostly naked, and it was obvious he was hoping no one would notice. His exposed skin was covered with bruises and welts.

The hero looked at Gorgon but spoke to the crowd. "What's going on?"

"Just explaining to these folks you were coming back from your mission as soon as possible."

"There was doubt?"

"There was." Under his breath Gorgon added, "You look like you got the shit beat out of you."

St. George bounced his eyebrows in agreement and turned to the crowd. His eyes flitted between the people slumped on the ground and the ones still standing. "Gorgon's right. Everybody needs to calm down," he said. "I'm sure things have been scary here, but it's going to get worse if everyone starts panicking and doing crazy things."

A voice shouted from the back of the crowd. "The exes spoke!" It launched a wave of cries and questions.

"But the Seventeens—"

"How are they—"

"The exes said—"

"What if they—"

St. George held up his hands until they quieted down. "I know there's a bunch of creepy stuff going on," he said, "but you have to believe me. There is nowhere in this city safer than right here, right now."

Stealth stepped out of the shadows behind some civilians and they shrieked. "St. George is telling you the truth," she said. "Return to your homes, protect your loved ones, and we shall protect all of you."

The mob was just a crowd now, and the crowd broke apart. People helped Gorgon's victims to their feet and carried the ones that couldn't walk.

"Make sure all the stage entrances are locked," called St. George. He helped Christian up and ignored the unsteady glare she shot at him. "Tonight you're in or you're out, people."

As they scattered, Stealth pulled the camera from her belt and summoned an image. St. George caught a glimpse of the monstrous ex, tight enough to make out the cross tattoo on its head. "This being seems to have some sort of history with you," she told Gorgon, handing him the camera. "He mentioned you by name several times."

Gorgon pondered the distorted face for a moment and

a grim smile formed under his goggles. "Well, fuck me," he said. "I guess he found his gamma rays after all."

"You know him?"

"Yeah." He handed the camera back. "That, my friends, is Rodney Casares, top enforcer for the SS. We've got grudges that go way back."

St. George glanced at the picture again before the camera went dark. "That's what you wanted to get back here for?"

"No," she said. "That was a confirmation. Gorgon, summon every guard, scavenger, and volunteer you can. Issue extra ammunition and prepare the walls for a full assault. Then meet us in the lobby of Roddenberry in fifteen minutes."

She gestured at St. George to follow her.

× × ×

Josh Garcetti checked on his latest patient, an appendicitis case. She'd come in on her own, he'd pulled out the offending organ, and now she was asleep. Her stitches were clean and tight, no seepage at all. He tried not to dwell on the fact that at one time he could've repaired her without a single incision.

He made a few quick marks on her chart, stepped out to the nurses' station, and made another set of notes on the night log. Then he turned to the cabinets and found himself inches from Stealth.

He stumbled back and the move yanked his withered hand out of its pocket. "Jesus," he snapped. "Do you have to pop out of nowhere like that?"

The cloaked woman said nothing.

Footsteps made him turn and St. George stepped in from the hallway. He was bare-chested and covered with bruises.

"George," Josh said with a nod. "What happened to you? What the hell's going on?"

"When we were discussing the recon mission," said Stealth, "you said you have had the virus hanging over you for two years. You were bitten less than fifteen months ago."

He blinked twice, then a third time. "That all? Feels like a hell of a lot longer. Sorry I don't have a computerlike mind like you." He shrugged and repocketed his dead hand. "Is that everything? Mr. Willis would love to get a few Vicodin so he can sleep."

Her feet shifted and she was between Josh and the cabinet.

He sighed and pointed at a row of bottles. "Do you mind?"

"The first definite sighting of an ex-human," she continued, "was twenty-two months ago. An unidentified woman assaulted a group of Seventeens in a parking lot. The attack that infected Rodney Casares."

Josh shrugged again, but his angry eyes flitted between the two heroes. St. George realized his hands had rolled themselves into fists.

Stealth still hadn't moved. She was tense but fluid. She was confident.

"Your wife died two years ago, didn't she, Regenerator?"

The doctor's glare settled on her even as his shoulders slumped, and St. George felt something twist in his stomach.

How Am I Supposed to Live Without You?

THEN

THEY'RE GOING TO kill me for this.

I was one of the most important heroes on this coast. When I first started out I was the Immortal, the man who couldn't be killed. A regular Jack Harkness, for those of you who watch BBC America. I've been shot, stabbed, beaten, crushed, impaled, and even eviscerated. And I don't even have scars.

Everything I was—everything I am today—is because of Meredith. She was the love of my life. People say shit like that all the time, I know, but there's just no other way to put it. I thought I was in love twice in college, once with a foreign exchange student, and once because I mistook phenomenal sex for love. There was one time in my early twenties when I wanted to be in love, wanted so bad to make this woman happy, but I just couldn't. It wasn't there. Not until Meredith.

Stupid and clichéd as it may sound for Hollywood, we met at a wrap party for a movie. Some low-budget Sci-Fi Channel thing. She was dating a grip. I was with a makeup artist. From the moment I saw her I couldn't take my eyes off her. Black hair, blue eyes, and a set of mismatched earrings. She'd lost one of each and just decided to make a set with what was left. We started talking at the bar, chatted all night, and pissed off both our dates. A month later we were both single. Two months after that we were together.

And two years after that she died.

It didn't happen quite like that. There was a lot more to it. Finding a Beverly Hills–adjacent place we both liked. Buying furniture. Teaching her how to drive stick. Rescuing a pair of stray kittens we named Lewis and Clarke. Proposing to her while we were getting lawn-bowling lessons.

And then there was the oddness of me developing super-powers.

Meredith helped with that, too. She was there for every part of it, keeping me sane. That first time, straining noodles, we both thought it was just dumb luck the boiling water didn't leave me with red skin and blisters. Then there was the broken glass we thought slashed my hand, but there wasn't even a hint except for the cut in my shirt cuff.

Of course, the one we couldn't ignore was the kid with the green bandanna stabbing me in the gut. I know now he was a Seventeen. Then I just knew he was the punk who made Meredith scream by trying to kill me.

We'd just seen Eddie Izzard at the Wiltern and were walking to where we parked, a few blocks up Oxford. She never liked parking in structures and called it a scam. The kid grabbed her arm, shouted for my wallet, and then he twisted her arm and she screamed. I lunged and pounded him until he was unconscious, and that's when we realized he'd stabbed me six times during our fight. Six bloody holes in my shirt, but not a mark on me.

When we saw the news reports about the Mighty Dragon, Blockbuster, Zzzap, and the rest, we both knew what I had to do. Meredith bought a full-body motorcycle suit and stitched on a logo, and for months I was the Immortal, the man who couldn't be killed. I was hit by cars and shotgun blasts. Threw myself off buildings. One night after a gang shoot-out I got home and pulled twenty-three bullets out of myself.

And then we made another discovery.

Mere cut herself with a kitchen knife while chopping broccoli. Nothing deadly, maybe a stitch or two. We laughed—it was bound to happen someday, she was so clumsy. And I held her finger and felt a tingle, a flow of my power, and she gasped as it closed up. The skin sealed together without so much as a pucker.

A medical resident who could heal with a touch. My success rate at the hospital went up. My popularity with my fellow heroes and police did, too. It took another month for my codename to change to Regenerator.

I teamed up with most of the heroes at one point or another. Midknight. The Mighty Dragon. Cairax. Even the police during a few standoffs. I was the ultimate support guy. With me backing you up, nobody could fail. Heck, with me there everyone was an immortal.

And then, with all this going on, *then* she died.

It was stupid. A stupid way to die. She'd been safe. So safe. It wasn't fair. That's what's important to remember. It wasn't fair for her to get taken away from me like that. That's what they'll need to understand. What happened wasn't right, so I didn't do anything wrong.

A broken finger. She died because of a broken finger. Mashed in a car door, broke the skin, heavy bleeding. If I hadn't been out playing hero I could've fixed it in ten seconds. Instead the neighbors called an ambulance and rushed her to the hospital.

And once she got there, the emergency room staff screwed up a test and gave her the wrong type of blood. She was A-negative and some idiot nurse misread a chart and gave her Rh positive blood. Blood that should've been screened out of their blood banks to start with, because it was tainted with hep-B. The mixed symptoms confused them and they spent hours pumping her full of poisons to deal with misdiagnoses, and filling her with more of the wrong blood. The odds of it happening are a million to one. I know this. Two horrible, freak mistakes that both fell on one person. As someone in the medical profession, I know this and I understand why they could've been so baffled. Hell, anyone who watches *House* knows why they were baffled.

It still wasn't fair. It wasn't right.

Meredith died in agony just as I got home and the neighbors were telling me she'd gone to the hospital for something minor. And so I did what anyone else would. What anybody with my abilities would've done.

It didn't take long to claim her body. The hospital staff knew how bad they'd screwed up and were willing to agree to anything. I talked about religious beliefs and they let me walk out the door with her body. I kept my hands on her the whole time, willing life into her nerves, every fiber, each individual cell.

My power let me see what had gone wrong. Let me reach in to fix her. But there was so much that needed to happen. Even more than I could do. I had to rebuild her, redesign her, so she could fix herself. Twist and tweak her blood cells to let them restore her nervous system and replenish her and fight the problem. Make them multiply faster. Make them stronger. Tougher. More aggressive.

Like a virus.

Sixteen hours after I got her home her eyes fluttered. An hour later her right hand twitched. I collapsed from sheer exhaustion after forty-two hours of forcing every bit of my energy into her, but not before I saw her lips move and heard her body shift.

I slept for thirty hours.

It wasn't her. I could see that as soon as I woke up. It was just a thing, still strapped to the gurney. The eyes were wrong. Flat. Meredith was gone. Dead. I'd just brought back her body, like some superpowered life-support machine, its jaws snapping at me. I should've destroyed it, but I couldn't.

It had her face.

So I kept hoping one morning her eyes would be normal again, that her skin would be warm. And she never was.

I had a funeral with an empty coffin. I went to work. I went out on patrol. I went to counseling. People everywhere told me how sorry they were for my loss and assured me things would get better if I just gave it time. That's all I needed was time. And then I'd go home and feed the thing that had been my wife.

One day, after six weeks of this, I came home and it was gone. Mrs. Halifax, our neighbor from two doors down, was dead on the dining room floor. She had a key, in case we needed her to feed the cats. There was a casserole dish near her right hand. Her right hand was six feet from her body, along with the rest of that arm where it had been gnawed through. She'd been gutted and eaten, by the look of her.

I called the police. I think that was when the denial kicked in. I'd been at work the whole time and dozens of people could vouch for me. There was no evidence, so I couldn't've done anything. Nothing but an empty stretcher in the living

room, which a grieving doctor could explain with no problem.

I did nothing wrong. The police agreed I'd done nothing
wrong.

That Saturday I heard about the woman attacking some
Seventeens outside a movie theater. The woman who clawed
and bit and ate an ear. The Channel 7 reporter said they put
over twenty rounds into the woman before she stopped.

They brought the body to our morgue. The face was gone.
Most of the left hand had been shot off. But it still had Meredith's hair, and the little scar under her right breast.

I made sure she stayed a Jane Doe.

Two weeks later I heard about another attack. Nine days
after that the Mighty Dragon told me Stealth had called in
Zzzap to help search the city for "some kind of infection."
By month's end we had an uprising. The month after that it
was a war.

Then the war was over. And Meredith was still gone. And
my powers were all but gone. And most of the world was gone.

They're going to find out. I try to slow down the tests,
contaminate the samples, corrupt the data where I can. But
there's only so much I can do.

Julie Connolly is a smart woman. Very smart. If the world
hadn't fallen apart she'd be a top doctor by now, I have no
doubt. I think she suspects. She doesn't know why I'm dragging my feet, can't believe I'd be messing with results. But it's
nagging in the back of her mind. I can see it in her eyes when
she looks at me.

They're going to find out.

And when they do, they'll kill me.

Twenty-Four
NOW

GORGON DROVE HIS FIST into Josh's stomach again.

The doctor slammed into the wall and his handcuffs chimed as he sank down to the lobby floor. "You have to understand," he coughed. "I wasn't . . . I just wasn't thinking right. Haven't you ever lost someone you loved?"

"Yes," growled Gorgon.

They stood in the Roddenberry lobby, the closest Cerberus could get to Stealth's office. As it was, the battlesuit rested on one knee, its head scraping the ceiling. Zzzap hovered nearby, lighting the entire lobby even as he charred the ceiling panels.

Josh coughed again. "And what would you do, Nick?" he said. "If you could bring Kathy back right now, if you had that power, wouldn't you use it? Wouldn't you try to do it?"

The goggles lowered to the floor.

"I did what any of you would've done," he told them. "George, wouldn't you try to save someone if you had the power? I tried to save the woman I love and I . . . I made a mistake. That's all. Just a mistake."

"You killed the world," said Stealth. "Billions of people are dead because of what you did."

"I didn't do anything wrong!"

St. George was standing off to the side, still bare-chested, kneading his scalp with both hands. "So now what?"

"What do you mean?"

He threw a glance at Josh. "What do we do with him? This is . . . Jesus, this is huge. This is war crimes huge."

"He makes Hitler look like a fucking saint," muttered Gorgon.

"Do we tell everyone? Do we lock him up forever? Do we . . ." St. George's voice drifted off.

"I think we're missing the big issue here." They all looked at Cerberus. "You started this. Can you stop it?"

Josh turned to her. "What?"

"This all stems from your powers. Can you undo what you did?"

"No." He shook his head. "No, of course not. I can't unheal someone. Don't you think I would've done that years ago if I could?"

This isn't healing, though, said Zzzap. *This is . . . this is just unnatural.*

"Unnatural," smirked the doctor. "You're a walking fusion reactor. George is bulletproof. Nick's a fucking vampire, for Christ's sake. And you're saying I did something unnatural?"

Gorgon was still looking at the floor. "Is it tied to you?"

"What?"

"You created all these things with your power. Even if you can't stop them, are they still linked to you somehow?"

Josh shrugged. "I don't know. Maybe?"

"There is a simple way to find out," said Stealth.

It was a scene from a Western. She pulled the Glock so fast, like a quick-draw artist, that there was no time to stop her. Josh's forehead burst before most of them even realized she had the pistol out. St. George was just starting to lift his arm when the doctor's eyes rolled back in his skull. Josh tipped over backward, hitting the wall just under the splatter. Blood poured out of his mouth and the ruined mass of his nose.

"What the HELL!?!" shouted St. George over the echo of the third gunshot.

Stealth looked at him as she holstered the pistol, and her voice almost sounded confused. "It seemed like the simplest solution to all our problems."

"You know, every time I start to think there's really something human under that mask, you go off and—"

Josh lunged up and took in a deep, rattling breath.

Oh, Jesus, said Zzzap. Stealth had her pistol back out.

Josh's eyes trembled and swung back down. The irises shrank, focusing on Stealth. The bloody hole swelled, filled in, and sealed itself shut. His nose wove itself whole again. The doctor staggered back to his feet, his hand shaking as he felt the back of his head.

Cerberus made a noise inside her armor that came out as a hiss of static.

There was a coarse, scraping noise as the back of his skull knitted together and his nose pulled itself tight. He spat out a mouthful of blood and a tooth he'd already regrown. "Oh, come on," he wheezed. "All I've been through and you think a few bullets are going to put me down? Don't you think I tried that?"

St. George glared at him. "You said your powers were gone."

"I can't heal anyone else," said the doctor. "Can barely even heal me. But it keeps me alive. Trust me, I've been trying for over a year. I'm here whether I like it or not." He leered at them with mad eyes.

"We'll decide what to do with him later, then," said Stealth. "Gorgon."

The goggles whisked open and his gaze pinned the doctor. Josh didn't try to look away. He sank to the floor as Gorgon dragged out his life. The doctor began to twitch on the carpet.

"That's enough," said St. George.

Josh spasmed for a few more moments before the lenses snapped shut. Gorgon drove his boot into the fallen man's head. "Just to be sure," he told them.

St. George shot him an angry look before turning to Stealth. "So what do we have?"

She threw a blueprint of the Mount on the lobby floor and crouched next to it. "The walls are still secure, the fences are all reinforced, so the most likely attack points will be the Melrose gate, Bronson, and North Gower."

"What about Van Ness or Marathon?"

"Too far east and north for a major assault," she said. "We can leave regular guard units there. If the Seventeens have done any reconnaissance of their own they will know Marathon is sealed."

"So's Bronson."

"Sealed to regular exes. If they are being guided by Casares we must assume they will be smarter and more resourceful. It is the next-closest gate after Melrose, the fence is low, and it is a very tempting target."

"I'd still like to see extra people at Van Ness," said Gorgon. "You doubt my strategy?"

"I doubt Rodney's going to approach it as strategically as you are. He's kind of an idiot when you get down to it."

"I was taking his lack of formal training into account."

Cerberus pointed a thick metal digit north of the studio. "Are we worried about Hollywood Forever?"

Inside the hood, Stealth's head shook. "The sheer height of the walls still protects us there. Regular numbers along that wall."

Gorgon tapped the blueprints. "If we break it down that way, we've got enough manpower for forty, maybe forty-five guards at each of these gates."

That's it?

He shrugged. "We don't have an army. Fuck, we barely have a militia."

The battlesuit straightened up as best it could. "How many weapons do we have? We could ask for more volunteers."

"Maybe another hundred rifles in good condition," said Gorgon. "If we can get people, we can use them."

I don't think we need to worry about the exes that much, said Zzzap.

They all looked at him. "Why not?"

Well, everything we've seen this guy do is either individuals or groups that are all acting the same way, right?

Stealth nodded.

I'm betting he's still got a human brain, said the wraith. *Or a human mind, at least. I don't think he can control lots of exes individually. It's too much input and output for him to handle. Like playing an RTS video game. You can work with one unit, or you can click on a bunch and make them all do the same thing. But it's impossible to manage more than two or three to do specific tasks.*

"Does he need to?" Gorgon shrugged. "They break open a gate and the exes are just going to do what he wants anyway."

Right, but I don't think we need to worry about anything too elaborate. He'll probably just move them to where they can do the most damage and that'll be that.

"A good possibility," said Stealth. "This makes splitting our forces more advantageous. Casares will have to split his attention to deal with all of us."

St. George nodded. "Keep him off balance on multiple fronts and he won't be able to focus."

"Correct. We know he has Cairax as an asset. The demon is still faster and stronger than humans, even as an ex, and also fireproof and bulletproof. Odds are he will focus some of his attention there." She looked up at Gorgon. "His main focus seems to be capturing you, however. You and I will be at the Melrose gate. It will most likely be the primary point of their attack and where he will be."

Gorgon nodded. "I can play bait. Barry?"

The burning silhouette turned to him.

"Remind me to bounce something off you. I thought of it a while back. It just seemed a little weird to bring it up if we didn't need to."

"St. George, you can monitor between Bronson and Van Ness," continued Stealth. "It is a larger area but you are the most versatile of us. Stay on alert for Cairax as well. Cerberus and Zzzap, you will guard the North Gower gate. If conditions permit, Zzzap can offer support to other crisis points. Cerberus?"

"Yeah?"

"I think it's time we re-armed you."

Inside the armor, Danielle smiled. "Finally."

× × ×

The North Gower gate was set up in the same way as Melrose. A truck had been tipped against the sliding fence to block one side, and another backed up to hold it in place. The other half was left open in case they ever needed an exit.

The walking dead filled the street as far as they could see in either direction. They packed every inch of the alley across Gower and the lower level of the parking structure. Dozens and dozens of exes stretched and clawed through the bars of the gate. Young and old, male and female, fresh and piecemeal. Where the truck blocked the entrance they flailed at the fiberglass walls with open palms. The sound was like an enormous drum.

"That's going to grate on the nerves," said Cerberus. She shifted her stance and the armor reset dozens of targeting factors for her. After all this time, the M-2s felt heavy on her arms.

Zzzap hovered over her, casting light over the gate and down Twelfth Street. *Could be worse,* he said. *Can you imagine if they all moaned like in the movies?*

On top of the guard shack, Lady Bee shook her head. "You don't know when to shut up, do you, hot stuff?"

What? I'm just saying, as sieges go—

"Stop talking," said the battlesuit. "Just stop."

A line of twenty guards stood by the gate, rifles slung over their shoulders. As one they stepped forward and rammed their pikes and spears through the bars of the gate. The dead stiffened as their skulls cracked and their brains were shredded. Then the humans pulled their weapons free, stepped back, and lunged at the gate again even as more exes staggered forward.

Lynne leaned against a lamppost, her dark hair fresh-shorn down to her scalp. She looked up at Zzzap. "Couldn't you just go out and burn them all up by touching them or something?"

The shape of his head twisted to point at her. *I could,* he nodded, *but I'd rather not.*

"Why not?"

It feels . . . creepy when things burn on me.

She tilted her head. "How so?"

Did you ever see Carrie?

"No."

The glowing wraith made a buzzing noise, and Lynne realized it was a sigh. *Okay,* he said, *imagine what it would be like to have someone dump a few gallons of cold, rotted pig blood filled with maggots all over you.*

Her face twisted up. "That's disgusting."

Yep.

Cerberus glanced up at him. "Wuss."

Lynne looked between the two heroes. "Is that what exes feel like?"

That's what everything solid feels like when I'm like this. Exes are worse because I have to think about what they are. The glowing outline shuddered in the air. *I'll do it to save lives, don't get me wrong. But I'd rather wait until that moment if we can.*

"Switch lines," called out Bee. "Let's not get tired before we have to."

Lynne gave them a quick nod and ran to the gate. The pikemen stepped back and handed off their weapons. She stepped forward with a new line and another score of exes twitched and dropped.

Cerberus glanced up at the brilliant figure. "That really what it feels like?"

No, he said. *It's actually a lot worse. I'm just not very good with words.*

× × ×

The Bronson gate had been barricaded for over a year. Each side was blocked with a huge truck pressed against the gates. Another set of trucks had been backed against them and their tires slashed, creating an alley for any exes that slipped through. Stair units and ladders against the fallen vehicles let patrols stand on top and watch the crowds of exes.

St. George dropped down out of the night sky and landed on a truck with a loud thump. He'd pulled on some heavy boots, gloves, and a leather jacket covered with stitch work and patches. He looked at the tense faces and trembling weapons. "How's everyone doing?"

The click-clack of countless teeth rose from outside the gate to fill the air.

Makana gave him a thumbs-up. "We're peachy," he said.

"You guys have it easy," he said. "No pike work."

"Rather be spearing 'em than sitting here," said a heavy man with short blond dreadlocks.

The hero looked out over the Bronson entrance. The short driveway was crammed with the dead. They beat at the trucks through the gate, and the impacts shook beneath their feet. At least four hundred exes packed the area between the gate and the street. Beyond them, they mobbed the street, a crowd that spread off into the darkness in either direction.

"Don't give in to fear," St. George said. A muffled cough in the back of his throat sent a few curls of smoke out of his nostrils. "If you're scared, that's normal. It's been a hell of a day. But if you let fear take over, you're as good as dead. Just remember to do your job and they can't get in."

A rail-thin woman shook her head. "What about the SS?"

"We'll take care of them, don't worry."

"But how? We can't shoot at people. We can't—"

"I said," he interrupted, "we'll take care of them. You don't need to worry about it."

"No point worrying anyway, right?" A young kid glanced up at the hero. He was sixteen at the most. and the rifle looked huge in his hands. "This is where we go down fighting."

St. George shook his head. "No. We don't lose. We're the good guys."

"So what? We all survive just because they can't hurt you?"

He sighed. "No, it isn't that." He gave the kid a pat on the back. "Stealth told me if we all survived tonight she'd have sex with me."

The kid's eyes bugged. "No way! Seriously?!"

"No," he said, shaking his head. "But it's a fun thought to live for, isn't it?"

They laughed.

His headset crackled. "St. George?"

"Go."

"Something big and purple at Van Ness. Thought you'd want to know."

"Damn it," he said, scanning the street. "How'd he get by us?" He looked at the guards. "You all good here?"

They gave him a round of thumbs-up and salutes and he threw himself into the air.

× × ×

Stealth crouched on the arch above Melrose gate with Gorgon. The exes had always been thick there, but now they grew denser by the moment. They packed the space in front of the gate and pushed back into the streets. Hordes of them staggered down Melrose and up Windsor.

Thirty people walked the walls and stared down at the hungry mob. Some of them manned scaffolding towers. The dead pounded and clawed at the stucco.

Another fourteen gate guards rammed pikes between the bars with a crunch of bone. They stabbed again and again, and ex after ex slumped against the gate. Their bodies slid down and vanished under the shambling, shuffling feet of the horde.

Derek's voice came from below. He stood on the wall at the side of the arch, his rifle held in one hand. "When do you want us to start sweeping?"

"This is not the attack," shouted Stealth, "just the massing of forces. Conserve your ammunition for now. Pikes only."

Another wave of crushed skulls echoed up to her.

"Demon's at Van Ness," said Gorgon. "Not the best way for us to start, with you being wrong right at the top."

"Thank you for pointing that out," she said. Her cloak draped across her shoulders and down over the edge of the archway. "Can you see any farther than four blocks under these conditions?"

He looked around. "Not really." His hand went to his mic. "All gates, let's get some flares up."

Across the Mount small comets shot into the sky and burst into stars. They could see for blocks now as red and yellow light bathed the surrounding neighborhood. Melrose was visible for a quarter mile past either end of the walls.

The walking dead kept coming. More and more, until the pavement vanished under a carpet of death. Thirty thousand dead eyes stared at them, and thirty thousand brittle hands clawed at the air. The exes pounded the walls, pushed at the steel fences, and rammed their arms between the gate's curling decorations.

In the distance they could hear engines roaring and horns blaring. The Seventeens were near.

Gorgon rolled his head in a circle until his neck popped. "Still feeling confident?"

"We are prepared," said Stealth. "We know their capabilities. It will be a challenge, but we are ready for whatever they have to fight us with."

And then all the lights went out.

Twenty-Five

NOW

THE FLOODLIGHTS AT North Gower flickered once and went dead.

A cry went out but Zzzap had already brightened. His light spread across the street. *No reason to worry*, he told them. *We're all grown-ups. Nobody's scared of the dark, right? Well, except Bee.*

"Fuck you," she said with a tight smile.

You wouldn't survive it, beautiful.

They all chuckled, and Cerberus gave him a nod. It was a clear night. Even without Zzzap, the waxing moon and the brilliant flares in the sky still made it easy to see. The pikes stabbed in again and dropped another handful of exes.

The pounding on the truck got louder.

Lynne looked up at the battlesuit. "Can you feel that?"

"What?"

The teenager looked around and rolled down her sleeves. "It's getting chilly."

Lady Bee nodded. "Temperature's dropping," she agreed. "What the hell's that about?"

The dead pounded on the truck, louder and louder. The living could feel the vibrations on their skin.

"They're getting stronger," said Cerberus.

"No." One of the guards shook his head. He had an ear up, listening. "It just sounds that way because they're syncing up. They're starting to beat in time."

The drumbeat on the truck became louder. The sound echoed across the Mount.

"They're *all* beating in time," muttered Bee.

A shiver worked its way through the crowd. Outside the gate, the chattering of dead teeth grew louder.

"Oh, God," a man shouted. His pike clattered to the ground. "Look at the sky!"

Far above, all three flares snuffed out like old matches. The stars vanished one by one. An inky shadow crept across the moon, across everything.

Inside the armor, lights flashed and power levels wavered. Frost formed on the screens. Cerberus staggered. She rerouted systems and tried to stabilize the batteries as her interior lights dimmed. "What the hell is going on?"

Every walkie-talkie let out a low, flat hiss of static. The guards screamed and the moon vanished behind a black shroud.

Zzzap extended his energies again and trembled as the darkness resisted. The shadows fought and forced his light back to his body. It was something he hadn't felt in over a year, and something he thought he'd never have to feel again.

Fucking son of a bitch, he said. *It's Midknight.*

× × ×

The drumbeat of the dead echoed across the Mount like a relentless overseer on an ancient slave ship. Gorgon's confident smirk faded. Even Stealth seemed shaken.

Below them, the exes parted to let the trucks drive up. Over a dozen of them, all spray-painted with different shades of green. Seventeens rode the roof and hung out the windows. At the head of the parade, Mighty Joe Young—Rodney Casares—rode in the back of a National Guard truck decorated with skulls and a large neon-green *17* on the hood. They whooped and hollered and fired their guns into the sky.

"Thank God," muttered Gorgon. "Something I can deal with."

Stealth sank down against the arch. In some way Gorgon couldn't wrap his head around, her black and gray cloak blended into the ivory material. She was ten feet away and he had trouble seeing her.

The gigantic ex waded through the dead, his eyes locked on Gorgon the whole time. They shifted and stumbled to clear a path for him. The drumming stopped. The chattering of teeth slowed and stopped.

"Just the man I was looking for," bellowed the Seventeens' leader. He stood in the intersection before the gates and flashed his tombstone grin.

"Rodney," called Gorgon. He crossed his arms across his chest and squared off his shoulders. Gunslinger pose. "Long time no see. Still ugly as shit."

"And bigger than life," he cackled. "Fucking awesome, isn't it? Life and death throw down in my body and I just keep getting bigger and meaner." He flexed a swollen arm the size of a beer keg.

Dozens and dozens of Seventeens trained their weapons on the Melrose gate.

"Tell you what," shouted the huge ex. He slapped his hands together and the exes shifted as one. A space opened around him, ten, twenty, thirty feet across when the dead stopped shambling out of the way. "Last chance. You come down, give yourself up, and I send everyone else away. You got my word."

"Yeah, you've been known for your word for years," called Gorgon. "Save the cheap effects, dipshit. You're still nothing special and you don't scare anyone."

"Oh, yeah?" Rodney spat out a mouthful of dark slime. "Want to see if your people scream when my army tears down these walls? Want to see who's scared then?"

The exes lumbered forward like a wave. Weathered hands closed on the bars. They all pulled. They all pushed. The hinges squealed.

Derek shouted and his gate guards leveled their shotguns a mere yard from the barrier. Their first volley went off at eye level and a score of exes packed against the gate dropped. Fourteen slides racked and the second volley dropped another dozen as they surged forward. Rifles went off along the top of the walls and another score of exes vanished beneath the mob.

Rodney waved his arm and the Seventeens shot back. A few people fell from the wall. Most of them dropped low and hugged the concrete.

"We can keep this up all week," shouted Gorgon over the gunfire.

"All week? This place be rubble by sunrise," yelled the dead giant. "We got the manpower, the firepower, the willpower! What you got? A couple freaks in costumes? You got nothing!!"

The Seventeens hollered and roared and punched the sky. The dead threw their arms up as well.

Gorgon stood up on top of the arch and looked down at them. Hundreds of Seventeens. Thousands of zombies.

"We've got brains, Rodney," he shouted with a grin. "And superpowers or not, you're still the same idiot you've always been. If you weren't, you wouldn't've brought an army of people who've never met me before."

"I'm gonna chop your fucking head off and shove it so far up your ass it's gonna come back out your neck!" bellowed the giant. He pointed a finger as thick as a baseball bat and a dozen Seventeens trained their weapons on the hero. "You got anything else smart to say?!"

Gorgon laughed and clapped his hands over his head. "Ladies and gentlemen of the SS," he shouted, "if you could give me your attention, please."

A good third of the gang members were already looking at him. Half the rest glanced up as Rodney yelled *"DON'T!!"*

The goggles opened and Gorgon cast his vampiric gaze out at the frozen crowd.

They shuddered and twitched as he tore their strength out. His body shook with the raw power of it, like the greatest sex of his life. Tier ten or eleven. Maybe higher. Weapons lowered and then clattered to the pavement.

Almost three hundred Seventeens collapsed in the street among the exes as the irises snapped shut.

Gorgon rolled his shoulders once and tried to settle the strength buzzing in his muscles. "Told you he was an idiot," he said to Stealth.

Shots echoed in the air as he leaped off the arch, dropped twenty feet, and drove a kick into Rodney's head. He rode the malformed skull to the ground and it made a satisfying crack as it hit the pavement. The hero slammed his fist into the giant's throat and followed it up with a strike to the solar plexus. He drove two-three-four more punches home, flashing the goggles on each one, before Rodney's arm swept him away.

It was like getting hit by a speeding car. Gorgon flew across the street, knocking down a dozen exes as he went.

"Your eye-magic don't work on me," said the giant as he stood up. "Not so tough when you can't make the other guy weak, are you?"

A handful of exes grabbed at Gorgon's arms and shoulders and he felt a tiny bit of his strength simmer away as he shrugged them off. "Man enough to test that?"

Rodney roared and charged.

× × ×

St. George landed at the Van Ness gate and Jarvis limped to him. "Moved past," shouted the salt-and-pepper man. He had one arm in a sling, and pointed north with the rifle clutched in his other hand. "Heading for Lemon Grove."

"Why didn't you—"

"Radios are out. We sent runners."

The hero nodded and hurled himself back up over the rooftops.

Lemon Grove had been a tiny pedestrian entrance, over a block north from Van Ness. When they'd moved into the Mount, they'd welded the rolling gate shut, jammed its drive chain, and boarded up the tiny guard shack with layers of plywood.

Two long, clawed hands gripped the top of the small gate and forced it back down its tracks.

There were six guards. On top of an office trailer, Ilya, Billie, and two others were picking off exes one by one. The

Marine was shouting into her walkie. The two guards on the roof of the shack were shooting at the demon on the far side.

"Oh, thank God," one of the shack guards said. "I didn't think anyone—"

"Radios are dead," St. George interrupted. "Stop wasting ammunition!" He punctuated it with a burst of flame.

They stopped firing and the gate squealed. One of the welds snapped with a sound like a cymbal.

"The demon's bulletproof. I've got him. Take care of the exes."

St. George leaped up into the sky and arced down to land just behind Cairax. He kicked two exes away and threw a few fists and elbows that shattered skulls. Then he latched onto the demon's tail and yanked.

The monster flew away from the gate as the hero swung it up, over, and slammed it into the crowded street. He leaped across the distorted body, dragging the tail with him, and shoved another ex away as he landed. He set his boots to the pavement and whipped the demon in a circle, swatting zombies away like flies. After two spins he hurled it across the street into the parking structure, decapitating a handful of exes on the way. The dead thing struck the concrete pillar like a wrecking ball and left a crater. It dropped to the ground in a heap of overlong limbs.

Behind the fence, the guards were cheering.

St. George waded through the exes, cracking heads and necks with each swing of his arms. Gunfire dropped the dead near him. He was halfway to Cairax when the demon lunged back up. Its head panned back and forth before something behind the twisted face focused on him and growled.

"Ahhh," he said. "Got your attention in there, big guy?"

Cairax lunged at him and he sidestepped. The nest of teeth cracked into the pavement next to his foot. He took the moment to grab a female ex by her coat and hurl her up at the demon. He grabbed two more and swung them like clubs, battering the monster in the head three times before the exes came apart.

The dead thing swept its arms together, knocking over its brethren, but St. George was already in the air. He shot a cone of fire into Cairax's face and the demon flinched.

"Rookie mistake," he called out. "Dead things aren't scared of—"

Cairax grabbed a dead man and hurled it up at the hero. The ex caught St. George in the side and he tumbled to the ground.

The demon moved like a snake, its spine rolling up and down as its head lashed out at him.

He swung a fist and caught it under the jaw. A tooth flew loose and Cairax staggered back from the impact.

The hero lunged up, dove in, and jerked back. A pair of exes held his coat. One was chewing on the leather, trying to work its teeth through a pocket flap. The other reached out with its free arm and grabbed a handful of hair.

He spun with his fist out and broke off the hair-puller's jaw. The fist swung back and shattered its skull. He shook off the leather-eater and a bullet exploded its head as it stumbled back.

A voice shouted something between the gunfire. Billie, up on the roof of the trailer.

He turned in time to see the demon's head lunge down again. The creature's mouth was a Venus flytrap of tusks and fangs. St. George threw his arm up out of instinct and the dead thing's daggerlike teeth punched through the leather sleeve.

Into his arm.

Agony, more pain than he'd felt in years, roared through him. The jaw hinged shut like a machine and one of the huge teeth scraped against bone as it pushed deeper into his flesh.

Cairax Murrain grinned and yanked him up into the air, shaking its head like a crocodile. St. George's shoulder twisted and he felt himself flail. He heard people screaming and realized through the pain he was one of them.

He coughed out a ball of fire and the flames cleared his head. He swung his legs, slammed his palm against Cairax's snout, and tore himself free. The sleeve shredded and just for a moment he saw white spots in the air. Blood splattered the ground, and he wondered how many pounds of meat were still in the ex's mouth. At least one of its teeth was still in his arm.

St. George landed on his knees and made an awkward lunge back to his feet. Claws slammed into his back and hurled him against a dusty Ford. His skull left a dent in the frame and the world blurred.

Rounds snapped and popped against the dead thing's leathery skin. It didn't notice. A ricochet caught an ex in the side of the head and it dropped.

The hero staggered to his feet and grabbed the demon's tail again as it lashed out. It dragged him across the pavement, tripping countless exes as it tried to shake him off. He twisted the length of muscle and felt bones snap under the leathery skin. Another car rushed up to slam into his back.

The barbed tail snapped like a whip and flung St. George back at the Mount. The mob of exes grabbed at his limbs, his coat, his hair. He shook them off, hurling bodies into the air, and got his feet back on the ground.

The ground was shaking.

Cairax lumbered forward, looming over the horde. Another swipe hurled St. George back again. He tried to focus, tried to make himself light, and slammed into the wall. He slumped to the ground and the exes swarmed over him.

Behind him, the demon roared in delight.

× × ×

"Holy Christ," said Billie as St. George hit the wall. She'd glanced back away from the street and was frozen. One of the other guards, a man with a dark unibrow turned and his jaw dropped. Ilya threw a look over his shoulder.

Looming over the buildings to the west, a huge sphere of blackness swelled, so dark they could see its edges against the night sky.

× × ×

Stealth heard the cries over the gunfire, saw the dark void swelling at the Gower gate, and knew what it was. The top priority was making Rodney lose control of whatever other dead heroes he had brought to the Mount.

She drew her weapons and leaped down into the crowd, her cloak spreading to slow her fall. The Glocks spat out two-four-six-eight rounds each before she landed in the space they'd carved for her in the mob. A quick split kick broke jaws on two exes. A sweep took down four and gave her a beat.

With one smooth motion she holstered both pistols,

swung the cloak aside, and grabbed the two ASP batons stored across the small of her back. A flick of each wrist snapped two feet of black chrome into position. The move flowed into a pair of strikes that shattered heads on either side of her. The batons whipped out again and beat out a drumroll of broken bones, making sure none of the dead things she'd knocked down would ever get back up.

She spun and smashed one baton through a dead brunette's forehead. The other cracked open a teenage boy's skull. Her boot lashed out to break the neck of a pink-haired woman. An old man. A small girl caked in blood. A businessman. A police officer with a gaping hole in its chest. Her weapons cut through the air as she marched forward and exes dropped around her.

A heavy Asian woman fell and revealed a Seventeen with a green bandanna wrapped around his head. He was dizzy, still trying to shake off the sight of Gorgon's eyes. He looked at Stealth, blinked, and tried to raise his rifle.

One baton struck the rifle barrel and jarred it from the Seventeen's hands, even as its twin swung back to crush another zombie skull. Her grip switched and the first baton bounced up from the rifle to catch him under the chin. His mouth sagged. She brought the other down and broke his wrist, then drove a kick into his chest. He hit the ground just as the pain reached his brain and he tried to scream through the fractured jaw.

Four swings bought her another moment. She'd worked her way out past the gardens flanking the gate. The guards on the wall were putting exes down one after another, but it was like dropping pebbles to divert a flash flood. The Seventeens were firing at the Mount, but it was random. They were children playing a game, not an army.

Near the center of the intersection, she saw Rodney Casares bring his massive fists around and Gorgon leap out of the way. He threw a punch that sent the monstrous ex staggering back. If the Seventeens were recovering, the hero was already losing their strength.

Stealth spun through the mob. Her weapons put down seven exes and three Seventeens. A spinning kick crushed another skull, the batons crossed to force down a rifle, and a head butt left a gangster reeling.

She lunged forward and thrust the batons into either side of an ex's head, a rough-looking man with a beard, and its skull caved in as the weapons collapsed back to their storage position. Her elbows sent two dead people stumbling back and her hands dipped forward to pull the Glocks out again.

Nine rounds dropped five exes, left two Seventeens screaming and clutching their knees, and gave her a clear shot at Rodney Casares, less than fifteen feet away.

She thumbed the selector and her right pistol emptied its magazine into the giant's head. Eighteen rounds clustered on the cross tattoo. The huge ex staggered back and fell.

A Seventeen screamed and brandished his Uzi. She put a round through his knuckles and the machine gun's magazine exploded in his hand. One of the trucks surged forward and two shots through the windshield brought it to a stop.

Gorgon glanced at her. "What the hell?"

"He has drawn Midknight down from the hills."

"Fuck."

"Oh, that's nothing, bitch," hissed Rodney.

The enormous fist sent Stealth sprawling. Her body vanished back into the crowd of zombies and gangsters.

The rounds had stripped away half his face down to the bone. His right eye streamed down his face and over the gigantic teeth. A flap of skin the size and texture of a fried egg hung loose from the bottom of his jaw.

"Now," rumbled the dead thing to Gorgon, "round two. Ready to finish this?"

× × ×

Under a veil of shadows, the exes shook the Gower gate. They pulled. They pushed. They pulled. The metal spars of the gate screeched back and forth.

Lady Bee fired down into the zombie mob from her perch. The muzzle flash was dim and the sound was dull. "Keep at it," she shouted. She traded out magazines and her AK spat a few more muffled rounds into the dead.

A handful of guards were cowering from the blackness. The rest were stabbing through the bars with their weapons.

Cerberus took an uneven step toward the gate. The battle-suit's left leg twitched and jerked forward. It made her limp. "It's Midknight and his damned EMP field," she shouted, her voice full of static. "Whatshisname turned it back on full force."

I know, yelled Zzzap.

One of the guards, the keen listener, lunged forward with his pike and stepped too far in the darkness. A withered hand grabbed his wrist and pulled him close enough for a second one to seize his forearm. He was dragged against the gate where dozens of hands and chattering jaws took him apart in seconds. His meat left bloodstains on the bars as it vanished into the crowd.

The battlesuit's eyes flickered. "Can you take him out?"

Zzzap flew up and looked out over Gower. It was a cold

blur to his eyes. Nothing alive. Nothing warm. Just a shapeless, shifting mass.

I can't see him, shouted Zzzap. *He's just another dead thing.*

At the squealing, shaking gate, someone else was screaming.

But only for a moment.

Twenty-Six

NOW

THOUSANDS OF THE DEAD swarmed the Lemon Grove gate. Gray hands tore at the bars and beat at the walls.

Billie and the others dropped exes from the trailer roof. Her M-16 barked and another shot blew the head off a dead man in orange coveralls. She looked down at the mass of figures against the wall. "Where is he?"

"They got him," wailed another man. "They got him."

"He's the fucking Dragon," she bellowed. "They didn't get him."

In the middle of the road, Cairax rose above the sea of exes and roared. The demon waded toward the gate. Its long fingers stretched and flexed.

Ilya tried to line up on a target and one of the other guards, Perry, leaped onto the trailer, shaking his scope. The man sprayed most of a magazine down at the exes before he even came to rest. He stumbled and pitched off the trailer onto the curved prongs topping the fence.

They pierced up through Perry's armpit and pinned him. He hung, howling, with a foot of steel arcing up through his shoulder and the rest of him dangling over the wall. His rifle fired off two bursts before he let go and it vanished into the crowd below.

The exes shifted focus. They reached up and grabbed feet, legs, hips, and started to tug. They sank their teeth into his flesh and tore off mouthfuls of calf and thigh. Billie emptied her rifle, but there were hundreds of them.

Perry screamed and they pulled harder and harder. There was a noise like wet magazines being shredded as he came apart. His right arm and shoulder blade stayed on the fence and he was yanked down into the horde of exes. He disappeared beneath the chattering jaws and his shrieks came to an abrupt halt. A few last exes clawed at the dangling arm and grabbed at the limp fingers.

Billie dumped a fresh magazine into the knot of dead people. Several of them fell, but she knew it didn't matter. "St. George," she hollered. "Get your ass up! We need you!"

Cairax grabbed the gate again and heaved. The rolling fence bent forward with a squeal and bounced back into place. The unibrow guard fired a burst into the monster's face. One of the men on the guard shack lashed out with his pike and the demon caught the end. It heaved the shaft up, flinging the man into the sea of undead. He hit the pavement screaming and vanished under a wave of hands and teeth.

Then St. George drove his fists up and the exes went sprawling.

The hero staggered to his feet. His jacket was covered with bite marks, his skin was pale, but he was still alive. He coughed out some fire and smoke.

Yards away, the demon glared at him and tried to hiss.

St. George grabbed a blue Metro parked near the curb, sinking his fingers through the body and the door frame. He heaved the car into the air and spun with it just as Cairax lunged. The demon's skull bounced on the hood and it staggered back. He threw the little car after it and sent the dead monster sprawling.

A cheer went up as the hero stumbled out to fight the monster. He gave them a ragged salute, drove his fingers through an ex's spine, and took a few unsteady steps after the demon. "If you need to take a breather," he shouted, "just put your hand up or something."

Cairax straightened up in the crowd of zombies, hefting a fallen phone pole. St. George ducked and the pole crushed dozens of exes in a wide arc. He leaped over the next swing and a handful of zombies were smashed into the burned remains of a Volkswagen. He flipped up though the air and got his arm around the demon's neck, wrestling past the thick collar.

The creature's long hands twisted back, grabbed him, and brought the hero hurtling into the pavement. They smashed him down again and again before flinging him against a light post. His body cartwheeled into the crowd and the dead stumbled after him.

Cairax marched forward, reaching up over the fence at the shooters. Billie and Unibrow sprayed bullets at its face. Ilya dropped half a dozen exes near it.

"HEY!"

The demon turned and caught the phone pole in the side of its head. The battering ram slammed it against the wall of the Mount.

"You dropped this!" shouted St. George.

The dead thing hissed and the pole crushed it against the wall again. Cinder blocks cracked behind its ridged back.

× × ×

Lady Bee fired down into the exes mobbing the gate. Even a few yards away, they were just shadows. She emptied her AK and traded out clips. "What am I looking for?" she hollered.

"An ex in a costume," bellowed Cerberus. "A blue and black costume."

She threw a few flares out at the endless hordes, but the darkness smothered them even before they fell into the crowd. "You're shitting me? In all this?"

Look for more dark, then, said Zzzap. *Look for where it's pitch black.*

Cerberus took another limping step and stopped. The battlesuit tried to turn its head and twitched like a junkie. Her feet shifted a few inches and froze. "I'm having tons of failures," she yelled. "The piezoelectric sensors aren't working. I'm locking up."

Bee dropped another handful of exes. "It's just dark everywhere," she shouted.

The wraith forced his way higher into the black air. He willed himself brighter and pushed out against the darkness. And again, the shadows resisted.

They pushed back hardest from the northwest.

Zzzap flew past Bee and the gate. He shifted in the air and let off another burst of light. Below his feet the black parted to reveal thousands of exes clawing up at him. They covered Gower like an open concert venue. The darkness rolled back and he resisted it again.

To the west.

Another burst guided him into the alley across the street. The consuming night had weight here. It pressed down on him, smothering his light like an ocean of ink. He let off enough energy to melt through steel and the shadows fled for a few moments.

At the heart of the darkness was a dead man, half hidden in the alley by a thick phone pole. Scores of other exes shifted and shambled around him, packed into the narrow space. The black and blue outfit hung on the desiccated frame and made the shoulder pads seem huge. Covering his head was a heavy mask designed to look like an armored helmet with a plume and a visor. The sleeves were tattered and Zzzap could see old bite marks across the withered gray flesh.

The thing inside Midknight glared out at the hero and gave one final push. The waves of darkness lunged in for a last attack.

The glowing wraith swept them aside with a wave of his hand. The shadows shattered as the air simmered. Zzzap brought his palms up and focused.

Beneath the visor, the ex's teeth started to chatter.

The blast was a foot across. It vaporized the ex-hero from the chest up, burned a hole through the apartment complex behind him, and went on for another two blocks before vanishing through molten pavement.

What was left of Midknight burst into flame, along with dozens of other exes in the alley. The dead hero crumbled into ash like charred logs. A roaring wind picked up around Zzzap as air thunderclapped in to fill the hole he'd burned into the atmosphere. The dust scattered and disappeared.

The moon and the stars shone down from above, and Zzzap felt the radio chatter filling the wavelengths around him. The gate lights swelled up to brighten that corner of the Mount.

He let his legs hang low and burned a path through the

exes, dropping a few hundred of them before he rose up over the Gower gate. The guards laughed and hollered.

"Holy shit, hot stuff," shrieked Lady Bee with a grin. "D'you think you got him?"

Nuke the site from orbit, he called out. *It's the only way to be sure.*

They cheered and the pikes lunged forward. The exes at the gate crumpled and fell.

He hovered in front of the battlesuit. *How are you? Back up?*

Cerberus shook her head. "Give me a minute or three," she said. "Surge protectors saved the mainframe but I need to do a full reboot."

Anything I can do to help?

The armored skull shook again and then her eyes went dark.

I'm going to check over at Melrose, he shouted to Bee. *I'll be back before you know it.*

× × ×

Gorgon could feel the strength ebbing. It had been a rush but he was at tier three now, tops. And the Seventeens were keeping clear of his fight.

Rodney swung and missed by inches. "Slowing down," he laughed. "Batteries are running out, huh?"

The hero ducked another punch, drove a kick into the giant's thigh, and followed it with a trio of punches into the solar plexus. Rodney caught him in the shoulder and he spun in the air. Dozens of dead fingers grabbed and held him as the huge ex lined up another punch.

Gorgon threw off the exes and ducked as the massive fist

sailed over him. He drove a punch up into the thick wrist and felt something crack.

"Kind of slow yourself, fugly," Gorgon shouted. "Your mind somewhere else, maybe?"

The monstrous ex rumbled and stepped back. "Think you're clever, don't you?" The exes all fell back as well, leaving Gorgon in another circle.

"Smarter than you, for what that says."

Rodney lunged again. The hero jumped up and drove his heels into the giant's chin. It was a weak kick. Tier three without a doubt. It pushed him back more than Rodney.

Gorgon grabbed his walkie and keyed the send button four or five times. And then huge fingers grabbed the tails of his duster and whipped him into the air. He flew, whirled, crashed into the mob of exes, the dead bodies cushioning his landing. Teeth were on his sleeves and got his arms up to protect his face. He threw out a few punches and kicks and they all backed away again.

"Okay," bellowed Rodney. "Fun's over."

Gorgon stood up and heard the crack at the same time his side burned. He thought the giant had broken one of his ribs. Then he looked down, saw the hole in the side of the duster, and felt the blood spreading.

There was another gunshot and his shoulder exploded with pain. His knees shook for a moment and he heard the Seventeens howling. He keyed the walkie again.

The giant loomed over him. "Still feeling tough? Still think you're better than me?"

"Fuck, it's not about what I think," said Gorgon. "Everybody here *knows* I'm better than you."

Rodney, the crowd of exes, and the sky spun around him and a beat later he felt the ribs collapse where the kick had connected. He hit the pavement and heard something snap inside the goggles. One of the lens sections tumbled in against his eye.

Rodney sneered. "This your big last stand, *esse*? This what you'd call being heroic?"

Gorgon spit out a blob of blood. "Nope," he said. "I'd call this round three."

He turned his smile to the bright sky as the last of the night fled and the sun raced around the corner. It incinerated a crowd of exes near the gate then shot back to hover above them. *Lay off the mic, for Christ's sake,* said Zzzap. *You sure you're ready for this?*

"Guess we'll find out."

Rodney scowled with his one eye. "What the fu—"

Gorgon pulled off his goggles.

For a moment, just the barest of instants, the man-shaped silhouette in the air dimmed. The false daylight flickered to gray and Zzzap sagged. Then his outline flared back up and he vanished up and across the Mount.

And Gorgon was on fire.

"OH, YEAH!" he roared. He couldn't even guess what tier this was. Fifty? One hundred? He could feel strength burning out of his eyes, mouth, every pore of his skin. "YOU STILL WANT TO THROW DOWN, YOU FUCKING FRANKENSTEIN WANNABE?!"

The hero lunged forward and his fist struck Rodney with the force of a train engine. The enormous ex hurtled back, smashing through a steel fence like a missile through a garden trellis. He shredded the roof of a dusty sports car and slammed into the minivan parked beyond it.

Gorgon bounded after him, covering twenty feet with each leap. "Come on!" he bellowed. "You and me, big guy!

It's what you always wanted!" He hurled the sports car into the air and the giant scrambled to dodge it.

A quartet of exes seized the hero's arms and neck. He crushed their skulls like paper cutouts and whipped the bodies away, sending everything behind him sprawling for half a dozen yards.

Rodney tore the axle from the sports car and swung it like a bat. He brought it whipping around and Gorgon caught the end. A quick shove and the steel bar cracked back into the giant's face. The hero hammered down again and sent the huge Seventeen sprawling.

× × ×

Stealth fought from her position on the ground while she reloaded the Glocks and tried to clear her head. She kicked and swept with her legs until the slides both dropped home. At this range, bodies dropped one after another with each shot, and she didn't pause to see if the blood spraying was black or red until she was back on her feet. She emptied the pistols to give her a moment of breathing room and swapped in another set of fresh clips. Her last set.

Rodney's strike had knocked her forty feet down the road. There were hundreds, more likely thousands, of exes between her and the gate. She would not make it back on foot.

The gate shuddered and a gap appeared.

Hundreds of exes backed by hundreds more pushed on the ornate double gate. Between the gunshots she could hear the terrible creak of the bars as they bent under the weight. The gap was already over a foot and opening wider. Derek, Katie, and a dozen others stood on the wall firing down into the horde and Stealth could see the pikes lashing out.

Something grabbed her shoulder. She spun and pistol-whipped the ex across the jaw. The backswing crushed its temple and the dead thing dropped. Another eleven shots opened the circle again and left a howling Seventeen with an arm all but severed at the elbow.

A few yards away a king-cab truck gunned its engine and moved for the gate. It pulled out into the wide intersection and its cowcatcher shoved exes out of the way. The Seventeens in the back howled and banged on the roof of the cab as it gained speed.

Her Glocks spat fire and dropped a score of exes as she charged the truck. The Seventeens saw her coming and shouted. Their aim was sloppy and nervous and she felt three individual rounds tug at her cloak for an instant each.

The last ex dropped and Stealth used its body as a spring-board. She holstered the weapons in midair and her kick threw the first Seventeen off the far side of the truck and into the mob of exes. Her boots clanged on the truck bed and she drove the heel of her hand into another man's chin.

They bumped each other, hesitated, and she took them apart.

One hand blocked a roundhouse punch, twisted the man's wrist around, and a strike slammed into his armpit to dislocate the shoulder. Her leg shot back, burying her heel in a woman's stomach. She grabbed a Seventeen's shoulders and the same knee flew forward as his head came down. A knife stabbed at her and she broke three of the fingers holding it and the wrist behind them. Her baton shattered the passenger window and she dragged the man out by his hair. The driver's nose hit the steering wheel four times before the Glock pressed against his head hard enough to force his right eye shut.

"You were heading for the gate," Stealth said. "You will continue to do so. Slowly."

× × ×

St. George slammed the Chrysler down on the demon and flattened it to the ground. The hero leaped into the air and dropped hard onto the roof. All four tires blew out and the last two windows shattered.

Beneath the car Cairax looked dazed. Most of its head and one arm stuck out beneath the passenger door, salted with broken glass. Its diagonal eyelids clicked shut a few times. The thing looking through the eyes went away and the demon's jaws started to gnash together.

"About damn time," said St. George.

Up and down the street he saw the shift. Thousands of exes slumped a little more, moved a little less, like a mass loss of confidence. The monster shifted under the car and reached up for him with a clumsy arm. The Chrysler groaned as the dead thing tried to push it out of the way.

The hero balanced on the swaying car and threw a glance back to the gate. "I think we're good," he shouted.

The claw latched onto his leg and yanked him off the car.

Cairax smashed St. George against the pavement, then swung him around. His head cracked against dozens of withered ankles and he was airborne again, just for a minute, before being slammed into the street again. His ears were ringing.

The demon tossed the car aside and glared down at him. A broad, thick-toed foot stomped down on the hero's injured arm. More meat pulled away from the bones and blood spurted across the monster's almost-hoof.

Something was thumping. St. George shook his head, shook it again, and the sound became clear. The dozen or so people behind the wall were chanting.

Chanting his name.

Even Cairax seemed to notice. It looked at the half-bent gate and then back at him.

St. George, the Mighty Dragon, pushed against gravity, shot up, and threw all his strength into a single punch. Dozens of oversized teeth sprayed out across the street as the monster's jaw shattered. A second punch crushed its rib cage and he felt the shredded muscles of his arm howl.

He threw a third, fourth, and fifth, knocking the demon back with each one. Both fists came together and he felt its sternum crack. Another thrust against gravity let him grab the leathery brow ridge in one hand and a tusk in the other. His boots braced against the monster's chest and he twisted its head with all his strength. The skull yanked to the left—

And stopped.

He could feel the muscles knotting up under the leather collar. Resisting. The saucer eyes glared at him.

It grabbed his wounded arm, squeezed the raw flesh, and flung him off. An enormous claw smashed him to his knees hard enough to crack the pavement. Exes pawed and grabbed and held him down while they gnawed at his skin.

Cairax wrapped its spidery hand around the fallen hero's hair, bent down, and roared with glee. The severed stump of its tongue waved before his eyes and something bumped against his chin. St. George's eyes glanced down and saw a glimpse of silver swinging back and forth from the monster's collar.

The Sativus medallion.

The thought crossed his mind in an instant. The hero

threw off the exes holding his arm. He tore the medallion away and sparks popped against the monster's purple hide as the silver links snapped.

Cairax Murrain twitched and pointed a talon at him. Then it trembled, opened its monstrous, sagging jaw, and collapsed in on itself in a swirl of dark flames and smoke.

In the demon's footprints stood an ex with a mop of black hair and a library of tattoos across its yellowed flesh. Pentagrams, long lines of Latin, and scores of Egyptian hieroglyphics. The heavy collar hung like a huge ring on the dead man's neck. The naked ex staggered and closed its mouth with a solid clack, then looked down at its tiny limbs. The thing behind its eyes looked confused.

"I'd explain what just happened," said St. George, "but I'd hate to ruin the trick for you."

The medallion let off a few black sparks as he crushed it between his fingers. Then he stepped forward and drove his fist through the ex's skull. It exploded like an old flowerpot and Maxwell Hale's headless corpse dropped to the ground.

× × ×

Gorgon grabbed Rodney's arm as the punch flew by and yanked the dead giant off his feet. A backhand slap sent the huge ex sprawling.

"Doesn't have to be like this," the hero yelled. He lunged forward, grabbed the oversized skull, and slammed it against the pavement. "You can still quit. Run away. Take your people and get out of here."

The monstrous ex snarled as another one of its matchbook-sized teeth dropped out. "Like that, *pinche*, wouldn't you? Making me lose face again?" He rolled away, grabbed a faded Boxster, and threw it at the hero.

Gorgon leaped over the car and hammered his fists down on the other man's shoulders, driving him to the ground. "Keep fighting and you'll lose it all, big guy."

Rodney pushed himself up onto his knees and chuckled. "Fight's over," he rumbled. "You're dead."

He hurled an oversized fist with enough force to crush a man. Gorgon leaped up, flipped around in midair, and found himself face-to-face with Banzai.

Her face was clean and pale. A few loose hairs wafted from her ebony braid. The dead woman looked at him with cloudy eyes and blinked twice. Her lips turned down ever so slightly as she glanced from his face to the ragged hole in her shoulder.

He stumbled. Just for a moment. "Oh, baby," he whispered.

And then she vanished in a gray haze. Enormous fingers wrapped around Gorgon's head and squeezed. Rodney lifted the thrashing hero into the air and the other massive hand pinned the flailing legs together.

"Sucker!" he howled with glee. "I've had your bitch, man. She's dry and tight and loved every minute of it."

Rodney twisted the hero, wrenching the hips around with a bubble-wrap sound, and let Gorgon's body drop to the pavement.

There were screams from the wall. Cheers from the SS. The gunfire picked up on both sides.

And then thunder hammered their ears.

A dozen windows shattered in nearby buildings. One of the trucks rushing the gate shook three times before exploding. A Seventeen lifted his machete to the sky and became a red cloud from the waist up even as the ex behind him spurted fountains of dark blood and meat.

Twin paths of fire tore up exes, pavement, and everything else they crossed. Rodney caught a line across his torso and shoulder that chewed his chest apart even as it pounded him back.

"Hey, death breath!"

The ground shook as Cerberus thudded out of the gates, the cannons on her arms smoking. "Want to try with someone your own size?!"

× × ×

The thunder echoed across the lot, and the unibrow man looked up from the bandage he was tying on St. George's shredded arm. The hero made a fist around the long, broken fang they'd pried from his biceps.

"Oh yeah," said Ilya before picking off another ex. "Definitely sounds like Judgment Day."

Outside the gate, a ripple of movement swept across the zombies. They stumbled in mid step. Their teeth began to clack.

St. George shrugged back into his patchwork jacket. "Ahhh, hell."

"What's going on?"

He looked out at the dead. They were flailing at the gate, pawing with no purpose. "I think we got what we wanted. Rodney's distracted and he's starting to lose control."

Billie looked out at the chattering horde. "Is that good?"

"Sort of. A few minutes ago we were surrounded by sixty thousand or so exes all obeying him."

"And now?"

"Now we're just surrounded by sixty thousand exes."

Her walkie squawked and Billie's face fell. "They need you at the main gate," she said. "It's bad. Derek says Stealth is missing. And Gorgon is down."

The hero's face hardened. "You have things here?"

"We can deal with exes," she said with a nod. "Go kick some ass."

St. George shot into the sky, tracing a high arc toward the Melrose gate.

It wasn't until a few hours later, looking back on the moment, that Billie, Ilya, and the rest realized he hadn't jumped.

× × ×

Cerberus stomped forward, the ground trembling with every step. She threw aside the exes mobbing the driveway. Her arms came up and the armor selected seven hundred and thirteen viable targets for her. The first pass with the M-2s tore a hundred exes into hamburger. She watched the ammo counters spin down to triple digits as the second pass destroyed two more trucks and cleared her path across the intersection.

Rodney lumbered toward the gate and the zombies came with him. They marched in perfect lockstep, heels slapping on the pavement. The Seventeens moved forward in trucks and on foot.

As one, the dead raised their arms to point at her. Bullets pinged and sparked against the armor.

"Come on, big girl," the dead giant shouted. He pounded on his ruined chest, and countless exes mimicked him. "You wanna give me my last chance to run away or you wanna fight?"

"You had your last chance," growled Cerberus. "You didn't take it."

The cannons roared again. Between the walls of the Mount and the nearby office buildings the sound itself was a weapon. The gate guards winced. Another two trucks vanished in clouds of shrapnel, and Seventeens screamed. More exes vanished in splashes of dark blood and rotted meat. Rodney staggered back as a hundred rounds punched through him like a swarm of high-caliber hornets.

The counters dropped into double digits, single, and the cannons clanged open. The silence was deafening.

Rodney stood up and coils of meat unspooled from his stomach. The intestines spilled over the ground and he reached down to tear them loose. "Someone hasn't been paying attention," he laughed. "Body shots don't do nothing and we don't get tired. Twenty minutes with your boy toy and I'm still fresh and ready to go."

He lunged at the armor and they met eye to eye. His massive fists clanged against the armored helmet. He drove his knee up into the battlesuit's crotch and jerked it a foot off the ground.

Cerberus brought her own knee up and heard his pelvis crack. She shoved him away and slammed her gauntlet into his ragged face.

He grabbed a gun barrel in his hands and twisted. Metal shrieked as he tore the cannon away from the battlesuit's arm.

Inside the helmet a handful of warnings flashed. Two subsystems shut down on their own to prevent shorts.

The giant lifted the cannon over his shoulder like a club

and grinned. His swing caught the battlesuit in the shoulder. The blow echoed inside the armor, rattling her teeth. Her viewscreens flared and sizzled with static.

"I'm death incarnate," he bellowed. "I killed the Gorgon. I killed the world. And it just makes me stronger!"

"Yeah, you're big and tough," Cerberus said. "And you know what else?"

She slammed her fist forward with a crackle of electricity. The arcs lashed at Rodney before the impact hurled him across the street. The battlesuit left cracks in the pavement as it raced forward, knocking exes aside, and sank its fingers into the giant's rib cage. She hefted him to his feet and a piledriver slammed into his face. Teeth sprayed across the intersection.

"You're meat," she roared. "I'm steel and you're nothing but a bag of meat."

The second punch shattered his cheekbone and one side of his face sagged like putty. She brought both fists down and his shoulder blades crumbled beneath them.

The broken giant looked up at her. "He meant something to you, eh?"

"Yes," growled the battlesuit.

"Ahhh." What was left of Rodney's face split in an evil, cracked grin. "Sucks to be you."

Cerberus grabbed his skull in her steel fingers and twisted. There was the sound of a tree trunk splitting, an ice shelf cracking, and the battlesuit tore the giant's head loose. She gouged out the one good eye, pulled back her arm, and sent the hunk of bone and flesh hurling into the sky.

The huge, headless body toppled to the ground a dozen or so feet from Gorgon.

And then . . .

× × ×

Things went mad.

Screams echoed across the broad intersection as the dead turned on their former allies. Exes swarmed over the Seventeens and the gangbangers vanished under scores of teeth and grasping hands. Some were caught off guard. Others went down fighting.

The entrance to the Mount had shifted from assault to feeding frenzy. The exes weren't focused or guided. They were just killing. Their teeth chattered like a tap school for the insane.

A truck lurched to a halt on the cobblestone driveway and Stealth smashed the butt of her pistol across the driver's head. She dragged him from the cab and threw him at the gate. The guards grabbed the dazed Seventeen and dragged him through the opening. A dead man with a mohawk grabbed at his legs, but the cloaked woman shattered the ex's skull with a baton slash.

One of the Seventeens' other trucks roared to life and plowed through the mob. Gangers clawed their way into the bed. More than one was pulled back by dead fingers. An old man with white hair and bloody teeth attacked a woman with dozens of braids. A gray-skinned Latina sank her teeth into a tattooed man.

The guards drove back the dead and fought the gate shut. Bodies clogged the opening. Some were struggling to get in, others were dragging them back.

Cerberus looked back at Gorgon's body, twisted and sprawled on the pavement, and saw a Seventeen swinging his rifle like a club at everything that moved. The boy was sixteen at the most, alone, and he was close to breaking. He was surrounded by hungry dead things.

Another truck turned and fled. It was all but empty. People shouted and waved and were ignored.

Cerberus reached out and grabbed the boy, hefting him up onto her shoulders. He shrieked and flailed until he realized he was safe. The battlesuit took four steps toward the gate, batting exes aside like flies, and pulled another Seventeen from the mob.

And then . . .

× × ×

St. George dropped out of the sky, leaving a trail of flames in the air behind him. He arced across the road until he was before the Melrose gate. The hero pushed down, forcing gravity to its knees and demanding it obey him.

And gravity, after a brief struggle, acknowledged his superiority.

St. George, the Mighty Dragon, hovered in midair over the intersection, floating above the mob. The tattered remains of his coat fluttered behind him. Smoke curled from his mouth and nose and wreathed his skull like a dark halo. Held out at arm's length was the prize he'd plucked in midair.

Rodney's head.

"THIS WAR IS OVER!"

His voice echoed across the street, over the chattering, and flames sparked in his mouth. He held up the severed head for everyone to see, then threw it down into the hordes. Exes staggered after the ball of flesh and bone.

"Anyone not wearing a green bandanna or scarf is welcome

to take shelter inside the Mount," he shouted. "I wish the rest of you the best of luck making it back to your compound."

Below him, the horde of living dead continued to rip and tear and claw at the Seventeens. The clacking of teeth drowned out most of their screams. Some of them fought their way into the remaining trucks. Many more were dragged back out and torn to shreds.

Close to the wall, a bald man with a mustache smacked an ex away with a baseball bat. Then he reached up, tore the green cloth from his arm, and ran for the gate. The woman next to him did the same with the bandanna holding her dark hair.

Guards on the wall set down covering fire where they could. Dozens of Seventeens battered their way to the gate, tearing off do-rags and patches. Cerberus knocked exes left and right as she marched across the cobblestone driveway.

St. George drifted above the crowd until he reached the gate. He settled to the ground and hurled the walking dead away like dolls. A baker's dozen of Seventeens stumbled past him and through the narrow gap of the gate.

The hero slammed his fist against one last ex, a skinny man in a filthy Santa Claus suit, and sent it hurling back. He took three steps back and the gate shut with a clang.

Cerberus braced a broad foot and three-fingered hand against the struts and gave Derek a quick nod. "I've got it," she said. "Go find another lock-bar."

Stealth had over a hundred Seventeens on their knees by the guard shack, fingers laced behind their heads. Ten or twenty of them were sobbing. So were a few of the gate guards.

Katie took a few deep breaths and looked up at St. George. "Am I wrong," she gasped, "or did we just live through that?"

St. George Kills the Mighty Dragon
THEN

THE CAPE WAS TATTERED, but I'd gotten used to it. Having it gradually fall apart ended up working like training wheels. It was shredded but I could fly better than ever. The next time I went out I was just going to trash it. To be honest, most of my Dragon costume was ruined. Runs, pockmarks, things smeared into it that were never going to come out.

Stealth had asked to meet me at sundown on top of the Kodak Theatre at Hollywood and Highland. It was a landmark. They held the Academy Awards here. Beneath me was a huge scrolling screen that had been blank for two and a half months. Kitty-cornered across the street, a fiberglass tyrannosaurus smashed through a building facade with a clock in its mouth. I had a certain sympathy for the thing that should've given up and gone extinct but kept fighting.

This used to be one of the busiest intersections in the city. LA's version of Times Square. Now it was the site of a seven-car pileup and the scorched wrecks of two National Guard Humvees. Highland was a vehicle graveyard as far as you could see in either direction. In at least a third of the cars things were clawing at the windshields. I could see another three hundred or so exes wandering between the metal corpses.

You have to kill them faster than they're killing you. That was the lesson we'd learned too late. Every person they kill comes back on their side. If they kill one and you kill one, your numbers have gone down and theirs have stayed the same. Zombies are like credit card payments. If you keep getting rid of the minimum amount, you'll never win.

And we weren't winning. No other way to look at it. I was sleeping three hours a night and still wasn't making any headway. Banzai was dead. Blockbuster was dead. Cairax was dead. Regenerator was crippled and powerless. Despite dozens of emergency bulletins and training seminars, the number of exes was still growing. It was almost inevitable.

The sun brushed the horizon.

"Thank you for meeting me."

Stealth stood a dozen or so feet behind me. As usual. God, she was hot.

"Well, it was this or use the time to eat a meal," I said. She didn't laugh, so I coughed and tried to brush past it. "What's up?"

"You are no longer hiding your identity?"

I looked at the black and green mask in my hand. The face of the Mighty Dragon. "Well, as I see it, it's moot either way. I'm pretty sure you already know who I am. Probably where I live and how I voted in the past three elections. As for everyone else . . ." I threw another look out at the darkened metropolis and shrugged. "I don't think there are enough people left to make a secret identity worth the effort."

She nodded. "I would like to discuss our options, George."

"What do you mean?"

Her hips were like a beautiful pendulum beneath the camo cloak as she walked to stand next to me. We looked out at the dying city. "Los Angeles has been lost."

As much as I knew it, no one had said it yet. We were still fighting, still holding blocks and stations. Cerberus fought her way over the hill with half a rifle platoon of Marines and cleaned out a good length of Sunset Boulevard in the process. Gorgon was keeping the base at Hollywood and Cahuenga safe, using survivors as batteries to keep his strength up. Zzzap was still trying to split time among four different cities.

"Yeah," I said. "I know."

"With that understood," she said, "I believe our energies are now best spent preparing for a prolonged siege. I have a secure area where we can protect a number of people. Certain preparations have already been made."

"Isn't there some sort of government plan we should be following? They must have something worked out."

She shook her head. "The State of California and the CDC each had three possible contingency plans for a major Los Angeles viral outbreak. All six have been rendered impossible either from lack of resources or because the outbreak has spread past the established containment parameters. Under ideal circumstances, their only option at this point is sterilization."

It took a moment for that to sink in. "Wait . . . you're talking about, what, they're going to nuke the city or something?"

The hooded woman nodded. "That is the CDC's fallback position for an epidemic this virulent and dangerous. However, the disease is already too widespread. Destroying every city in the country would not eliminate it, and there are not enough pilots left to perform the number of required missions."

"So . . . what are they going to do?"

"CDC in Atlanta stopped responding to queries seventeen hours ago. Zzzap has investigated and can see no signs of life from their command building. He believes it has been overrun or abandoned."

"Abandoned?"

"Air Force One has gone to radio silence. The governor is missing and his mansion has been destroyed by rioters. We are operating on our own."

"Jesus." I heard something click on the rooftop and realized I'd dropped my mask. She kept talking in the same calm voice, as if the end of the world was something she dealt with all the time.

"There are still thousands of survivors scattered across the city. People who have endured in fortified buildings or complexes. Individuals, families, and in a few places I have seen groups of several dozen. Our first priority will be to assess these survivors and gather them to a single, secure location."

"What were you thinking?"

She pointed southeast. "You are familiar with Paramount Studios?"

"Yeah, of course."

"Just under thirty acres of area. Five major entrances, two minor, all easily sealed. Two underground tunnels. The walls are eight feet at their shortest point, in the northeast corner, and are topped by outward-curving spikes. It is an ideal fortress."

I tried to picture the big, wrought-iron gates. "Couldn't

you say that about most of the studios? I think Universal City is bigger."

She shook her head. "I have made several observations and believe Paramount has the best combination of existing resources, defensibility, and long-term potential."

"And where do we fit in?"

"There will be rogue elements inside and out. We shall serve as protectors and wardens until some system of government can be reinstated."

"You and me?"

"All of us who are left here in Los Angeles. Myself, you, Gorgon, Zzzap, Midknight, Cerber—"

"Midknight's dead."

She twitched. "What?"

"Yesterday. You didn't know? He was overwhelmed at one of the checkpoints near the Hollywood Bowl." I scratched the back of my neck. "He's already walking again."

"I see."

"Thought you didn't make mistakes?"

"Everyone makes mistakes. I merely make far fewer than most."

"To be honest, I was surprised he made it this long. His power was kind of defensive, you know? Not much good against exes."

"You disposed of him?"

I shrugged and made a fist around my hair. It was getting long in the back. On the ground, my mask stared up at me. I knew I wouldn't be picking it up. The Mighty Dragon, dead on the roof of the Kodak Theatre. Another ex-hero.

"I took him up into Griffith Park," I told her. "That's where I've been dropping our people if they turn."

"He is dangerous if his powers are still active."

"They are," I said. "He probably is." I looked back out over the dead metropolis and let a few streamers of smoke thread their way out of my nose.

"George?"

"I had to put down Blockbuster last week, you know. I was the only one strong enough to break his neck."

"He was doing a phenomenal amount of property damage as an ex," she said. "He walked straight through seven blocks of Beverly Hills. Over forty-three structures were leveled."

The day was almost gone. The sky was burning up, and shadows stretched across the city. I hadn't watched a sunset in over a year.

"It's been a very long summer," I said. "I didn't feel like killing anyone else I knew. If you like, I can take you up where I dropped him and you can do it. He'll be easy to find."

She didn't respond, and for a moment I thought she'd vanished again. "That will not be necessary," she said.

"Good." I looked her in the face. "So, what's your plan to save Los Angeles?"

"You are a symbol among heroes and civilians alike. They will all accept your recommendations and follow where you lead. We can begin to contact survivors and guide them to the Mount."

"The Mount?"

"A simple abbreviation. It conveys a sense of stability and defense rather than reminding them of the illusions film creates."

"Good point."

"I believe we can have the majority of the city's survivors there in four to six weeks. With a few simple questions and reviews, we should be able to create a balanced and optimum population. Doctors, teachers, engineers, and others who will have the most long-term usefulness. I believe we can then prepare—"

"No."

She twitched again. "What?"

"No." It was a moment of clarity. One of the first ones I'd had in several weeks of hard decisions and acceptable losses. "If we do this, if you want my help with it, it isn't some stupid selection process where we pick and choose a few hundred who we decide are worth it. We just save everyone we can."

"The studio lot cannot support thousands of people."

"Not as it is, no. But we could adapt more of the buildings to housing, plant gardens, do things to make it work. I won't be part of a plan that involves leaving most people outside to fend for themselves."

"A limited selection is our best hope for survival."

"If that's our best hope then we shouldn't survive."

Her head shifted ever so slightly. I had enough female friends to recognize the gaze I was getting.

"Look," I said, "this is going to sound really stupid, but you have to understand something." I passed my hand across the red-scaled suit. It was stained and fraying but it still glimmered in the fading sunlight. "You called me a symbol, and you're right. This suit stands for something. It isn't me living some childhood fantasy or anything like that. It's about hope."

"Hope?"

I took in a deep breath, and smoke twisted around my head as I let it slip through my teeth. "Do you know what my favorite show was when I was a little kid?"

The look again. "I would have no idea."

"*Doctor Who*. British sci-fi show."

"I am familiar with it. Christopher Eccleston, David Tennant, and Matt—"

"No," I said. "The new show's great, but I grew up on the old one. The low-budget, rubber monster show with Tom Baker and Peter Davison. I watched it on PBS all the time as a kid."

I looked out at the dark ruins of Hollywood, at the stumbling shadows dotting the streets as far as you could see. The only other living person within half a mile was standing behind me, her eyes boring into my head.

"The Doctor didn't have superpowers or weapons or anything like that. He was just a really smart guy who always tried to do the right thing. To help people, no matter what. That struck me when I was a kid. The idea that no matter how cold and callous and heartless the world seemed, there was somebody out there who just wanted to make life better. Not better for worlds or countries in some vague way. Just better for people trying to live their lives, even if they didn't know about him."

I turned back to her and tapped my chest. "That's what this suit's always been about. Not scaring people like you or Gorgon do. Not some sort of pseudosexual role play or repressed emotions. I wear this thing, all these bright colors, because I want people to know someone's trying to make their lives better. I want to give them hope."

She was quiet for a long time. "I see."

"Good. Because I won't let you do what you're talking about doing. I'm not going to cherry-pick people who you think will be 'useful' and leave everyone else to die."

She stared at me for a long moment. I could feel her eyes even through the mask. Then she nodded. "If you feel this is the right path, I shall trust your judgment."

I let out a breath I didn't know I was holding and nodded back.

"It will require more work," she said, "but we should be able to rescue the majority of the survivors."

"Thank you."

"As I was saying before, with your reassurances we should be able to gather the majority of the survivors to the Mount within four to six weeks. That number should hold even with the expanded scope of this venture."

"How can we promise them it'll be safe?"

"You and Cerberus can reinforce the entrances."

"With what?"

"Production vehicles and trucks. Either of you can tip them and move them into position, giving us solid walls at any gate. Once the facility is sealed, Zzzap can search all of it in an hour. We could have the lot clean and secure in two days' time."

"How do we keep it clean, though? I've seen the movies. People could come in infected."

She shook her head. "There is no evidence the virus can pass except through blood contact. All survivors will be strip-searched for bites or injuries before being allowed to enter."

I mulled over the idea. "That won't go over well with a lot of folks."

"It is necessary. Keeping the Mount clean and free of infection must be our primary concern."

"And us? Pardon the reference but . . . who watches the watchmen?"

"You, Zzzap, and Cerberus are all effectively immune since the exes cannot reach your respective bloodstreams. The three of you will observe and examine the rest of us for bites or possible infection."

I raised an eyebrow. "You're going to submit to a strip search?"

Stealth tilted her head, and I could feel the icy stare. "I will allow Cerberus to examine as much of my body as she deems necessary. There is no way an attack on my head or face could be hidden."

"Okay, then," I said, banishing that set of thoughts. "What do we do if they don't want to come?"

"You think they will doubt us?"

I looked out at the city. "I think people are doubting everything right now. After a few months of martial law and the walking dead, we're going to have an uphill battle making them believe anything's okay."

"I have no doubt you can convince them they will be completely safe within the Mount," she said. "The populace of Los Angeles all but worships you as a saint."

Epilogue
NOW

ST. GEORGE STOOD on the water tower and looked out across the darkened city. The sky was getting brighter but the night still held its ground in places. Some of the exes had wandered away, but thousands still mobbed the walls of the Mount. He could hear their teeth echoing in the air.

"I imagine this view was impressive in the years before."

Stealth stood behind him, one leg raised on the steep cone of the tower's top.

"It was," he said. "I came here once or twice."

He stepped off to the side, taking the antenna in his hand for balance. She took a few lunging steps up to stand next to him and nodded at his sling. "I was under the impression you were confined to bed."

"One of the joys of superpowers. You can almost always go somewhere the doctor can't chase you."

"Are you going to recover?"

"Yeah." He lifted his bandaged arm. "The wounds weren't that bad. Well, all things considered."

"And the virus?"

St. George shook his head. "Doc Connolly's amazed. She's wanted a blood sample from me for a year now. Apparently my immune system's so powerful it's killing everything Cairax dumped into me. My white blood cells are a cure for hepatitis, malaria, HIV, pretty much anything you can think of."

"I am not surprised."

The hero nodded. "It just sucks there's no way to get at them once I'm healed."

"Always the giver," she said. "Always the saint."

"Was that a joke?"

"Perhaps."

"I guess today's a miracle on several levels, then."

The mountains to the east burned red. They watched the shadows shrink. Automatic lights flickered and went out across the Mount, and over on Stage Four Zzzap relaxed a little in the electric chair.

"So," the tall hero said, "what are you going to do with Josh?"

Stealth bowed her head to examine the dark gardens below the water tower. "I do not know," she admitted. "Word of what he did will leak to the populace, yet I am no longer confident I can decide the punishment for a crime of such scale."

"And he can't be killed," added St. George.

"Yes. Which limits our options. Cerberus has locked him in a cell for now. I believe she wants to starve him."

He lifted his chin. "We shouldn't do that."

"I agree."

"Thank you."

"There are larger issues to consider," said the hooded woman. "The Seventeens are broken. We are now the only significant force left in Los Angeles."

"How many people are still back at their little kingdom?"

"Almost nineteen thousand. Now with minimal protection and resources."

"No way we can fit them all in the Mount."

"None at all."

The tallest buildings in the city were already glowing. St. George looked at the distant cluster of Century City and imagined the work crews he'd seen. "Zzzap and Cerberus could head down there," he said. "Give them power for a while, and she's a definite morale boost. We could get by with the generators and solar cells."

"An adequate temporary solution. We will need a long-term one, however."

He smiled. "If you're saying that, it means you already have one."

"Gower Street Studios is six blocks north of us. Ren-Mar is four blocks to the west. They are substantially smaller, but it would be possible to adapt the stages there into housing much as we did here. We could do the same with Raleigh Studios."

"You always said Raleigh was too hard to defend. And it's still not enough room."

"It is a start."

He looked at the roads outside the Mount's walls. "You know," he said, "we could do what they did. Use cars to block off streets. We could expand our perimeter, get all four stages inside one wall. One safe zone. It'd take some work, but we could do Sunset to Beverly, Vine to Western."

"That would be almost a square mile. Difficult to patrol."

"Not with another nineteen thousand people."

"It would take close to a year."

"Probably."

Stealth looked out over the lot. "Do you think the general populace would be willing to begin such a project?"

"To have some hope," he said. "A real purpose? Yeah, I think they'd all be up for that. I think they'd do almost anything so they can think the future's going to be better."

To the west, the night was concentrating its darkness for one last hurrah. In the east, the black had faded to dark blue and now light blue. Across the Mount a few birds chirped and sang.

"Will it be?"

"What?"

"I am not an optimist by nature, George. Will the future be better?"

He looked down at their home. "Yeah," he said. "I mean, that's what it all comes down to, isn't it? We can sit in here and worry about what might happen or we can go out and do what we can to make a difference." He shrugged. "We're superheroes. We'll make it better. That's what we do."

She followed his gaze and nodded. "Karen."

"Sorry?"

The cloaked woman continued to look across the Mount as the shadows faded away. "My name is Karen."

St. George started to open his mouth and thought better. He gave her a nod as the sun broke over the distant mountains.

"All right, then," he said, stepping into the air. "We've got work to do."

Acknowledgments

It still amazes me that a few random conversations could somehow combine with a handful of superheroes I made up in grade school to create a novel in just a few months. Let alone a novel someone else would want to read. Of course, it could not have happened so fast without some help from a few people. With that in mind, allow me to give some very heartfelt thanks . . .

To Ilya, who figured out how to defend a movie studio from the undead and gave me more information on how to do it than I could ever use in one book.

To Doug, who loaned me his own childhood creation, the Awesome Ape.

To the owners, staff, and players of a small world known as M'Dhoria. You wouldn't be reading this if that world still existed, so I tried to make it live a little here.

To Jen, Larry, Gillian, and Marcus, who read early drafts of this novel, offered some thoughts, and convinced me I wasn't entirely wasting my time. Double that thanks for David, who deserves to be paid far more than the few drinks I get to buy him when we're in the same city.

To my mom, Sally, who read countless pages of bad sci-fi,

fantasy, and *Star Wars* fanfic (long before such a term existed) and yet still always gave me the encouragement to keep at it. Even when it horrified her on many levels.

And finally to Colleen, the wonderful love of my life, who is always there to be a sounding board, a critic, a line editor, or to deliver either reassurances or a swift kick (depending on what the given day calls for).

—P.C.
Los Angeles, January 16, 2009

Peter Clines grew up in the Stephen King fallout zone of Maine and started writing science fiction and fantasy stories at the age of eight with his first "epic novel," *Lizard Men from the Center of the Earth*. He made his first writing sale at age seventeen to a local newspaper, and in the years since then he's ghostwritten two books, published a handful of short stories, and the first screenplay he wrote got him an open door to pitch story ideas at *Star Trek: Deep Space Nine* and *Voyager*. After working in the film and television industry for almost fifteen years, he wrote countless articles and reviews for *Creative Screenwriting Magazine* and its free *CS Weekly* on-line newsletter, where he interviewed dozens of Hollywood's biggest screenwriters and upcoming stars. He currently lives and writes somewhere in Los Angeles.

Read on for a taste of Peter Clines's

EX-PATRIOTS

PETER CLINES

Prologue
NOW

THE NIGHT BREEZE swept the black cloak away from Stealth's body. As the folds of fabric opened up, they revealed the array of straps and sheaths crisscrossing her skintight uniform. Her boots shifted on the water tower's sloped peak until the warm wind died down and her cloak and hood settled around her again.

Her featureless mask looked down at the figures gathered around the base of the tower. They filled the streets of the modern-day fortress that had come to be known as the Mount. Some of them staggered and made awkward lunges at each other. Many of them were eating. Shouts and cries echoed up to her.

She shook her head and turned to the man hanging in the air near her. "This is a waste of time."

"No, it isn't."

St. George, once known to the world as the Mighty Dragon, floated next to the tower and ordered gravity to ignore him. A solid six feet tall, his body was well muscled but leaned toward wiry. His leather jacket, the same golden brown as his shoulder-length hair, was decorated with sutures and grafts. At this point it was two jackets stitched into one. A five-inch tooth was tied to the coat's ragged lapel with thin straps.

Stealth glanced over her shoulder at the building that served as her office and the de facto town hall. "We should be drawing up schedules for this week's construction. The north wall is close to done."

"It can wait," he said. "They all need this. They probably don't even know how bad they need it."

"So you keep insisting."

Below them, the celebrating people packed the streets and alleys. Families gathered on the rooftops. They cheered and laughed and called out to one another. Even the guards along the wall seemed more relaxed.

"You're grumpy," said Claudia. She picked her nose while she stared at Stealth.

Inside her hood, Stealth turned her head to the little girl perched on St. George's left shoulder. "I am practical."

"She is very grumpy," St. George told the child, "but we're working on it." He pulled his arm across her legs like a seat belt and spun around in the air.

"Go higher!" yelled Timmy from the other shoulder.

"Actually," said the hero, "I think time's up for you guys. Down we go."

"No!" the boy shrieked.

"Good-bye, grumpy lady," said Claudia with a wave.

St. George drifted down to the crowd and handed the kids off to their parents. Dozens of little arms reached up but he waved them off. "No more rides for now," he told them. "Show's going to start soon."

A few yards away, the blue and silver form of Cerberus

waded through the crowd. The battle armor towered over the tallest citizens of the Mount. Most of their heads didn't reach the American flags stenciled across its gleaming biceps. The metal limbs were extended out, and gleeful children swung from each massive forearm.

The titan's armored skull looked up at the sky with lenses the size of tennis balls, then back to St. George. The armored suit was androgynous, but after working with its creator for so long George tended to think of it as female. He gave her a thumbs-up and got back a nod from the helmet.

He looked up to the star-filled sky and keyed the microphone on his collar. "Hey, up there. You ready to do this?"

Far above the Mount, one of the stars swung back and forth through the sky, tracing zigzags and figure eights across the night. Barry's voice echoed in St. George's earpiece. "Yep."

"No problems?"

"No, of course not. What could go wrong?"

"Didn't you say something yesterday about setting fire to the atmosphere?"

"Well . . . yeah," Barry said after a brief pause. "But the chances of that happening are really minuscule."

From inside the Cerberus armor, the voice of Danielle Morris echoed across the channel. "You could set part of the atmosphere on fire?"

"Not part of it," said Barry. "Look, the odds are slim to none, seriously. There's a better chance of one of us getting— wow."

"What?"

"I just got struck by lightning up here. What're the odds of that?"

"Quit it," growled Cerberus. She set down the children who were climbing on the armor.

"Trust me," said Barry, "everything's going to be fine. Make your little speech."

St. George gave the armor a smile as he drifted upward. Another round of cheers broke out as he spiraled into the air, and several bottles saluted him. Matt Russell's home brew reserves would be gone after tonight. The hero gave the crowd a wave and soared back to the top of the water tower.

Stealth was watching the walls when he landed next to her on the sloped peak. "Are you certain all guards are on duty tonight?"

"Yes," he said. "And so are you or you would've already dealt with it. Try to relax for one night, okay?"

She said nothing.

"Ladies and gentlemen," boomed Cerberus from below. With the suit's speakers at full volume she was louder than a bullhorn. The voices quieted.

"A year ago," she continued, "we'd barely been in the Mount for eight months. We were all still working around the clock just to make this place livable. There was no time for fun. No time for celebration. It was all about survival." She paused and let the echo of her voice fade. "And not all of us survived."

The crowd murmured its agreement, and a few more bottles were raised.

"So this year, we wanted to make sure everyone remembered the day and everyone had time to celebrate. We're alive. We're together. Happy Fourth of July."

There was a rumble of thunder and a bright red flower of light filled the sky. A moment later a white blossom appeared next to it, followed by a blue one. Cheers rose and spread out across the Mount. Hundreds of children screamed with joy. The lights faded and four more bursts went off in a row. The sharp thunderclap of a distant cannon echoed in the sky.

Barry's voice came over the radio again. "I thought you said you were going to do the President's speech from *Independence Day*?"

"No," said Cerberus, "you kept saying I should do it. I ignored you."

"That's such a great speech."

"Weren't you about to blow up again or something?"

Above the Mount, the night sky lit up with another burst of light. The applause echoed for blocks. St. George keyed his mic again. "How long do you think you can keep this up?"

"I can probably do another ten or twelve like this," said Barry, "maybe a dozen quick ones as a grand finale. You can't have fireworks without a finale."

"Not going to be too much for you?"

"I had a big dinner." Two more bursts lit up the sky, followed by another thunderclap. "Besides, this is totally worth it for the view. I can see most of North America. The top of South America, too, I think."

"Wow," said Cerberus. "How high up are you?"

"Pretty high. I just dodged a satellite."

"Wait," said St. George. He looked up at the sky and tried to spot Barry's gleaming form between the stars. "You're out in space?"

"Technically, yeah," Barry said over the speaker, "but I was joking about the satellite. I'm right about at the Karmann Line."

"Are you . . . okay with that?"

"Well, it's not like I need to breathe or anything. And this way we've got the ozone layer between me and Earth, just in case."

"Just in case what?"

"Hey, I'm letting off a lot of energy here. Some of it's going to slip into the more dangerous wavelengths. Can't be helped."

"It is a wise precaution," said Stealth. She'd listened on her own earpiece without looking away from the Mount's defenses. "As you were, Zzzap."

"Yes, ma'am," said Barry. They could all hear his grin. A pair of gold flowers exploded across the sky and another cheer came from below.

St. George looked up at the display and pretended not to watch the woman next to him.

"If it matters so much to you that I take part," she said, not lifting her gaze, "please just say so."

He shrugged. "I just think it would be good for you, too. You need a morale boost as much as anyone else. Maybe more."

"I do not find it as easy as some to set aside my responsibilities for a few hours of frivolous entertainment," said Stealth. "Especially to celebrate the anniversary of a country that, in most senses, no longer exists. There are always more pressing concerns." She looked out across the dark metropolis.

He followed her gaze. Each burst of light illuminated the city. Beyond the high walls of the Mount, past the barricaded gates and the rows of abandoned cars in the streets, he could see the other inhabitants of Los Angeles.

The ex-humans.

The more distant ones staggered aimlessly. Closer to the

Mount, where they could see the guards, they clawed at barriers and reached through gates. They made slow swipes with emaciated fingers. Not one of them reacted to the thunderclaps. Not one of them looked up at the brilliant display in the nighttime sky.

Not one of them was alive.

From the top of the water tower he could see tens of thousands of the walking dead—maybe hundreds of thousands—stumbling through the streets in every direction. During the flashes of light, he could pick out some with twisted limbs and many more stained with blood.

The sounds of celebration and the echo of Zzzap's fireworks almost hid the chattering. The constant noise that reached everywhere in Los Angeles, that echoed off every building and down every street. The mindless click-clack of dead teeth coming together again and again and again.

If Stealth's estimates were correct—and they almost always were—there were just over five million of them within the borders of the city.

St. George sighed. "You can really kill the mood sometimes, you know that?"

"My apologies."

The Doctor Is In

THEN

I WAS IN my private lab, gathering the notes for my one-thirty lecture. My teaching assistant, Mary, was dividing her time between searching for the flash drive that contained my PowerPoint slides and organizing a pile of correspondence and journals that had spilled onto the floor from my desk. To her credit, she'd let the papers fall and grabbed the photos of my wife and daughter.

My beard was scratching against my collar. I'd wanted to have it trimmed before the start of the semester and lost track of time. Now I was heading off to my fourth lecture and it still was a shaggy mess of too-much-silver hair. Eva hates it when my beard gets too long. It was short when we met in grad school. I needed to stop by the campus barber before I ended up looking any more like Walt Whitman.

I heard the door open behind me while I packed my briefcase, but thought nothing of it until I heard my name.

"Doctor Emil Sorensen?"

The speaker was a young man I didn't recognize. He wore a well-tailored suit he looked uncomfortable in. A double-Windsor-knotted tie. Tight, cropped hair above sharp eyes.

I'd seen this ploy many times. Every professor sees it at

least once or twice a semester. There are a few different names for it, but here the faculty calls it the VIP play. An undergrad tries to look or sound important to put themselves on equal footing with their instructor. Then they explain the extenuating circumstances behind a certain grade or exam result. They drop the names of people who would be disappointed because of it. Which all leads, of course, to the suggestion they should be allowed to resubmit a paper, retake a test, or—in some bold cases—simply have their grade changed to something acceptable.

I was running late and it was too early in the semester for such schemes. "You have ninety seconds," I said. "Can I help you with something?"

Even as I spoke, two more men stepped in behind the first. They were larger and more solid than him. One carried an attaché case. All their suits matched.

Mary stopped looking for the flash drive. Her gaze shifted from me to the trio of men.

"John Smith," said the man. "I know it sounds like a joke, but that's really my name. I'd like to speak with you for a few moments, if I could." He had a broad smile I knew from fundraisers and alumni dinners. A practiced smile, but not a well-practiced one.

"This really isn't the best time. I have a lecture in about ten minutes on the other side of campus, and—"

"I hope you'll forgive me," said Smith, "but I took the liberty of canceling your lecture."

It took a moment for the words to sink in. "Who the hell do you think you are?"

"John Smith," he repeated. The smile faltered as his hand fumbled with a leather wallet. He opened it to reveal a golden badge and a set of credentials with his photo. He was smiling in the photo. "Agent Smith, technically. I'm with the Department of Homeland Security, seconded to the Defense Advanced Research Projects Agency. Could we speak alone, sir?"

He said the last with a nod to Mary. She looked at me with wide eyes. We all spoke a bit too freely at times, and on a college campus paranoia and rumors about the Patriot Act ran like wildfire. "Doctor?"

I tried what I hoped was a reassuring smile. "Why don't you go see if there are any stragglers at Bartlett Hall," I told her. "Let them know this delay doesn't mean they're off the hook for next week's test."

She gathered her own papers and paused to make sure I saw the flash drive she'd uncovered. The smile graced Smith's face the entire time. He gave Mary a polite wave as she slipped out between the two larger men. They closed the door behind her.

"So what's this all about?"

Smith's face relaxed. As the smile faded, he gained several years. Not a young man, but cursed with the face of one. One of the other biochem professors had the same problem. A young face in a college town meant always being carded at the store and never being taken as seriously as your colleagues.

"You're a very impressive man, Doctor Sorensen," he said. "You've got more doctorate degrees than I've got years of education. Physiology. Neurology. Biochemistry. A forerunner in molecular nanotechnology and—"

"I know my own credentials."

"From what I've read, you got cheated out of the Nobel Prize last year."

"It's not about winning prizes," I said. "Besides, the gene-modification techniques Evans and the others developed are brilliant. They even helped my own work."

"Of course," Smith agreed with a polite nod. "You've received several grants from DARPA over the past twenty years. If I read the file right, your contract's been renewed a record-breaking seven times. In fact"—he gave a forced chuckle—"you started working for the government just before my eighth birthday."

"Can you please get to the point, Mr. Smith?"

The smile faltered again. "Well, Doctor, the fact is they want to bring you on full-time and put you in charge of—"

"Not interested."

His face dropped. "You don't even know which project I was going to say."

"It doesn't matter," I said. "I'm comfortable with my arrangement the way it is."

"Are you sure?"

"Why wouldn't I be?"

Smith reached out to the side. The man with the attaché case opened it and placed a file folder in the waiting hand. "You've seen some of the headlines, I'm guessing?" He walked past me to the table and spread out some clippings and printed articles.

THE MIGHTY DRAGON PATROLS LOS ANGELES

"APE MAN" STOPS ROBBERY

SHADOWY FIGURE HUNTS RAMPART DISTRICT CRIMINALS

I'd seen most of them before. A few of my grad students had been saving news stories and images for me since the

Mighty Dragon had first appeared in June. I guessed we had twice as many articles as Smith did. Copies were on the flash drive, which reminded me to pick it up and drop it in my pocket. "Have you seen the ones about the electrical man up in Boston?" I asked him.

His eyes lit up like a child. "I have. What do you think of them?"

"I'm intrigued, of course, but until I see more concrete proof than a headline in the *Post* or some grainy photos on a blog, it's not going to occupy a lot of my time."

"But you've had your students saving news stories for you." His smile came back.

"What are you getting at, Mr. Smith?"

He avoided my eyes and looked around the lab. "I hate to sound suspicious, Professor Sorensen, but . . . well, some folks at DARPA have been wondering if you've had some success with your human enhancement research that you haven't told us about."

I felt a twinge of panic. Maybe Mary's paranoia wasn't that misplaced after all. "You think I had something to do with these people?"

Smith shrugged. "To be honest," he said, "I think they'd be thrilled if you had. It'd put the United States far ahead in the superpowers race."

"The what?"

"They're not just here, Doctor," he said. "People with superhuman abilities are appearing all over the world. Did you see Vladimir Putin on the cover of *Time* last month?" Smith shook his head.

"I saw the picture," I said with a nod. They'd titled it "Superman of the Year." Putin had been bare-chested in front of the Kremlin, holding a car one-handed over his head. "I thought it was Photoshop propaganda."

"Most people did. Thank the CIA for that. But superhumans are popping up everywhere." Smith slid some more photos from the file folder. "England's got the Green Knight and the Scarecrow. Japan's got a whole team of super-samurais. There're two guys in Iran calling themselves Gilgamesh and Marduk. Hell, we got satellite footage of a dragon flying over Baghdad this morning. Wings, horns, tail, everything."

"A dragon?"

He shrugged. "Some of the agency folks think it might be some kind of metamorphosis or something." His tongue tripped over the word. "That something, maybe someone, changed into—"

"I know what metamorphosis means."

"Right, sorry. Anyway, don't you see, Professor? That's why we need to get you back on Project Krypton. No more consults, no more outside evaluations. We want you working full time with us on this. And you don't want to miss out on a chance like this, do you?"

"No," I found myself saying. I knew Smith was right. Eva and Madelyn were going to be angry with me. I'd promised them I wouldn't take on extra projects this year. "I thought Krypton was done for good?"

"The Secretary of Defense likes it. He brought it back two years ago, but it's been kept pretty quiet. The Future Force Warrior project gets most of the headlines on *Wired*, anyway."

"Then why bring back Krypton?"

"Well, Future Force is doing well," he said, "and they're also hoping to have that new exoskeleton project in the public eye in the next seven or eight months. But when it comes down to it, the Vice President, the Secretary, and the Joint Chiefs want to see the real deal in our corner and they think you're the man to do it."

I furrowed my brow. It's a bad habit. Eva says it's giving me wrinkles. "Our corner? I'm not sure I understand."

He gestured at the papers and images on the table. "All these other superhumans are answering to their country's government," he explained. "Almost every one of them. Some are even on payroll. I mean, think about it, Doctor. There's no point in having superheroes in the United States if the government doesn't control them.